WRITTEN OUT

Recent Titles by David Armstrong

The Kavanagh and Salt series

UNTIL DAWN TOMORROW
THOUGHT FOR THE DAY
SMALL VICES
A KIND OF ACQUAINTANCE *
WRITTEN OUT *

Stand alone novels

NIGHT'S BLACK AGENTS
LESS THAN KIND

available from Severn House

WRITTEN OUT

A Kavanagh and Salt Mystery

David Armstrong

This first world edition published 2009
in Great Britain and in the USA by
SEVERN HOUSE PUBLISHERS LTD of
9–15 High Street, Sutton, Surrey, England, SM1 1DF.
Trade paperback edition published
in Great Britain and the USA 2009 by
SEVERN HOUSE PUBLISHERS LTD

British Library Cataloguing in Publication Data

Armstrong, David, 1946–
  Written Out.
  1. Kavanagh, Frank (Fictitious character) – Fiction.
  2. Salt, Jane (Fictitious character) – Fiction.
  3. Novelists – Crimes against – Fiction.
  4. Police – England – Shropshire – Fiction. 5. Detective and
  mystery stories.
  I. Title
  823.9'14-dc22

ISBN-13: 978-0-7278-6779-7   (cased)
ISBN-13: 978-1-84751-159-1   (trade paper)

All Severn House titles are printed on acid-free paper.

Typeset by Palimpsest Book Production Ltd.,
Grangemouth, Stirlingshire, Scotland.
Printed and bound in Great Britain by
MPG Books Ltd., Bodmin, Cornwall.

To Gill

'The good thing about writing fiction is that you can get back at people . . .' Tom Oliver out of John Grisham

PROLOGUE

For fourteen years, Sarah and Will Cassin had lived half a mile from the centre of Hereford in a red-brick, three-storey Victorian house with a little back yard and tiny front garden.

When the house had been built by a local seed merchant in 1864, the only things to trundle past the bay window were the carts that delivered produce to the local shops and, for those wealthy enough to own them, the horses and horse-drawn carriages that carried squires and farmers, tradesmen and well-to-do ladies to and from church and to conduct their business in the town.

Nearly 150 years later, the house remained, but just about everything else had changed. Very few people walked anywhere at all these days, and even fewer went to church. People might buy a loaf or a newspaper in the town, but most shopping was done in retail parks or supermarkets miles away. Almost every house in the town now had two cars, one for the commuting breadwinner, another to ferry children to school and visit Sainsbury's or Tesco.

Through the successive post-war property booms, much of the land that had once skirted the town and separated it from outlying villages had been built on as, keen to escape the noise and growing populations of the nearby towns and cities, people made for market towns just like this one which then, of course, themselves became the micro-cities that those same migrants were seeking to escape.

And, with every newly built house on Meadow Rise, Spinney Lane and Linden View, came another two, or sometimes three, cars.

Will Cassin taught geography at the local college and knew a good deal about demography and the falling birth rate in the indigenous population, but as the traffic thundered past his house at every hour of the day – and nowadays late into the night, too – he sometimes found those facts hard to believe.

The Cassins' street of houses that had been erected with

timber scaffolding – the sand, lime and bricks delivered to the builder with a clatter of hooves – had stayed more or less that way for fifty or sixty years. And even then, for the next thirty or forty years, throughout two world wars and right up to the 1960s, the street had seen only a very few Morris Minors and Vauxhall Victors parked there. But these days, those same houses shook as the ceaseless traffic rumbled by, and it was on this account that the Cassins had, for the last five or six years, been in the habit of parking their car (Will cycled to his work at the college every day) in the quieter road just around the corner from their house.

But all of this, wearisome though it might be, was fairly academic until the house next door to the Cassins, the corner property, lived in by an elderly couple for many decades, was sold in probate to a developer.

The new owner, a man from Ledbury, gutted the house, installed an en-suite bathroom, a downstairs loo, dimmer switches and ceiling spotlights and a kitchen with dishwasher and a range cooker, just as the TV make-over shows said that every speculator should. He covered the floors with 'wood' laminate, every wall with woodchip paper painted beige, and within two months the house was sold at a handsome profit.

The woman – a short, dark-haired divorcee – was from the area, and two grown-up boys were hers. Her partner was a burly Scotsman with a gold ring in his left ear, and if his accent didn't declare his roots, the tattoo of a rampant lion on his bulging forearm certainly did: he was from the blue side of Scotland's largest city, a Glasgow Rangers follower.

On the day that they moved in, the Cassins said hello to their new neighbours but received the barest of greetings in return. They put it down to the stress of moving.

In December they sent a Christmas card but it, too, went unacknowledged.

Until some three years previously, Sarah had taught English at the same college as her husband, but since their son had graduated and left home and, more importantly perhaps, since her second selection of poetry had been accepted for publication, she had given up lecturing to devote herself wholly to the business of writing. Even with teaching the occasional residential poetry course, the fact that she now earned about a tenth of what her lecturing job had paid was of no importance compared with her earnest wish to write full time.

The note on her windscreen told her in no uncertain terms not to park outside her new neighbours' house. And it wasn't just the note itself; it was the uncouth tone of it. Was Sarah imagining too much to think that the capital letters scrawled on the envelope there had been written with rage and anger?

For the first time in all the years that they had lived there, the Cassins felt ill at ease in their own home and Sarah was shocked to discover just how unsettled she was by the antagonism that she felt. Obviously, she'd read about this kind of thing happening and, now and again, if some neighbourhood dispute got really out of hand, it might end up in tragedy and the ensuing violence make the TV news. But not here, surely? Not amongst what had always been friendly, neighbourly people? There was a war in the Middle East, and many people had no clean water to drink in some of the most populous countries of the world, and yet here was she, unable to sleep as she fretted about their new neighbours' bullying behaviour over a parking place.

But no amount of rational thought could give her peace of mind, and she was shocked and distressed by how completely her equilibrium had been rocked by this absurd situation – an awareness of which only made her feel worse.

As Will left for work one morning, he looked in utter dismay at Sarah's car. It had been gouged down one side, a deep scratch, from bonnet to boot and across both doors. When a policeman called on her later that day, Sarah said nothing about the dispute, fearing an escalation of hostilities if she was suspected of suggesting that their neighbour might have been responsible for the vandalism.

And anyway, when she told the policeman that her husband was a teacher, he was certain that the perpetrator would be an aggrieved student, some youngster who must have reckoned his essay had been harshly marked, or imagined himself the victim of some other trifling injustice.

He gave Sarah a crime number but told her it was unlikely the offender would ever be caught. He then knocked on every door in the short street to ascertain whether anyone had seen or heard anything the previous night. They hadn't.

The night before his wife was due to leave home to tutor

a poetry course in Shropshire, Will had been for his regular
Sunday evening drink with friends in one of the town's only
pubs that didn't have music, fruit machines or a pool table.
The three men sat there and chatted as they completed the
crossword in the Sunday newspaper and drank three pints of
the local brewery's bitter.

Walking home, as he was crossing the deserted car park at
the top of the town, someone stepped from the shadows and
struck Will Cassin a fearsome blow to the side of his head.
He reeled and fell to the ground. No-one had hit him since
he'd been at school. Blood poured from his nose and his ear.
The side of his head throbbed with terrible pain. Before he
could get to his knees to look up, a kick to his side broke two
of his ribs. Cassin had never experienced such agony and he
curled into a ball to try to protect himself from what might
follow. 'Please . . . not me, please,' he mouthed, convinced that
he was the victim of mistaken identity. But as he put his hand
to his face where the tears and blood were streaming in a
warm mess, another kick came at him, this time smashing
into his cheekbone. He tightened even further into a ball and
pleaded again for mercy.

And then, as suddenly as the attack had begun, it stopped.
There was an interminable wait and Cassin sobbed as his
whole body shook with fear and he awaited the next blow.
But this time, all he heard was the man taking a step away
from him, the slight clatter of something falling to the ground,
and then his assailant striding away from the scene.

A few moments later he heard the throb of a vehicle starting
somewhere nearby and it driving off.

PART ONE

ONE

Shropshire

For novelist Tom Oliver it was just another week away. Away from what, exactly? Away from his north London flat, his TV and books; away from coffee in bed at eight a.m. with Radio Four's *Today*, and tuna salad with *The World at One* five hours later.

He'd made this journey twice before, and he had an uncomfortable sense that his present feeling – a slight but all-pervading sense of melancholy – was very similar to what he might have experienced the last time. And, for all he could recall, the time before that, too.

Oliver had never had any truck with things mystical, or even things mildly esoteric but, as he drove along the trunk road he did find himself with teasing thoughts about the possible existence of some sort of field force. Ley lines, call them what you will, might, for all he knew, straddle this bit of the A49 just north of Ludlow.

Maybe hereabouts there was some ancient track, the residual power of which was still so potent that it penetrated the skin of his well-made car and permeated his being so completely that it was able to affect his mood?

He turned up the music on the CD player and dismissed the thoughts as the fey nonsense he knew them to be. He was melancholy, he knew very well, simply because he was, even now, only a few miles from the place where he would be spending the coming week.

But why? Why this maudlin state? Why, as the old joke went, the 'long face'? Surely not on account of the prospect of a few days to be spent with writers – invariably young and sometimes attractive writers – in the midst of Shropshire countryside? What, exactly, was the man's problem?

After all, compared with his usual daily life – a life in which he would have been ashamed to admit that he could, and sometimes did, in the middle of the seething, bustling

city in which he lived, occasionally go for an entire day
without exchanging a single sentence with another human
being – surely the prospect of such a week was not
unwelcome?

He turned on to the B4368 and followed an elderly couple
as they snaked along the lane in their immaculate green
Rover. A tractor and trailer hauling cattle beet came the other
way and obliged both cars to slow as it passed on the narrow
road.

'"Clunton and Clunbury, Clungunford and Clun, Are the
quietest places Under the sun,"' he mouthed. That was the
thing about Housman; he was one of those writers, like a
prophet of the Old Testament, a purveyor of saws and proverbs,
whose couplets people somehow just knew, often without even
knowing they were uttering the man's work.

There was no helpful sign on the main road announcing
the centre, and the first time he had tutored a course here, a
couple of years ago now, he'd ended up in the village a further
mile down the road. He'd pulled in at the MOT testing garage
with its three white triangles on a blue background and asked
for directions, like many before him and since, no doubt.

Oliver slowed as he approached the dangerous bend where
he had to leave the country road. The Rover in front of him
pulled sedately away. Still no sign for the venue. Odd. After
all, you could barely light a cigarette in a public place, or
switch on a library computer without the thing having a
worthiness certificate, but on this tight bend, and with no
warning sign of the place, you could easily get yourself killed
before you'd even arrived at the centre.

Oh, well. '"Clunton and Clunbury, Clungunford and Clun,"'
he said again as he carefully turned off the road. The Saab
lurched through the puddles on the rutted lane, over the tiny
humpbacked bridge and on up towards the big house at the
top of the drive.

At the area reserved for parking and unloading, he would have
chosen to sit quietly for a moment but, glancing in the mirror,
the sight of a taxi in the distance trundling up the long drive
behind him urged him into action. He got out of the car, took
one of his bags from the rear seat and slipped through the
front door of the imposing stone house.

There was no-one in the dining kitchen, with its L-shaped table arrangement and pine benches, but there was milk open on the table and steam still wafting from the electric kettle in the kitchen proper.

From the sitting room down the hall he could hear the murmur of voices. He knew where the tutors' bedrooms were and made his way stealthily up the stairs.

On the landing, he tapped the door of the bigger room (the one he had never been able to occupy on his previous visits). Nothing. He went in and turned the key in the door behind him.

He slipped off his shoes, creaked as softly as he could across the oak boards, and stood by the dressing table at the window. The passengers in the taxi below, two men and a woman, were fumbling with purses and wallets. The driver stood idly by, aware that a three-way split like this was unlikely to lead to his receiving any kind of tip.

Quite unexpectedly, the woman in the group looked up to the window and glimpsed Oliver standing there, watching. He felt as if he had been discovered doing something inappropriate and, at a loss, half raised a hand in acknowledgement, smiled weakly, and stepped away from the casement.

As the driver's door slammed shut and the man reversed back down the drive to a turning place, Oliver slipped off his jeans and jumper and lay down on the double bed in his boxer shorts and tee shirt.

Only the previous week, crime writer Jay Tyler had apparently reclined in this very place. It was of course possible that the popular novelist had taken the smaller room next door, but, given his standing, Oliver somehow doubted this and so, content with his groundless speculation, he imagined the writer lying here, stretched out, just as he himself now was.

Rather more intriguingly, perhaps, if the information in the course booklet was correct, only a couple of weeks before Tyler's stay, romantic novelist Lynne Baines had slept here, too.

Tom Oliver might not be up there with Tyler or Baines, he mused, but right now, he was in the same room and lying on the same bed as these estimable writers, and in this, at least, he was their equal.

TWO

London

'**F**rank . . .' said DC Salt.
        'Yes, honey?' said the detective inspector.
        'Would you mind not singing?'
'Singing?' said Kavanagh. 'Was I?'
'Yes, I assure you, you were,' she said, and handed him a tea towel.
'You know,' he said, 'have you noticed, Salt, you never hear anyone whistling anymore?'
'I have noticed, actually, yes. I think I've even heard it discussed on the radio.'
'Really?' he said irrepressibly jauntily. 'I wonder why that is. Can you remember what the conclusions were?'
'No, I don't know what the conclusions were, Frank, and I have to say, for myself, whistling's not anything that I miss terribly . . .'
'Really?' he said. 'I used to quite like it, people going down the road whistling. When I was a kid, everybody used to do it in Birmingham if they were happy. It was almost like a sign, I suppose. Milkmen . . . bus conductors . . .'
'Must have been great,' she said with sly sarcasm.
'Yes, it was OK,' he said innocently, refusing to rise to the bait.
'There aren't any milkmen any more. Have you noticed that, too?' she offered.
'Aren't there? None at all?' he queried.
'Nor bus conductors,' she said, ignoring his determination to see the very best in everything this morning, and then added, 'Not that you'd know. When's the last time you went on a bus, Frank?'
'Do you know, Constable, it's only a little feeling I'm getting – call it my copper's instincts if you like – but I think you're determined not to have a happy policeman in your kitchen this morning. Could I be right?'

'I'd be happier if you could just not whistle, Frank, which would be marginally worse than you singing . . .'

'It's not by any—' he began.

'And if you were to even consider asking me what time of the month it is,' she interrupted, 'you'll be out of the door, and I assure you, I will never, ever see you again.'

'Well, I certainly wouldn't want that, would I?' he said, finally feeling deflated by the exchange.

She continued to wash the breakfast things with undue care, and he took them from the draining board and dried then in reciprocal silence.

Eventually, feeling a little guilty, she said, 'So, what are you going to do with your week off?' But then couldn't resist adding pointedly, 'Without me?'

'Even I can't fix your leave patterns, Salt,' he said wearily.

'No,' she said. 'I know you can't.'

'What I should do is a bit in the bathroom, give it a coat of paint and finally fix the tiles. But what I'll probably do is nip up to Lancashire and see my old mate Davey Whisker. There's a midweek Preston game we could go to, and then . . . and then, I'm not sure really. A bit of this and a bit of that. Go over and see Mum one day, of course.'

Salt dried her hands and, with a huge effort of will said quietly, 'I'm sorry, Frank. I'm a bit off this morning. Work's been hard this week.'

'Sure,' he said. He chucked the tea towel on to the work surface and offered her his open arms, an offer which she declined.

'Are you ready?' she asked, returning to brisk mode. 'Shall we get down to the deli?' And with that she picked up her bag and jacket.

'Sure,' he said, and began to hum the bit he almost always hummed from *La Bohème* as he joined her in the hall.

She stopped, her hand on the latch, turned and looked at him, and they left the house in silence, walking just a little apart from one another.

THREE

Shropshire

F ew visitors can have failed to notice that housekeeping at the Osman Writers' Foundation came a poor second to the main purpose of the place – and the thing for which it had originally been endowed – but aspiring poets and dramatists, chock-full of energy and teeming with creativity, were unlikely to be troubled by matters domestic in such a febrile atmosphere. The people who came to spend a week here were not a bunch of IT geeks looking for the air-conditioned comfort of a city-centre conference hotel, and as American-born centre director Keira always pointed out in her welcoming address, she wanted people to treat the place as their home from home. 'It's not a hotel,' she would say. 'Think of it as a slightly shabby, comfortable country house.'

Slightly shabby, thought Oliver as he looked at the dust on the dressing table beneath the window.

Dozing there for another half hour as the mild October afternoon turned to dark evening, he was aware of a car's arrival, then another, and of voices down below outside the window of his room. And then, just a few minutes later, the sound of his co-tutor – the poet Sarah Cassin, he imagined – noisily moving about as she unpacked her things in the room next door.

It was just before six o'clock by the time he fully woke and switched on the bedside radio. He pulled on his Levis as Big Ben tolled and the news headlines were declaimed between the bongs. He looked tired and he was in need of a shave, but instead, he merely washed his face, put on a clean shirt and slipped into comfortable shoes.

But he was still reluctant to go downstairs and started instead to unpack his workshop folders and the (lamentably few) printed pages from his 'work in progress'. Hanging his jacket in the wardrobe, it was clear that the base of the thing hadn't seen a vacuum cleaner for a very long time. Tom Oliver had reached an age where he saw no discrepancy in being moved by the power of language – the electricity that flowed through decent prose – as well as the more discordant but equally powerful note of a Dyson vac.

The voices in the sitting room below were intermittent and confirmed the notion of strangers who had been arbitrarily brought together: staccato bursts of muffled conversation, a little over-excitable laughter, and then the edgy silence of reflection and embarrassment.

He could almost sense the tension there. He really should join them. Instead, he sat disconsolately on the side of the bed and listened to the news headlines summary.

Ten minutes later he tapped on the sitting-room door. His outré politeness was intended as a declaration of solidarity, an announcement that – for the next few days, at least – he was one of them. 'Hello, everyone,' he said, peering round the door. 'I'm Tom. Tom Oliver.' The group, waiting nervously in the sitting room, volunteered their names, which he instantly forgot, and he went round the dozen people sitting there and shook each of them by the hand.

He registered only Neville, a man with nasal hair and an unkempt beard whom he identified as someone almost certain to prove troublesome during the next few days.

Without even being aware that he was thinking it, he dismissed four of the seven women present as being without any kind of romantic possibilities whatsoever. The other two might just about squeeze under the bar (admittedly, a bar that was set pretty high these days), and the third, a young black woman, was so young and handsome that, even by his elastic standards, he judged her far too youthful and attractive to conceivably wish to have anything to do with a man of his age.

'So, here we are,' he said superfluously and took a seat, aware of the silence that his own late arrival had actually exacerbated. Mischievously, he thought about entrenching, just sitting there beside the standard lamp and saying absolutely nothing. Someone would break, and eventually have to say something no matter what the risks of appearing foolish. But it was just as likely that one of those present, perhaps someone on an anti-anxiety prescription drug, unable to deal with the tension, would have some sort of seizure on the spot.

No, he'd get the ball rolling in just a second, after he'd had his moment of silent assertion. After all, he may not be the most famous writer in the country, but he was certainly the most famous writer in this room.

'Have you come far?' he enquired of a woman directly opposite him, and then added, 'Er, sorry . . .?' prompting her for her name once more.

'Jeannie,' she said.

'Jeannie.' And he repeated the question.

'I've come up from Bath.'

'Really,' he said, and then, addressing the group and treating the woman's information with complete indifference, 'What we have to do of course is not reveal too much just yet, otherwise our getting-to-know-one-another session after supper will be redundant . . .'

There were slightly forced smiles. The idea of not exchanging titbits of information with and about one another was laughable: things had felt awkward enough in the room as it was without further sanctions on the laboured exchanges being implemented.

But they were saved from further difficulty as at that moment the sitting-room door opened. Centre director Keira stood aside and ushered in a woman wearing a long blue, coarsely woven skirt, sandals and a poncho around her shoulders. 'Hello everyone. Hello Tom,' said Keira brightly. 'May I introduce your other tutor, Catherine. Catherine Wooley.'

Amidst the general murmurs of slightly surprised greeting, Tom Oliver looked at the buxom woman and acknowledged her quietly with the one word, 'Catherine.'

FOUR

I t was remarkable to Tom Oliver just how many would-be writers never opened the arts pages. Few of those in the room, therefore, were aware of just who the woman – who was now smiling warmly and greeting each of them by the hand – actually was.

Keira remained standing at the open door and when Catherine Wooley eventually squeezed onto the sofa between two women, she began, 'Well, the bad news is that Sarah, Sarah Cassin, the poet who you were all expecting to be here . . . I am afraid she has had to pull out. Sarah's husband had an accident last night and she is unable to leave him as he needs her care.'

There were a couple of token expressions of sympathy for the plight of someone about whom they knew nothing, but mostly what followed was silence.

'These things have occasionally happened before, of course, but very, very rarely and we naturally do everything in our power to ensure that the writer that you are promised, and that you sign up for, is the person that you get.'

The remark seemed a little utilitarian, given the circumstances, thought Oliver.

'However, every cloud,' she began with renewed vigour (again, the phrase was rather tactless, he thought), 'I was eventually able to contact Catherine here who, fortunately for us, doesn't live so very far away, and she kindly rearranged everything she had planned for this coming week and agreed to step in.'

Most of those present recognized the delicacy that was required to negotiate this particular situation: if Keira suggested that Catherine Wooley was able to come without any difficulty, the clear implication would be that her diary was devoid of appointments for an entire week. 'How far is it, Catherine?' asked Keira as an aside, hoping to deflect attention from the group's gloomy thoughts of a stand-in writer's barren diary.

'It's about twenty miles,' volunteered the poet.

'Anyway,' continued Keira, 'I'm sure you all know Catherine's work. Her first collection won the most-promising-newcomer prize in *Poetry Now* magazine,' and here she read from the scrap of paper in her palm, 'as one of the most significant voices in women's poetry writing today.' There was an awkwardly long pause as Keira tried in vain to straddle the gap between the assertions of that early promise and the subsequent plateau which had been Wooley's poetic home since. 'Catherine was runner-up for the Staffordshire Potteries Prize the year before last, and,' she glanced down at the scrap of paper again, 'her new collection is due out with the Stiperstone's Press in . . . when is it out, Catherine?' she asked.

'Early next year,' said Wooley vaguely.

'So, as I was saying,' continued the centre director, 'we are extremely lucky and very privileged to have Catherine, and I know you will all enjoy working with her.'

As she looked around the room, she sensed a little disquiet about the late change, but didn't detect signs of imminent mutiny. Emboldened, she went on, 'Right, I think that I should leave you now. You've already met Tom, of course, so why not have a little chat with Catherine and we'll all meet at supper in an hour, where I can let you know how the week will pan out, discuss cooking arrangements – very important – and answer any questions that anyone has. OK?' And with that, she turned and was gone.

As Catherine engaged in conversation with the people on either side of her on the chintzy sofa, Tom Oliver immediately followed Keira to the kitchen.

'Keira?'

'Hi, Tom,' she replied.

'I'm at a loss . . .' he began.

'Sorry?' she said.

'Catherine. Catherine Wooley. Why? Why didn't you tell me?'

'Didn't you get my messages?' she asked.

'Messages?' he said.

'I left messages on your answerphone at home.'

'When?' he demanded testily.

'Today, first thing, as soon as I heard that Sarah couldn't make it. I phoned.'

'I've been in Wales, in the Black Mountains for the last three days,' he said irascibly, as if his absence from home was Keira's fault. 'At the cottage I rent; I often go there when I'm working on a new book.'

'I'm sorry,' she said, 'but I couldn't do any more. Your mobile was unobtainable. Was it charged? Switched on?'

'Was there no-one else?' he interrupted, ignoring her questions.

'It was very short notice,' she said, and took a step closer to him. 'Between ourselves, Tom,' she whispered, looking to the door, 'and promise me you'll never say anything, I did try two other writers before asking Catherine.'

'And?' he said.

'Geoffrey Portman's in Belgium on a British Council tour, and Terri Walker – she's often tutored here before, and she'd have been ideal – she's doing two readings in Scotland this week.'

'I just can't believe it,' he said.

'What is it, Tom?' she said, failing to understand his consternation. 'It was unavoidable, and frankly, we were lucky to get anyone at such short notice.'

'You don't know, do you?' he said. 'You really don't.'

'Know what?' she asked, intrigued.

'Catherine Wooley and myself. We have . . . history.'

'History?' she repeated, incredulous. Catherine Wooley had never been in the slightest bit circumspect about her sexuality, and it was sexuality of a sort which Keira assumed would have precluded her having 'history' with Oliver or, for that matter, any other male on the planet.

Oliver quickly disabused her of the assumption. 'Not *that* kind of history,' he sneered. '*Literary* history.'

'Oh, I see,' she said. 'Go on.'

'A few years ago, Catherine "reviewed",' and here he spat the word out, 'a novel of mine.'

'Really?' said Keira. 'But she's a poet,' she added, genuinely baffled.

'Exactly,' said Oliver. 'Some fool of a literary editor's idea, no doubt.'

'She reviewed it . . . not well?' ventured the director warily.

'Her review – if that's what you can call it – was completely ill-informed and extremely disparaging.'

'I see,' said Keira as, for the first time, she began to recognize the possible consequences of her actions.

'One phrase sticks in my mind,' Oliver continued, reliving the painful experience. 'She suggested that the book – which had some sort of mystery at its centre – was like "a so-so episode of Morse". Those were her actual words,' he added bitterly.

'Morse?' queried Keira, Colin Dexter's maudlin detective never having been quite the hit in her former home of Boston USA, as he was in the UK.

'Inspector Morse. He's on television,' he said scathingly.

'I see,' she said.

'A television programme?' he went on witheringly. 'It's no more than an hour's plot with pictures. Where is the *writing*? My book was three hundred pages of prose, dialogue, description, carefully constructed characters . . .' He started to choke on his own splenetic words and, unable to continue, poured a glass of water and drank it down in several big gulps.

Keira looked on, at a loss as to what to either say or do. The man looked broken, and yet unapproachable, too. There was danger in him, as well as abject despair. 'Morse,' he finally said, his voice cracking with emotion.

'I suppose it *was* only one person's opinion,' suggested Keira as she tried to ameliorate the man's anger.

'Yes,' he agreed, 'but unfortunately, an opinion expressed in the biggest circulation Sunday broadsheet in the land.'

There was silence between them, a reflective moment, and not the best moment for the sound of laughter to come down the hall, especially as, given her husky guffaw, it was only too clear exactly which person it was coming from.

'And that was it?' she asked gingerly, suspecting that Oliver's story was not quite finished.

'No, that was not "it",' he said pointedly, risking offending the very woman whose solicitous enquiries suggested that she was at least sympathetic to his plight.

'Yes?' ventured Keira.

'There was an awards ceremony a few months later. I had been shortlisted for something – which I didn't win – and she was there as prizewinner on some poetry magazine thing.'

'And?' said Keira tentatively.

'I had drunk rather a lot; she was being congratulated by the white-pumps-with-dinner-jacket lispers. I went and told her what I thought of her mealy-mouthed doggerel and, more to the point, what I thought of her critical faculties when it came to reviewing a proper writer's work.'

'Oh dear,' said Keira, wincing at the thought of the exchange and the repercussions of what she had unwittingly done.

'Yes, it got very ugly. We've avoided one another since then,' he concluded.

'I see,' she said.

'And you've never heard of any of this?' he asked, intrigued.

'Never,' she confirmed, and thought for a moment. 'I suppose I was still in America then,' she said, 'doing my Masters at Amherst.'

They stood there for fully half a minute, each of them considering the situation and weighing the very limited options available to them.

'I just don't know what to say, except that I'm most terribly sorry,' she began.

'It's not your fault,' he said, more conciliatory, but without a great deal of conviction. 'The thing that I don't understand,' he said, 'is what was her attitude when you told her that it was me teaching the course, the person that she would be sharing it with? She must have said something, surely?'

'Of course, I told her it was you, and that Sarah had dropped out. I think her exact words were: "Are you sure? Will that be OK?" and of course I assumed that she meant, what with you doing the fiction segment and she now doing the poetry, rather than Sarah, you know, would you complement one another. I said I was sure it would be fine. It's all writing, after all, isn't it?' she added rather hopelessly. 'But obviously, her question was a bit more pointed that that.'

'Obviously,' he concurred sourly.

Eventually, Keira asked quietly, 'What do you think would be best, Tom?' She had already had one tutor drop out, and was now very possibly about to lose another. It would hardly be surprising if, for the first time in the centre's history, there followed immediately an exodus of fee-paying students.

Her second thought was of a week spent in an intimate but poisonous atmosphere, something like being locked in an unhappy and sexless marriage.

Whilst it was not unknown for co-tutors to have a low opinion of one another's work, and even, occasionally, to fall out over some difference of opinion during their week together, this situation was unprecedented and could go down in creative-writing folklore as the most tremendous gaffe on the young centre director's part.

Oliver considered just what his contractual obligations were and, more importantly, what the centre's were to him. He'd never even bothered to read the two-page contract, merely signed a copy and returned it weeks ago. He imagined it would have had all the usual stuff about dealing with folk with disabilities of one sort and another; how to conduct oneself with people from ethnic minorities – how to respect their rights and wishes with regard to food and prayer, all that sort of thing – but he was certain that there was going to be nothing whatsoever about a situation such as this. Almost certainly, then, the thousand pounds (plus expenses and board and lodging) would never materialize if he were to pack his bags, get in his car and drive back to his north London flat.

And a thousand pounds for five days' work was a third of what he had received from the publisher for his last novel, a book that had taken him the best part of fifteen months to write.

'I think I should do what I can,' he said plaintively.

'Really? Are you sure, Tom?' she said, taking her elegiac tone from him. 'That's wonderful.'

He nodded sagely, not exactly happy, perhaps, but feeling a degree of satisfaction in assuming the unaccustomed role of victimized party.

'Do you think we should all – the three of us – speak together? Perhaps have some sort of meeting?' asked the young woman.

'I don't think that will be necessary,' he said. 'She can conduct her workshops, and I'll do mine. With luck, we'll have little more than mealtimes to negotiate. And I'm prepared – for the students' sake, of course – to be civil. If any of them happens to remember the event – it was after all written up fairly extensively in the arts pages – they'll imagine it's all water under the bridge. After all, they've paid a good deal to be here, and we owe it to them to concentrate on their progress. As writers.'

He was quite surprised at how easily this sententious tosh issued from his own mouth. Even more surprising was how the young woman opposite him appeared to be buying it, hook, line and sinker.

'It's so good of you to be this understanding, Tom. I really can't thank you enough.'

'We'll get through,' he said. 'I'll do my best.' And he left the room.

FIVE

London

Crouch End Broadway on a Saturday morning in October is almost certainly one of the safest places in London to be, and even though Kavanagh's apparently irrepressible good humour had eventually been worn down by Salt's lack of equally good spirits, the day had to be got through just the same.

In the deli they bought ciabatta, antipasti, and that Italian creamy cheese that Kavanagh could never remember the name of. But things were strained as they struggled to find their usual harmony on this morning: they both knew very well that it was simply one of those occasions when they'd have been better off apart until the current relationship clouds had blown over.

Their plan of a buffet lunch back at his flat – followed by an hour in bed, perhaps – would have been delicious, but now he secretly wished that he could have been on his own, watched Football Focus and just put his feet up on the big sofa with a cup of coffee and a piece of toast and Marmite.

But neither of them said as much, for they were both old enough to know that this was sometimes how relationships were and anyway, generally speaking, he and Salt got on very well. How long was it now? Ages. They'd been colleagues for three years – more – and lovers for over two. They just hadn't yet relinquished the safety net of their separate flats, hers on Ferme Park Road, his here in Crouch End, just off the Broadway.

And it was at times like this, rare though they were, that he (and she, too, presumably) knew that they had definitely done the right thing. Like every couple in the world, they had their tricksy moments, and this was just one of those times: work pressures, family issues, his tendency to a slight loopiness at full moons, a hyperactivity that could make him crabby, but also agitated and productive.

And there were the couple of days before her period was due when her skin felt different to his touch and her demeanour was, just like today, almost unrecognizable from her usual amenable self.

'Shall we get a coffee?' he said without much enthusiasm as they stood in line outside an ATM.

'Do you want to?' she replied.

'Not bothered,' he said, 'just thought you might . . .'

'We haven't long had breakfast. And we've got lunch here,' she said, gesturing to their delicatessen bags.

This said it all, he thought. When things are out of shape, everything's awry, and we can't even breeze into Starbucks, get a coffee and a muffin and sit there for half an hour while we chat or share a read of the paper together. But it was no good trying to force relationship issues: when things were awkward, they were awkward, and no amount of trying to move them on would work. By tomorrow, it would all be different. 'Yes, sure,' he said. 'Let's get home.'

'I'm sorry,' she said again, and this time he did take her hand in his and smiled a forced smile.

As he folded into his wallet the fifty quid he'd withdrawn from the machine, there was a smash of glass just across the road from them and everyone on the pavement looked round. Someone in a black four-by-four had reversed into a parked Mercedes saloon. People watched as the owner of the damaged car emerged from the florist's on the corner carrying a big bunch of lilies and advanced on the driver of the Jeep that had done the damage.

'Come on,' said Salt, 'ignore it,' and tugged Kavanagh's hand. He took a few steps but voices were now being raised and the man with the flowers was delivering himself of a stream of expletives as he moved closer and closer to the Jeep driver's face.

Eventually, the man had had enough of the abuse and put his hand on the driver's throat and pushed him firmly away. The driver of the Mercedes dropped the lilies in the gutter, went to his car and reached into the footwell. Kavanagh knew only too well that he hadn't gone there for his insurance documents. He took his hand from Salt's, said, 'Won't be a second,' and ran across the road.

'Frank, just leave it,' she called to his back.

'Oi,' shouted Kavanagh, grabbing the man's arm and forcing him to drop the baseball bat he had clutched there. 'Just you take it easy, mate. It was an accident. I saw what happened. Now just calm down.'

'What the fuck's it to do with you?' said the man.

'Pol—' began Kavanagh at the very moment the man pulled himself free and swung a fist that glanced Kavanagh's ducking head.

'Oh, God,' cried Salt and ran to the scene, calling at the top of her voice, 'Police! Police! Stop that now,' as she punched the buttons on her phone and dialled 999.

The driver of the four-by-four had seen and heard enough and drove off at speed down the Broadway, the owner of the Mercedes shouting further abuse at him as he went.

SIX

Shropshire

At dinner at the Writers' Centre that evening, Romilly, the attractive young woman on Oliver's left, asked him, reasonably but directly, 'Do you like teaching these courses, Tom?'

The question was overfamiliar, and the use of his forename (even though he'd already made it clear that it was what he wanted the students to call him) disconcerted him. But the woman was so very young, and she had such an extraordinarily nice bosom, that Oliver merely glanced at her and smiled before answering.

The truthful answer would have been: 'Yes, if I could guarantee that there would be pretty women like you on them.'

And it's just possible that his candour might not have been unwelcome, and she might not have been displeased to hear it as an answer, but he didn't say it. For it was equally possible that she would have left the table and immediately reported him to the centre's director for inappropriate behaviour, or even sexual harassment for all he knew.

Of course, behind her question he imagined there was also the perfectly reasonable assumption that, rather than being here, he should, actually, be in his study, writing.

But no, it wasn't really – at least it wasn't very often really – the truth of the matter. Pilots flew aeroplanes; bricklayers buttered the bricks in the palms of their hands with sloppy mortar, but writers were only infrequently to be found sitting at their desks, writing.

Writing was time-consuming, usually poorly rewarded, and often difficult. No, the thing about writers was that most of the time they didn't write at all.

And people like himself, 'mid-listers', that arcane name given to the great swathe of anonymous authors, the writers who were the silent rump of it all, these people generally wrote only reluctantly, with resentment in their ink, and often with malice in their thoughts.

'Mid-list' writers were the invisibles, the *Unterme* of the literary world. They went uninterviewed and una ledged. No features about them in the Sunday broadsheets – their first car, their best friend, that embarrassing holiday romance, favourite restaurant, club or pair of shoes. The books pages of the papers weren't cluttered with reviews of their new titles, for this was space almost entirely reserved for notices about coming young things.

'Do I like teaching these courses?' repeated Oliver, still smiling, his head slightly inclined towards the young woman. 'Well, it's nice to get away from the word processor now and again. And, you know, it's important for a writer to keep in touch with the real world.'

There was no more truth in the answer than there would have been had he claimed he was a hip-hop DJ, but the words slipped out so effortlessly, and had been uttered so often as a pat response to desultory enquiries over the last few years, that it no longer even occurred to him that it was wholly without truth or foundation. It sounded plausible and made him sound a little bit more interesting – and interested in others – than otherwise might have been the case.

He was here because it was very much easier than being at home and trying to fashion a novel, something which became more difficult with every passing year.

And anyway, this was the countryside. It should, theoretically at least, be nice to be in the Shropshire hills for a few days, a place where shopkeepers often still said thank you, and sometimes even asked you how you were as they handed over your chocolate or cigarettes.

So why this abiding sense of unease, he wondered? It's true that it was about this time last year – he'd been tutoring a course here at the centre, and recalled the trees just beginning to turn, as now – that his six-month-long affair with Alice had entered its final death throes; a year or so before that he had broken up with illustrator Stella. A couple of years before that it had been Michelle. Or was it Lauren? Half-a-dozen years, just as many failed affairs.

The young woman sipped her wine and pressed a paper serviette to her lips. He picked up his glass and asked her solicitously, 'Does that answer your question, Romilly?'

'Yes,' she said, smiling warmly. 'It does, Tom. Thank you.'

SEVEN

'Just what do you think you're doing here?' said the woman.

Tom Oliver felt like a child being castigated by a teacher or an overbearing parent. He had got up early. It had been many years since he'd had what people called a 'good night's sleep'. But there must have been a time, surely. As a teenager, he must have stayed in bed till noon. Didn't everyone? Even with his mother beavering about the place, vacuuming or dusting. Jesus! What a suffocating lack of privacy that Willesden semi-detached had afforded them. No wonder that as an adult he'd become a man filled with secrets and confusion. Little wonder that he was a writer: the misery of it all was almost worth it for the solitude.

And if he didn't sleep well at home in his own divan, Oliver certainly wasn't going to sleep well away from home, no matter how comfortable the bed and quiet the room.

And here at the centre, in the middle of a black Shropshire night, yes, the room had been quiet, indeed. People had travelled long distances – one woman from Norway, another from the highlands of Scotland – and, being only the first night, there were no high jinx; the group didn't yet know one another well enough for that. People drank a glass or two of wine at supper, there had been the getting-to-know-you hour in the sitting room, the welcoming address and housekeeping information from Keira, and then the course briefing by Wooley and Oliver.

Given the last-minute drafting in of Catherine Wooley, Oliver imagined that any awkwardness that the students might perceive between the two writers they could reasonably attribute to them adjusting themselves to their new situation as an unexpectedly late-billed double act.

In fact, whilst Oliver had still been seething – he was not a man not to bear a grudge – 'Cath' infuriatingly seemed simply to have placed their unsavoury incident in her delete box. But now, seeing herself as the aggrieved party in the whole episode, Wooley appeared to have effortlessly segued into the role of magnanimous victim, something which, of course, might have been designed merely to even further infuriate Oliver.

No matter. Although inwardly incandescent at her Lady Bountiful persona, Oliver had maintained decorum and had been as good as his word to Keira. He appeared civil, occasionally smiled weakly, and even did some acquiescent head-nodding at her suggestions to the group for their initial poetry writing exercise.

By eleven-thirty that first night, then, everyone was in their rooms, and although he imagined very few people were asleep, all was quiet. Later in the week, once alliances and friendships had been formed, things would be different, of course. There would be more drink, trips to the pub, subsequent revelry and even the odd creaking board, perhaps, as this or that person slipped into another's room and bed for an hour or two.

Oliver had made a cup of instant coffee in his room, carried his walking boots downstairs and slipped out into the autumn morning.

He stood beside the old wooden handcart at the side of the door. Its iron-bound timber wheels had disintegrated long ago and been replaced with incongruous-looking cycle wheels, but the timber handles and top planks were original, worn smooth by a century of work on the estate. The final resting place for the thing, it was now home to a couple of compost bags full of nasturtiums. The watery stems looked frail and ready to break, but the few remaining flowers were vibrant in darkest red, startling orange, streaked yellow and gold.

The trees around the house were still, a grey-barked holly's dark green leaves bright with berries, the only sounds the croak of a pheasant, followed by its clattering flight away from imagined danger, and the crows' disputatious early morning tree-top greetings.

He walked a few steps further on and, through the line of alders in the distance, glimpsed the placid lake a hundred yards from the house, a shroud of mist lying on its surface.

He ambled away from the house and up the sandy track that snaked between the towering larch and pine. Half a mile up, instead of following the track around another bend, he climbed through a rough copse that took him down the other side of the hill. Ten minutes later he came upon a rickety fence with a single strand of rusted barbed wire hanging there with a drystone wall beyond it, much of which had fallen in heaps.

Gingerly, he negotiated the big stones and made his way into a clearing, and something man-made. These stones had been quarried and fashioned; there had once been some workings here, maybe even a rough dwelling. On the ground were a couple of sheets of corrugated iron, pitted and rusted and holed from years of lying there. Intrigued, he knelt down, pushed one of the jagged sheets aside and peered down into the darkness of an abandoned mine shaft.

'What exactly are you doing here?' said the woman again, this time even more forcefully.

He was shocked by her appearance. She must have been sixty-five, possibly even seventy, he reckoned, and although she was no more than five-feet three inches tall, her voice was determined, unwavering and strong. She carried a stout walking stick in her hand. Her dog, a border collie, stayed by her side but watched Oliver closely, its head hung low. 'What do you think you're doing here?' she repeated.

'I'm sorry,' offered Oliver, 'I'd no idea . . .'

'This is private land,' she said, cutting him short.

'Really?' he said, completely taken aback by the woman's aggressive manner.

'Are you from the centre?' she went on. But before hearing his reply she continued, 'Guests are expected to stay on the path. All of this land is private.'

'I'm sorry,' he said again, more to try to humour the woman than because he felt any contrition.

'You're at the centre?' she asked once more.

'Yes, I'm a tutor. Tom. Tom Oliver. And . . . yourself?' he ventured tentatively.

'I'm Margaret Osman,' she said.

'Really,' he said. 'Well, I'm pleased to meet you.'

The woman declined to reciprocate his civility.

'I'm sorry I strayed from the track,' he continued, eager to appease her. 'I'd really no idea.' In spite of herself, there was something engaging about the woman's irascible nature that the writer warmed to.

'Don't let it happen again,' she said. 'Sadie,' she said to the dog, and turned to leave.

'I suppose it's on account of your husband that I'm here at all,' he called to her departing back.

'No doubt,' she acknowledged, and walked away through the damp grass and foxgloves.

EIGHT

'Hi there, Tom. How are you today?' said Keira brightly as she rummaged amongst the cereal boxes in the cupboard above her.

'Keira,' acknowledged Oliver quietly, suggesting that her tone did not quite fit his mood. Just because he had undertaken to make the best of the difficult position that this woman's ineptitude had placed him in didn't mean that he did not feel it was his due to receive some continuing understanding of the situation.

'Are you OK?' she asked, sensing his prickliness. Frankly, the week's course now back on track, the students already going industriously about their business, the matter was, at least as far as she was concerned, resolved, and she'd all but dismissed it from her mind.

What, after all, were other people's travails? Think Auden and poor Icarus's fate. As the grizzled writer said about Brueghel's painting of the myth, who gives a toss about a boy falling into the drink? The folk on the 'delicate ship . . . Had somewhere to get to and sailed calmly on.'

Keira had her Polish cleaning girls to supervise, then Shirley the housekeeper to liaise with and finally gardener and odd-job man Leon to instruct. But more importantly, right now, she had her own breakfast to organize.

And anyway, Oliver was a writer, and writers, as she knew only too well, were often difficult. She spent her working life cosseting them, fulfilling their needs, and trying to make their time here at the centre run smoothly.

'Would you like some tea, Tom?' she asked.

'I'll make some coffee,' he said, reaching past her for the cafetière.

Through the open door in the big kitchen diner, Catherine and Lizbet, the Norwegian woman, were already breakfasting at the same time as poring over some of the Scandinavian's writing.

'Are you alright?' asked Keira again.

'I'm OK,' he said, like a doughty child who, after a grazing fall still feels entitled to a little more attention.

'Good,' she said, hoping to bring an end to it, but then fatally added, 'It's just that you seem a bit quiet this morning?'

'No, no, Lizbet,' came Catherine's husky voice from next door. 'Really, it's *so* very good . . . the metaphor of the waves there, it really works.'

Oliver winced. 'I just met Margaret Osman,' he said to Keira.

'Really?' she said, as bearded Neville and Jackie, a smartly dressed divorcee whom he had befriended, brought in their cereal bowls and coffee cups.

'Yes,' he continued, spooning coffee into the pot. 'In the woods.'

'Did she speak?' asked Keira directly.

'Sort of.'

Keira looked at him. 'Yes?'

'She berated me, actually,' he said.

Neville and the woman at his side looked across from where they were stacking plates in the dishwasher. 'Sounds interesting,' said the man, feeling that his intrusion was better than continuing to feign deafness whilst only a few feet away from the writer.

'Well, that's something; she often doesn't speak at all,' continued Keira.

'Really?' said Oliver.

'Yes, she'll pass people on the track and not say a word. Maybe she's wrapped up in her work,' she added.

'What work's that?' he asked.

'She's a sculptor,' said Keira. 'It's how she and Richard first met. She was commissioned to do the bronze of him. You know, in the vestibule?'

'No,' he said. 'What bronze?'

The other woman put a couple of slices of bread in the toaster.

Keira went through to the hall and came back a moment later with a bronze statuette in her hand. At only seven or eight inches high, Richard Osman's features were immediately recognizable as those of the fiery 1970s' playwright.

Oliver held the piece from him as the tutees, by now feeling included by proxy, also came over to examine it.

'I didn't know that she was an artist, too,' said Oliver, handing the statuette to the woman.

'So, what did she say to you?' asked Keira. 'You say she told you off?'

'I'd wandered into a copse at the top of the hill. There's some old mine workings there. A shaft and a fallen building.'

'Yes, I know the place,' said Keira. 'I think they explored it for lead or something years ago.'

'Anyway, she told me in no uncertain terms that I shouldn't be there. That I should stick to the path. I couldn't see that I was doing any harm,' he added defensively.

'Of course not,' she agreed.

'What about the old man?' asked Neville as the toast popped up.

'Richard?' said Keira.

'Yes, I haven't heard anything about him for ages. Wasn't he in poor health? Or is he . . .?' he began tentatively.

'No, he's still alive,' she said. 'He had a stroke about four years ago, before this place was signed over to the trust. It was his home, before he and Margaret were married,' she added.

'And now?' said the man.

'She does everything for him. There'll never be any improvement, apparently.' She lowered her voice. 'It's really just a matter of time.'

The woman smiled sympathetically and patted the statuette on the head. She placed it on the work surface and began to butter the toast.

Oliver took his coffee into the breakfast room and said a stiff 'Good morning' to Catherine, who was cradling a mug of something in both her hands, her big, pink-framed spectacles pushed up onto her forehead. He smiled at young Romilly, but took a seat near the window with two of the men on the course. Malcolm was halfway through a creative-writing MA at Keele University, and at six-feet four and with a thirty-two-inch waist looked more like a basketball player than a writer, or at least any of the shuffling, overweight writers that Tom Oliver tended to meet.

Terry, a tax inspector, originally from Cork, but now living in west London, had told everyone present the previous evening that he had written four unpublished novels and that his writing was the only thing that kept him sane, given his 'soul-destroying' job.

Even in a painfully self-conscious, first-night, mini-biography, Oliver had winced at the cliché, but the Irishman's self-deprecating manner meant that Oliver felt unthreatened by him – his essential criterion for liking anyone – and the writer had warmed to him.

At just before nine, Catherine got to her feet, drained the fruit tea in her mug and announced brightly, 'Right, hey ho, it's off to work we go.' She gathered her folders, a couple of slim volumes of her poetry, and headed off to the study space in the converted barn a short way from the main building. The rest of the group, carrying coffee cups, water bottles, A4 pads and laptops, followed in her wake. Romilly, the last person to leave the room, gave Oliver a fleeting smile as she did so.

At lunch, a buffet affair that Keira laid out just after noon, there were plates of cold ham and chicken, pickles and locally made chutneys, hummus, tuna, fresh breads, salad and fruits.

Oliver had already come down from his room a couple of times, but there had been no-one around and, keen to foster the impression that his own morning had been every bit as industrious as theirs, he had slunk back upstairs until he heard a gaggle of them arriving in the kitchen.

He was relieved to note that the mood amongst those who wandered around the tables and filled their plates – acknowledging him in the most desultory way as if, as a non-team-player in this morning's exercise he had already, for the time being at least, been sidelined – did not seem particularly energized. Neither could he detect signs of grumbling dissatisfaction, he admitted, the sort of disquiet that would have made his day, but people were certainly not looking brimful with excitement about whatever rhymes their poet mentor had been encouraging them to conjure during the previous two hours.

Folk filled their plates and sat around the table. A couple of them took chairs outside into the early afternoon sun. Keira and Oliver sat together on the stone steps that led down to the barn. The only person still working was the gardener. Dressed in combat trousers, a dark tee shirt and boots, the young man was forking up the last of the annuals from the border in front of the house. He wore his dark hair long and had the ruddy complexion of someone who spent a lot of his time out of doors. 'Are you going to have something, Leon?' called Keira.

'Yes, just finish this,' he said as he dropped another clump of wilting border flowers onto the barrow at his side with a pleasing thud.

Afternoons were given over to one-to-one tutorials, individual writing or reading and walking 'for inspiration' – the latter phrase printed in the course brochure without either exclamation marks or inverted commas.

Oliver had already been left samples of the work of two students to read prior to their thirty-minute meetings with him later that afternoon. He had learned early on in his work as a writing tutor that the cardinal rule was always to restrict the amount of writing that you allowed anyone to submit. Like salt in the soup, you could always ask for a little more, but not the contrary.

In the little cardboard box that passed for his in-tray at the foot of the stairs were a short story by Romilly and the opening chapters of Neville's science-fiction novel.

Giving Tom Oliver a science-fiction novel to read was a complete waste of time and he knew that he would have no choice but to confess to its hirsute author that he'd never had any idea what the genre was either for or about. And anyway, rather more worryingly, on account of his deep antipathy to this type of book, he knew very well that he wouldn't recognize a best-seller even if it had fallen on his head.

Notwithstanding Oliver's instructions that only one chapter should be submitted for initial reading, Neville had left not five pages, but five *chapters* of his science-fiction trilogy. Oliver had spent fifteen minutes before lunch reading some of the words there with total incomprehension, but compared with this complete bafflement, the subsequent tutorial proved to be a painless affair.

He willed himself to pay attention to what was being said by Neville, whose nasal hair moved worryingly whenever he exhaled, but his resolve proved fruitless. Listening to the man's drone was like hearing someone else's dreams or, perhaps even a little worse, trying to feign interest in a complete stranger's horoscope for the coming week.

Oliver was no genius, but nor was he a completely stupid person. No matter, after ten minutes' dogged concentration, he was still without the slightest idea what Neville was talking about and, unable to maintain this level of rigour, he decided to stop listening to the man's actual words and merely follow his intonations.

Thus guided by the rhythms of his speech, Oliver inter-jected whenever he felt that it might be appropriate. He offered a 'Yes' or a 'Right' or even, occasionally, an expansive 'Yes, right' and these sympathetic interjections seemed to give Neville all the encouragement he needed to continue his monotone delivery.

After twenty minutes of this Neville closed his folder and the men nodded sagely at one another for several seconds. Oliver then pursed his lips and said, again, nodding his head, but this time also opening his hands in supplication, 'What can I say, Neville? What can I say?'

Without another word, the man got to his feet and shook Oliver by the hand just as firmly as he had done when they had first met the previous evening. And although he might just as well have been speaking Mandarin for the previous half hour for all that Oliver had discerned any meaning from his words, Neville appeared perfectly satisfied as he left the room.

NINE

Oliver stood at the sitting-room window and watched the ripples on the surface of the lake a hundred yards away as the Polish cleaning girls stood on the jetty, wisps of smoke rising from their cigarettes.

There was a tap on the door.

Oliver had never had difficulty dealing with those people he disliked or was indifferent to. No, the people who made him self-conscious, tongue-tied and maladroit were people he either admired or coveted. And in spite of the several decades that separated them, Romilly fell into both categories.

If science-fiction writer Neville's work had been incomprehensible, Romilly's was only too clearly that of an extraordinarily talented young writer. Oliver had read her short story with a pencil in his hand, ready to mark with arrows and asterisks his suggestions for cutting or rearranging words and phrases. But no, this woman's voice was naive yet knowing, her prose lean and spare with nary a redundant word, and Oliver read her work with the poignant combination of sadness and resentment that he always felt when confronted with exemplary writing, irrespective of its source. His pencil remained in his hand, and not once did he mark those pages.

'Come in, Romilly,' he said, using her name merely for the pleasure of hearing it on his lips. 'Please, have a seat.'

He sat back in the armchair adjacent to her, stretched out his legs and crossed his ankles as he tried to look relaxed, but the posture felt absurd.

He'd conducted tutorials such as this many times before, but here, right now, he felt disabled by Romilly's very presence.

Of course, he knew from his experience of doing this sort of thing that a role is everything: if he had passed this attractive young woman in the supermarket aisle, she would not even have looked up from her trolley.

Now, she was not only here to listen to his every word but, with pen in hand and pad on her lap, she was even preparing to jot a few of those words down.

Taking heart from her attentive demeanour, he cleared his throat behind his hand as he prepared to try to say something – anything at all – which might justify her diligence. He sat forward and leaned over her work. 'I think it's a wonderful story, Romilly. It's so well written.'

'Thank you,' she said, glancing up and briefly meeting his look. 'Do you really think so?'

'Really,' he said. 'I do, and it's always difficult – well, it doesn't happen very often, of course – but the better a writer's work, the less there is for me to say really, do you see?'

'Of course,' she agreed, looking away and feeling embarrassed at both his praise and the fleeting look that was again exchanged between them.

'Maybe an ellipsis here, rather than those two words?' and he pointed to a paragraph on the page that lay between them.

She leaned forward and, as she looked at the text, he inhaled the scent of her skin. 'Yes,' she acquiesced.

'And the opening is so good with this apostrophe. It's arresting, which is what the reader wants, of course . . .'

How much he yearned to incline another foot towards her and lift the hair from the nape of her neck and lay the back of his fingers on that smooth, dark skin.

She'd told the group the previous evening, in an unassuming voice, that she was a trainee on a financial magazine and had a degree in journalism. Judged on any normal scale, he knew already that she was much more innately intelligent than he. But whilst the work of a writer might be a complete mystery and of no interest whatsoever to ninety-nine per cent of the population, to the remaining one per cent, writers were people to whom normal judgements did not apply. Right now, at this place and time, the little stack of some of the books that he had written during the last ten years or so beside them, it was he who had the imprimatur of office.

The book on top of the pile, *Getting it Write*, with its awful punning title, the one about the business of actually being a writer, had not been a best-seller, of course, but it had limped along, and had even been reprinted.

And it was on account of this book, he suspected, that this very course was fully subscribed.

Having exhausted every avenue of comment surrounding Romilly's short story, he leaned back in his chair once more and tried to appear relaxed. He considered asking her to read him a page so that he could more fully appreciate the story's movement, a shameless ploy that would have allowed him the secret pleasure of watching her, but he decided against it, fearing she might see through his wish to observe her in this way.

'Do you have any plans?' he asked, a deliberately open-ended question which was calculated to be vague enough to allow her to reveal something, anything, about her personal life: perhaps the man in whose arms she lay at night, the person with whom she sat and watched TV, even the person who kissed those lips.

'Plans?' she said. 'Work, do you mean? Or my writing?'

'Well, for me, of course,' he said, 'it's all one and the same. Are you thinking of a career in journalism, or do you want to be a writer?' And, before she had a chance to answer, he added, 'I'm sure you know how tough getting published can be, even for someone as talented as yourself . . .'

'I'd never thought of my writing as a career,' she said.

'Your voice is so . . . particular . . . so distinctive, it would be a shame not to use it,' he interrupted.

'I've been writing since I was in the sixth form. I have to. I can't really stop myself,' she added, aware of the naked force of the comment and its overtones of an almost sexual impetus.

'It's like that for most real writers,' he added, including her in this coterie group.

'You think I could be a writer?' she asked and glanced up at him but looked away as soon as their eyes met.

Oliver thought of the writers he'd met who didn't have a quarter of this woman's talent, the dozens that he'd 'taught' at places like this – even a few at week-long schools in sunny foreign spots – who had the absolute conviction that they, too, would one day join the ranks of the published, no matter how utterly bereft of ability they were. 'Yes, I do, Romilly,' he said.

'That's very nice of you to say,' she said, unable now to quite use his forename in what was, after all – in spite of her obvious sense that something else entirely was going on between them – a teacher/pupil situation.

There was a protracted silence.

He eventually stood up and said with hollow resolve, 'Well, I guess that's us done . . .'

He would have liked to have said, 'Would you like to go
for a walk down the lane?' or, perhaps, 'Shall we get married,
Romilly, you absolutely divine young woman? Ignore entirely
your youth and beauty, and my sour, vindictive nature and all
of the years that separate us.'

'Thank you,' she murmured. 'It's been really useful.' They
stood awkwardly together a moment longer. Maybe she didn't
want to go? Maybe she, too, had seen the absurd possibility
of something beyond the embittered, misanthropic man?

'I really enjoyed *Get it Write*,' she added, gesturing to the
book on the sofa.

'Really?' he said, even forgiving her mangling of the title,
a crime which, in any other circumstances, he would have
punished with contempt. 'Thank you.' He extended his hand.
She put her fingers on his for a second and said, 'Goodbye,
Tom. Thank you so much.'

TEN

London

'Inspector?'

'Sir?' said Kavanagh.

'Could we have a word, please? My office. In about ten minutes.'

'Of course,' said Kavanagh and continued to write up the report on the unfortunate bit of business down at Crouch End the previous weekend.

'Come in, come in,' said ACC Hyland in his customary manner and with his penchant for repeating things, a verbal tic that his subordinates often privately mocked, but which none of his advisers at Scotland Yard had yet felt able to share with him.

'Kavanagh, slight problem . . .'

'Yes, sir?' said the inspector. 'What's that?'

'The incident at the weekend . . .'

'Yes?' said Kavanagh.

'The man's making a complaint . . .'

'A complaint?' said Kavanagh, surprised. 'What do you mean? Who against?'

'Against you, of course, Frank.'

'I'm sorry, sir? I stepped in to defuse what was looking like something that was going to turn ugly. It was a Saturday morning and there were shoppers and families around and, I might add, dozens of witnesses . . .'

'Yes, I know Frank. You did the right thing and you did what any decent copper would have done.'

'Quite,' said Kavanagh. 'So what's the problem?'

'Unfortunately the man's claiming you didn't identify yourself. No uniform, not even a cap or a badge . . .'

'We were out shopping, sir. It was a Saturday morning and we'd just come from the cash machine. Of course I wasn't in uniform; I wasn't even on duty.'

'Warrant card?' said the ACC.

'The guy was about to set about the other fella with a base-ball bat, sir. There was no time for anything but to restrain him. You'll remember, if you look at the side of my face here, I very nearly stopped a full fist for my trouble. I should be bringing a charge against *him*.'

'Of course. I know, Frank. Trouble is, his point, and his solicitor's take on the situation, is that he swung out on account of him thinking you were a member of the public getting involved, and so he's claiming self-defence against you attacking him.'

'I identified myself as soon as I could. Salt did, too. I followed the book.'

'Of course you did, Frank, and of course it'll be cleared up in no time, but you know how it is. Right now it's open season since the Stockwell tube incident, and . . .'

'And what?' said the inspector.

'The fact is, Frank, I don't think this is the best time for you to be taking any leave . . .'

'A week?' said Kavanagh. 'What difference will that make?'

'Not even a week,' said Hyland. 'It'll be dealt with quickly, but it's no time for you not to be around to answer whatever comes up. And, more to the point, if you take leave and the press get hold of it, it'll go one of two ways, and both of them are bad. You – and that means me in this situation – don't care, and are just buggering off somewhere on holiday, or you've something to hide and you're lying low.'

'This is absolutely absurd,' said Kavanagh.

'I couldn't agree more, Frank. It's ridiculous. But we live in crazy times, we both know that, and so, if you don't mind, for all of our sakes, delay your leave for a few days until it's been sorted out. The complaint's minor and unsubstantiated so, for the time being, I see no reason for you not to continue with normal duties.' And, before Kavanagh could respond, Hyland added, 'That'll be all, Inspector. Thank you very much.'

Kavanagh left the ACC's room, stood in the corridor outside and said, 'Bollocks.'

Hyland emerged only seconds after him. 'Frank?'

'Sir?' said Kavanagh, hoping his boss, admittedly rather out of character, was going to say it was some sort of wind-up and call after him, 'Have a nice holiday,' but he did nothing of the sort.

'Frank, I meant to say, you're aware that DS Soames is in hospital for tests?'

'Of course,' said the inspector. 'We share an office, sir.'

'Well,' said Hyland, ignoring the sarcasm, 'things aren't looking terribly good for John. Susan, his wife, phoned. They want to keep him in for a few days. It shouldn't be for long but they're not happy, apparently; something to do with his chest . . . So, if anything urgent comes across Soames' desk, will you make sure it gets dealt with promptly? Many thanks.' And with that he turned back into his office.

ELEVEN

Shropshire

The following morning, it was Tom Oliver's turn to troop down to the barn where he would conduct the first of his novel-writing workshops but where, in fact, his priority was simply to outshine anything that Catherine Wooley had done the previous day.

He'd slept badly and had fitful dreams about Romilly. Whereas initially he'd been entranced solely by the young woman's beauty, a day later he'd found himself beguiled by her exceptional work. And now, he was in a stupor of excitable infatuation, a state made more risible by the fact that all of this had happened in a mere thirty-six hours.

Unfortunately, the feelings that he was experiencing were by no means unfamiliar: Oliver knew only too well the lovesick symptoms of obsessive longing, a state of being he found so conducive that he almost sought it. More often than not, of course, these love suits ended in woe and lamentation but, occasionally, and always to his complete surprise, he had just enough success to keep him pursuing relationship dreams.

And whilst mere common sense suggested that many of the more attractive women in the world were already spoken for, Oliver's experience had repeatedly taught him that men are extremely foolish creatures and, even when blessed with a companion who is pretty, intelligent, insightful and caring, he will continue to roam the prairies, restaurants and bars of the world as, still not content, he seeks yet another mate.

This being so, there is always a pool of recently discarded, but perfectly nice and often kindly women to be found on those very same prairies, in those same restaurants and bars.

Down in the high-ceilinged barn with its huge roof trusses, Oliver set the writers an exercise and – like hounds in pursuit of a fox – they trailed it with gusto.

He watched surreptitiously as Romilly set to work, but left

undisturbed he too was soon lulled into that reverie of compo-
sition that he knew so well. In spite of everything, in spite of
his cynicism and the daily disappointments, it was still Tom
Oliver's favourite place to be.

And he knew from experience that if he appeared to be
engaged in his work, fiddling with this chapter or planning
that, his students' pens would also scrawl across their pads,
their fingers tap their laptop keys.

He had given them half an hour to come up with a page
of narrative, involving at least two characters, one of whom
must be deaf, and after twenty minutes they were still toiling
away.

Instead of calling them from around the barn back to their
desks, Oliver watched as the sun slanted through the tall,
arched windows. He felt a sort of benign indulgence as, heads
bowed with concentration, almost everyone scribbled away.

Romilly had tucked one of her legs up onto her chair underneath her thigh, and he gazed at her with absolute longing.
At that very moment she glanced up from her work and caught
his look. Oliver felt almost blessed as she smiled warmly and
then turned back to her work and began writing once more.

After lunch Oliver made his way down to the sitting room to
give feedback to six-feet-four MA student Malcolm, who was
already sprawled in the armchair there.

Stoke-born Malcolm was not only doing a full-time MA in
creative writing, but had visited more writing centres and read
more books about the writing and publishing business than
Oliver had any idea actually existed. The man seemed to feel
that if he acquired enough travel stamps in the equivalent of
his writing passport he would, like one of those football fans
of yesteryear who used to collect badges from every away
ground to which they had followed their team, simply by a
sort of osmosis, somehow acquire the skills of a novelist.

But the portents for Malcolm's career as a scribbler were
not good.

He'd attached a Post-it to the front cover of his story, which
was itself enclosed in an opaque plastic wallet (the sort of
thing favoured by earnest but generally low-achieving school-
girls for their home-economics coursework assignments), and
written on the little pink square of adhesive paper there, in a

hand so tiny that Oliver had to reach for his travelling magnifying glass as well as his spectacles to read it: 'I hope you won't be too offended by the enclosed, Malcolm.'

In fact, the story didn't offend Oliver at all. Yes, it was filthy, but it was neither bestial nor paedophiliac filth, and Oliver doubted that it would have made it into the pages of either *Fiesta* or *Readers' Wives* back in the 1970s, the last period during which he had occasionally subscribed to those publications.

'I hope you didn't find it too . . .' began the quietly spoken Malcolm.

'Not at all,' said Oliver gamely. 'The thing is, Malcolm, as writers, our first duty to our readers is to be honest, no matter what the cost to ourselves.'

The thing he would have wished to say but didn't was that it was clear from the facts of his story that Malcolm might conceivably, with a good deal of further study, one day make a gynaecologist, but that he would surely never write a publishable book.

'It's not easy, Malcolm, of course, but we have to write from the heart and not be afraid what any other person looking over our shoulder might feel about what it is we're doing, even if that person is . . . our own mother.'

Malcolm nodded his agreement.

'Unless, of course,' continued Oliver, thinking this might be an opportunity to establish his familiarity with postmodernism, something with which Malcolm was sure to be on rather more than his own very shaky terms, 'unless we are writing a book in which our mother, herself . . .'

'Yes?' urged Malcolm, intrigued.

'Unless our mother,' reprised Oliver, 'is observing those events, and possibly even commenting on them, and that commentary happens to be the very point of the book . . .'

'Yes, of course,' said Malcolm earnestly, making notes in tiny handwriting with his slender fingers as Oliver spoke.

'Yes, it's good stuff,' said Oliver with a conspiratorial flourish. 'And you know, I don't mean to be crass but, between ourselves –' and here he lowered his voice to a whisper – 'as men, and as writers, a little knowledge of the market is no bad thing. Sex sells. Always has done. It's a cliché, we know, but it's true. Just look at the ads.'

'Absolutely,' said Malcolm, extending his huge hand. 'And you think I'm on to something here?'

'Think?' said Oliver, as his own hand was enveloped. And then he said again, 'Think?'

TWELVE

That Wednesday evening, a writer of something called 'crossover' fiction was booked as the midweek guest reader. Oliver had heard the term but dismissed it as yet another twenty-first-century publishing ploy. Apart from the inauspicious notion of Simon Jackson writing crossover fiction (his books were apparently written to appeal to both teenagers and adults, the titles published with two different covers to appeal to both markets), Oliver had never heard of either the man or his gimmicky books.

Just before supper, Keira introduced Jackson to the group. Oliver, as the undisputed senior partner, as it were, greeted the man with a brief handshake and a token civility and then took a seat as far away from him as possible.

As Jackson chatted to Keira, Oliver made witty and knowing remarks to the cluster of folk down at his end of the dining table, remarks and witticisms designed entirely to appeal to the sensibility of Romilly who sat only a couple of places from him.

Whilst there were no wholly accepted modes of dress for male writers, there were some generally recognized parameters, but Simon Jackson was clearly wholly unaware of the conventions, turning up, as he had, in a crumpled dark suit and an unironed striped shirt, the top button of which was actually fastened.

After dinner, the entire group wandered down to the barn, wine glasses in hand, a couple of them stopping en route for a quick cigarette outside.

'We're delighted to have Simon with us this evening,' began Keira, even as the straggling smokers took their seats. 'His work may not be as familiar to some of you as it might be . . .'

You bet, thought Oliver.

'. . . but I think you'll enjoy his original and very distinctive brand of fiction . . .'

Oliver raised an eyebrow and exchanged a quick smile with his adversary Catherine across the other side of the room.

'. . . fiction that's finding an ever-growing market, not only with teenage boys, that group of readers who writers always find most difficult to reach . . .'

'And why should we even try?' murmured Oliver.

'. . . but with growing numbers of adults, too, readers who savour the integrity of his storytelling.'

Oliver sighed heavily and then immediately covered his mouth in a fake yawn, raising his other hand in apology as Jackson glanced at him.

'Thank you. Over to you, Simon,' ended Keira, and there was a round of polite applause.

Without a by-your-leave or any of the usual falsely modest introductions; with no account whatsoever of his crap schooling, constantly bickering parents, or long childhood illness that had left the poor mite bedridden and with little to do but access his imagination, Jackson began to mumble, almost inaudibly, in a thick Yorkshire accent.

'I'll just read you a bit from the new one,' he said into his chest, and without mentioning the title of the book in his hand, nor showing the cover; without any introduction to any of the characters nor a context for the extract, he began to read.

Oliver settled himself back in the easy chair and smiled indulgently as he looked at the shambling forty-year-old there. It had taken him years to acquire the skills required to give a decent reading and Oliver warmed to Jackson as he resolved right there and then to use his performance as an object lesson in exactly how not to do it.

But almost immediately, the atmosphere in the room changed. Yes, the man was still muttering quietly into the top of his shirt, but the audience had started to listen carefully to what he was saying. First one person, then another, put down their half-filled glasses and actually leaned forward. The man's prose was dry and tight and undercut with humorous asides, asides which Oliver willed not to be funny, but there was no gainsaying it: people were smiling. Not himself, of course, but there were ripples of amusement around the entire room. The clearing of throats had stopped, and the man's determinedly undemonstrative voice now permeated the place.

Jackson wasn't working the crowd; the words he'd written were doing the work for him. Oliver again looked across to Catherine Wooley seeking the solace of a temporary suspension of antipathies but saw on the winsome poet's face only a look of entranced admiration.

He glanced across at Romilly in the forlorn hope that she alone might be resisting Jackson's prosy charm. But she too was similarly engaged with the man's reading and, much more alarming for Oliver, she had quietly left her place on the sofa and was now sitting to one side of Malcolm's long legs on the floor. And worse – much worse for Oliver even than hearing Jackson's apparently effortless prose – the lanky MA's hand was resting lightly upon her bare shoulder.

Oliver wanted to get to his feet, cry, 'Foul,' and protest that there had been some kind of mistake. This was wrong. The man was an (inept) pornographer, a literary retard. Romilly was clever, gifted and beautiful, and Oliver had felt certain that she was warming to him, and with that warmth, as everyone in the world knew, there was always the chance of being reborn amidst the possibilities that a new relationship offers, no matter how remote that possibility.

Jackson stopped reading with no more ceremony than he had begun and there was spontaneous applause and even a muffled shout of approval from someone in the staid group. Oliver was ashen-faced.

Jackson read three more very short passages and then asked if anyone wanted to ask him anything. Oliver had done the same thing fifty times himself but had often had to prompt someone in the audience to venture a question.

Several hands immediately went up, and he answered half-a-dozen questions, one after the other, effortlessly weaving in a little story here, an anecdote there, in not one of which was he himself the centre of attention.

Eventually, at half past ten, half an hour beyond his allotted time, Keira said that she would have to bring things to a close, but that if anyone wanted to buy one of his books, she felt sure that he would be pleased to sign them. She finished her vote of thanks and then in a sombre voice added, 'Simon asked me to say nothing about this, but I would like you to know that he's waived his fee for this evening and asked that it be donated to Save the Children.'

'You *bastard*,' murmured Oliver with feeling. 'You absolute bastard.' And the room erupted in further applause.

Catherine smiled and clapped along with the others.

No sooner had the applause subsided than there was a clamour around the man and the table at his side upon which he had (discreetly) displayed copies of his most recent book. Some people were buying two copies at a time. In the previous three days here, Oliver had sold one out-of-print novel and two discounted paperback copies of *Getting it Write*.

'Oh, God,' he groaned.

THIRTEEN

Something extraordinary was happening. As far as Tom Oliver was concerned, there was something patently absurd about Romilly Thorne's involvement with lanky Malcolm. The man was coming on to her. That was fair enough, maybe. But the beautiful young woman, unless Oliver was mistaken – and he rarely was mistaken when the driver of his thoughts was jealousy and rejection – was responding to him with warmth.

Oliver had hoped that, against all odds, he had been succeeding in ingratiating himself with her. Of course it was possible – likely, even – that he would not have been able to draw her into his own sticky web and that at the end of this week she would have melted away back to her London life and he to his, never for them to speak again. But that this towering man should beguile her was absurd. It simply could not be happening.

Why hadn't he lambasted the man's neo-pornography for what it was when he had had the opportunity? He'd crushed writers before, people whose aspirations irked him, or whose work offended his sensibility. Why hadn't he done it to this man? Ironically, he suspected it had been his own infatuation with the young woman that had made him much more charitable than his usual self. And this was his reward. The quietly spoken Midlander now filled Romilly's landscape and had swiped him entirely out of the picture.

Oliver barely slept all night as he imagined floorboards creaking, doors quietly closing and bed springs moving to the rhythm of bodies yoked together.

The following morning he scowled past the barn where he could hear the students engaged in their final poetry 'jamming' workshop with Catherine (she had brought her tabla with her) and sloped off up into the woods in a bitter frame of mind.

In the afternoon, he held the last of his one-to-one tutorials with Ruth, a Cornish woman who had left him the first chapter of her crime novel to 'peruse'.

He had a duty to be civil to the woman. It wasn't, after all, her fault that he had become smitten with an unobtainable young woman, and then had his nose put out of joint by the previous evening's guest writer.

'Ruth, come in, have a seat,' he said, almost relieved to be in the company of someone who, although clearly female, and blessed with a very large bosom, was of absolutely no sexual interest to him whatsoever. 'Your novel outline,' he immediately began. 'It's really interesting—'

'Interesting?' interrupted the woman a mite tetchily, justifiably wary of the pejorative nature of the word.

'Yes, interesting,' he said, 'but I think it has a good deal to recommend it,' he went on more reassuringly.

'Good,' she said, having negotiated the concession, and settled back on the sofa, her bosom swaying to a halt some little time after the rest of her ample body.

'The only thing is,' he added thoughtfully, 'the only thing that occurs to me is . . .'

'Yes?' she said, sitting forward and craning her neck to look at her own work.

'Is this an area with which you are . . . familiar? Do you read much crime?'

'I don't really like it, as such,' she averred, 'but I do know that it's one of the biggest-selling genres in literature, and so I thought, well, if I'm going to write in any area, it might as well be this one.'

'I see,' he said.

'Actually,' she continued, 'it was John – my husband – who suggested it, so I mustn't really claim the credit. John works with figures and he thought that if I wanted to increase my chances of success it would obviously be best to write in the most popular area. And also, I don't know if you know this, Mr Oliver . . .'

'Yes?' he asked, intrigued as to what the woman was possibly going to share with him. 'Please?'

'Crime readers, apparently, are very loyal. Once they have started to read your work, and have got involved with your characters, they tend to stay with them and so you have a more or less guaranteed future readership . . .'

'Yes, I believe that is so,' concurred Oliver. 'Anyway, as I say, I think that your work is very . . . engaging, but I'm just a bit concerned that some of the language and, you know, the sorts of crimes, and the people who commit and investigate them these days, I wondered whether you might do a little research? Do you ever watch *Crimewatch* or see current films?' he asked soberly.

'*Crimewatch* would give me nightmares,' she said. 'And we don't go to the cinema any more. It's all bad language. There's no need for it whatsoever. It's just laziness, an excuse for not finding the best word . . .'

'Really?' he said. 'And what if the best word is a swear word?' he asked.

'If the best word is a swear word, the writer must have a limited vocabulary,' she responded gamely.

'But what if the swear word is the very word that that character might use in that situation?' he pursued obstinately, ready to swear at the woman himself.

'Then I would change the situation,' she said.

There was a stand-off, a moment's silence. 'Have you read any of my books?' he asked slyly, knowing that their exchange was now irretrievably doomed.

'I did try one,' she responded hesitantly.

'And?' he asked, almost certainly ready to kill her there and then in the sitting room if she dared to so much as traduce his work.

'I . . . I . . .' she stuttered, recognizing somehow that the exchange could lead to her immediate demise. 'I think it had to be back at the library, before I could finish it,' she said.

'A library copy,' he sneered. A few seconds later he said, 'Gosh, is that the time, Ruth? You must excuse me, but I have another appointment.' And with that he got to his feet.

'The sub-plot?' she ventured, resolutely sitting there and refusing to leave.

'Yes, you need one,' he said.

'Another one?' she said, both deflated and surprised.

'Another one would be good,' he agreed, with no idea whatsoever what she was talking about. 'Yes, another one would be very good.'

She made the slightest shuffling movement on the sofa, which he took as a sign that he could finally escape and walked towards the door. 'I'll see you at supper,' he said and strode away down the hall.

As he turned towards the stairs to his room, bearded Neville intercepted him and said solicitously, 'Tom, do you have a moment, please?'

'No,' said Oliver, and walked up the stairs.

FOURTEEN

Following Simon Jackson's sell-out performance on Wednesday evening, Oliver now approached Friday with considerable foreboding. What should have been the apotheosis of his week – a chance to shine with a triumphant reading from his latest work – had been usurped by the mumbling Yorkshireman.

Catherine Wooley might have nurtured few illusions about her standing as a contemporary poet but Oliver still cherished an unshakeable belief that any critical acclaim that he lacked was solely on account of a reading public who lacked the wit and intelligence to recognize his writing for the thing of beauty that, in his view, it clearly was.

And whilst he knew it was not a good idea to make important decisions at times of stress and difficulty, he also knew he had only a very short time to wrest back the initiative that he had so clearly lost. He decided that he would storm the citadel. He would give the reading of his life, and not from just another of his campus novels, but from his work in progress, never uttered before in public, *How Not to Get Hurt in Love*.

After supper, as they took their seats in the barn, Romilly gave him what might have been construed as the apology of a smile. Was it possible that with that one quick parting of those lovely full lips she could be saying quite as many things as he imagined? That she was sorry to have left the possibility of their relationship a wholly undiscovered country? That she was even sorrier that she had hurt him greatly by taking up with the six-foot-four pornographer, Malcolm, before his very eyes? And that, yes, she loved his work and valued immensely his perceptive admiration and encouragement of hers?

Possibly not. But it's what he had to content himself with.

Wooley and Oliver sat awkwardly at the front of the room feeling as if they might be about to be humiliated, pelted with fruit and eggs, or even shot. Keira thanked them for the 'fantastic week' that they had been responsible for, thanked the group for being one of the best that they had ever had at the centre, and thanked the Polish cleaning girls, Ilona and Renata, for all their hard work, and gardener Leon (sitting at the back of the room) for his. Plenty of wine had been drunk at supper and there was some drink-induced applause.

Catherine began. She chose several poems from her soon-to-be-published selection and read them with the sort of voice that has successfully turned ninety-seven per cent of the population off poetry for the last five hundred years. The conclusion of each reading was greeted with an awkward silence followed by a little half-hearted clapping.

Half an hour later, and with two of the fifteen people in the room by now apparently asleep, it was Oliver's turn.

He'd been working on what he coyly referred to as his 'relationship book' for the previous ten years and, as he well knew, the manuscript was little more than an autobiography. Trouble was, these days no publisher was going to be interested in the autobiography of a writer that most of the population had never even heard of. To get a publishing deal you had to be a footballer with a drink problem, a haughty model from a council estate who'd been 'discovered' in a shopping mall and grown into a coke-using monster, or a particularly unsavoury politician.

But he remained convinced that his 'relationship' book – no more or less than the story of the women with whom he'd had affairs during the dozen years since his last marriage had collapsed – would, given the chance, find a market.

Oliver craved the indulgence of his audience and asked them (always a good ruse) if they would tell him 'honestly' whether they, as writers themselves, thought there might be a book in this work in progress.

But of course, the real point of the reading was not merely to ingratiate himself anew with the group as the perceptive writer that he was, but to demonstrate unequivocally to Romilly that she should be feeling some pangs of regret that she had chosen to realign her affections.

'The book's written in diary form,' he began, 'a stream-of-consciousness account of one man's relationship life.'

He read a couple of short extracts to set the insightful,

comic tone that he had aspired to, but there was little reaction and no laughter at all inside the room.

After twenty minutes, and with a growing sense of desperation at the lack of any sort of response to his prose except for some fidgeting, yawning and muttered exchanges that he tried in vain to ignore, he eventually said with an attempted flourish, 'Right, here we go with a final extract taken from near the end of the book . . .' He started to recount his pièce de resistance, his witty account of the brief, sexual affair he'd had with a pretty but wholly unsuitable Indonesian dental nurse who he had met through a dating agency. But only half a page into the story, his mouth drying with every sentence, he glanced up to see faces that registered nothing but bemusement. He hurried on.

'We were never really suited,' he read aloud. 'She had entered under the column marked "Reading: *Daily Express*".' He paused for laughter. None came. The words on the page began to swim and blur before him. 'Eventually we chatted on the phone, but the only topic of shared conversation was porcelain bonded crowns . . .' There was a slight giggle from someone in the room.

Encouraged, he risked everything and began to recount the details of the only time the ill-matched couple had shared a bed. But just a few paragraphs in, he glanced across at Romilly. She was no longer smiling and her eyes were fixed firmly on the floor. The room remained eerily quiet.

He closed the manuscript and said, 'Thank you. Thank you very much,' and actually wanted to cry.

Malcolm began clapping slowly and, eventually, encouraged by the man's tipsy good humour, several other people clapped along in a desultory way.

'Are there any questions?' asked Oliver, hoping against hope that he might simply have stunned the audience with the power of his prose.

Norwegian Lizbet eventually raised a hand and said flatly, 'What do you really think about older people having sex, Tom?'

Oliver winced and began to mumble something incomprehensible in reply, his stuttering response lost in a hubbub of general conversation – none of which, he was sure, had anything whatsoever to do with the reading he had just given.

He stood at the front of the room a lonely and isolated figure as people shuffled away.

As was always the case on this last evening, the plan was that everyone should go to the pub a mile away. It was only ten o'clock. Even in his wretched state, what was he supposed to do? Sit alone in his room for hours? (People always stayed very late, the landlord glad to shovel up the extra fifty or sixty quid that they would spend after closing time.)

He agreed to go, but sat silently wedged into the back of one of the taxis beside the two Polish girls – who ignored him as they chatted away in their own language – and Terry the Irishman exchanged pleasantries with the driver up front.

At the pub it was clear that, just as he had slipped entirely out of the reckoning, dithering poet Catherine had now been taken fully into the group's bosom and was at the centre of all the laughter and demob-happy revelry. He was like a stranger amongst these people, quiet and awkward, and the longer they stayed in the pub, the quieter and more awkward he became. If he tried to say something funny or clever, it was met only with the silence of embarrassment.

A little after midnight, the Polish girls, Keira and most of the writers left the pub but, desperate to try and retrieve something from the wreckage of the week, and this awful evening in particular, he stubbornly remained with Romilly, Malcolm, Leon and Terry.

He bought another round of drinks and again tried to offer something cynical or casually wise to assert himself. But even the couple of old soaks at the bar – locals who stood here every night – ignored him and played instead to Romilly's effortless tipsy charm.

It was half past one when they started the long walk back to the house.

Oliver watched from behind as Malcolm took Romilly's hand in his and Terry and Leon made their own halting way down the dark lane between the high banks on either side of them.

Back at the centre Oliver said, 'What about a nightcap? I've a bottle of malt in my room.' There were no takers and most people went to their rooms. Oliver mumbled something about getting more cigarettes and trudged up the stairs as Leon made coffee.

In his room he lay down, his head spinning.

He lit a cigarette and, half falling from the bed, leaned across to the ledge and opened the window. The smoke poured out and, after several long drags, he flicked the butt away into the night and reached for the notepad beside him. Lying there, his head propped awkwardly on the pillow, his knees drawn up, he moved the biro across the page until it refused to counter gravity any longer and became merely a metallic scratch on the paper. 'Why not just fuck the woman you can fuck, rather than fuck about with the women you can't?' he wrote, a few words that would surely one day find their way into the mouth of some character in one of his as yet unwritten books.

A plane droned by overhead. He watched the tiny wingtip beacons and imagined he could see the pricks of light along the fuselage windows. Cocooned inside, on their way to Majorca or Cadiz, were people tapping out their texts, playing on their games machines and reading books and magazines. And here was he, silently below. The plane's noise faded and it disappeared beyond the window sight line.

He looked at what he had scrawled on the pad as the bile in his gut rose. The afternoon had been miserable, his reading this evening a humiliating ordeal, and his maudlin thoughts this late night were truly horrible. And yet, at the end of it all, these few words, this sour little epigram, were a tiny something saved from the wreckage.

He could wait no longer. He rolled from the bed, staggered down the stairs and out of the front door. He needed to be ill, and then, perhaps, he would have one last cigarette.

PART TWO

FIFTEEN

Shropshire

Sergeant Jeff Earle drove over to the centre from the police station at Craven Arms that morning. Things were quiet. Clungunford and Clun really were quiet places.

He tapped at the door at the same time as opening it. 'Hello, Shirley?' he called.

He could hear the vacuum cleaner and stood listening to the hum and creak above him. Then he sat down at the big L-shaped table and waited.

Five minutes later, the vacuum stopped and he heard the housekeeper carrying it slowly down the stairs.

'Morning, Shirley,' he said, getting up with a sigh.

'Jeff. Do you fancy a cuppa? I was just going to have one.'

'Be lovely,' he said. 'No sugar.' He patted his stomach.

The squat woman filled the kettle and stacked crockery as he spoke.

'How's things?' he asked.

'Oh, alright. My back's no better.'

'Tell me about it. I can hardly get out of the car if I've sat in it for an hour. Good job there's not many robbers to chase round here . . .'

'And how's Carol?' asked the housekeeper.

'She's alright. We've had the grandson over for a couple of days. It wore us out really, but it's nice to have him. How's the old man?'

'My old man?'

'Well, no, I meant the old man here, really, but how is Tony? I've not seen him for ages.'

'Nor me. If he's not in the garden, he's out fishing. Better than under my feet I s'pose.'

'And what about *this* old man? Osman?'

'He's much the same, I think. I never see him, either.'

'And her? Mrs Osman?'

'I only ever see her when I take the shopping down to the house on a Saturday, and that's about it.'

'So, this thing that's gone missing, then?' he asked, folding back the pages of his notepad.

'It's the little statue from in the hall. Did you ever see it?' she asked.

'Can't say I did.'

'It was part of the furniture. Been there for years. I don't even know if I should have phoned.' She lowered her voice, looked towards the back kitchen door. 'Keira doesn't seem bothered. She says it'll turn up.'

'You think it's been nicked, then?' he asked.

'I don't know. All I know is it's always there, and then this morning, when I was dusting, I noticed it's gone.'

'When did you last see it?'

'I don't know to be honest. You know how it is, when something's just always there, you don't even see it properly any more.'

'My missus could change the wallpaper in the front room and I wouldn't notice,' he said, 'as long as the telly was still there.'

'I thought you were supposed to be a copper, Jeff.'

'I *am* a copper,' he said defensively. 'And a good one. I can tell you a dodgy fella or a nicked motor; I'm just not much good with things that don't move.'

'If you say so,' she said.

'So what's it like then, this statue?' he asked.

'It's of the old man, Mr Osman. It must be bronze or something; it's very heavy.'

'Bronze, eh? So it's going to be worth a bit, then?' he suggested.

'I don't know, but I should have thought so,' she said. 'Something like that, made specially.'

'How big is it? How tall I mean?'

'About that.' She gestured to the coffee jar on the work surface beside her. 'Perhaps a bit bigger.'

'About eight or nine inches, then?' he said, holding his hands apart and framing the jar at a distance.

'You tell me,' she said.

'Anything else about it?'

'It's been on that dresser in the hall since I've been coming, the last ten years at least. And when the Osmans moved out of here down to their house it was left as a sort of reminder, I suppose, for all the writers coming here, just whose house it was, and why they could be here at all.'

'And so you noticed it was gone today?' he said as he wrote the information in his pad.

'This morning, first thing. The girls come in and strip the bedding and sheets and towels ready for the laundry as soon as the guests have left on a Saturday morning, and then I come in on a Monday and vacuum and dust and get the place ready for the new ones this afternoon.'

'Mmm,' he said as he wrote.

'No sugar?' she asked as the kettle came to the boil.

'Well, somebody's half-inched it,' he said, getting slowly to his feet and arching his back.

'Do you think so? One of the writers?' she asked.

'Who else?'

'They're not those kind of people, Jeff. You could leave your purse open here. It's not that kind of place. You know that.'

'Well, they're the only ones who've been here,' he replied conclusively.

'Here's your tea,' she said. 'Milk's in the jug. I'd better get on. They'll start arriving before four and I've a dozen beds to make yet.'

'Thanks, Shirley. Where's Keira? I'll need to speak to her. Get all their details. See if she noticed anyone who looked like a suspect.'

'Are you serious?' said the housekeeper.

'Course not,' he said. 'But I'll need to know who was on the course and where they live, all that sort of thing. Got to keep me records up to date and log it all for the crime statistics, fill in the forms for the Home Secretary.'

'And then?'

'Then I've just got to catch the bugger,' he smiled, and sipped his tea.

'Will you really have to interview them all?' she said. 'Is that what you do?'

'I don't think my boss would like that. They come from all over, don't they?'

'Always,' she agreed. 'London, Manchester, Scotland. We had a woman from Norway last week. Just to be on the course.'

'So, where's Keira?' he asked. 'Is she around?'

'She's down in the village, gone for fresh dairy and bread. Shall I leave a note for her? Tell her you want to speak?'

'Yes, thanks. Have you got her mobile number?'

Shirley jotted the centre director's number down and handed it to the policeman. 'You might get her in the village, but up here you'll only get her on the landline; there's no signal.'

'Sure. So who was teaching here last week, then?' he asked.

Shirley took a copy of the course booklet from the shelf and thumbed through it. 'Tom Oliver and Sarah Cassin. *"Beginning to write: come and be inspired by two established writers working in entirely different disciplines. Make a start on that novel you've always promised yourself you'll one day write. Or do you fancy penning an ode, a sonnet or a haiku? Then this is the course for you. Just bring a pen, a pad and your imagination to the beautiful Shropshire countryside and spend a week working with real writers."'*

'Never heard of them,' said the policeman as he copied down their names from the booklet.

'Do you read much, then, Jeff?' she asked.

'Jack Higgins,' he said. 'Read 'em all. Jack Higgins, and what's that other fella, the South African bloke?'

'No idea,' she said. 'Actually, Sarah Cassin couldn't come in the end and Keira had to get another writer in. I've forgotten who she said it was, but another woman. A poet. Her name's escaped me. But it went alright, I think. Everybody seemed happy enough when I popped up on the Wednesday.'

'Wilbur Smith,' he said.

'Sorry?'

'That's the other one I like, the South African bloke, Wilbur Smith.'

'Oh, right,' she said as she gathered her cleaning materials from the cupboard at the far end of the room. 'I wonder what's happened to it? You know, the statue.'

'It is a mystery,' said the sergeant as he got up and arched his back once more, 'but I don't think it's gonna be on *Crimewatch*.'

SIXTEEN

London

One of the problems with living in a basement flat is that you can hear the couple upstairs when they have sex. Some people, of course, don't mind. The other problem is that when the shower floods or the cistern fails, the people downstairs are the first to know about it, and this, they always mind.

An hour before he had left for the cottage he occasionally rented in the Black Mountains, more than a week ago now, Tom Oliver had thrown some things into the washing machine and clicked the dial. One of the very few drawbacks about living alone, Oliver reckoned, was that you could never quite get enough clothes together to make a coloured wash. Half his white tee shirts were now grey, the other half were pale pink.

He'd lugged his holdall and folders and books for sale to the car, and then driven round Regent's Park, through St John's Wood and out along Western Avenue past the Hoover building. He never once thought about the old washing machine, by now on its final spin cycle, and by the time he joined the M40, the clothes lay there in his flat on Gloucester Avenue, tangled and damp, the little red light glowing on the front of the machine.

Forty-eight hours later, in the middle of Monday night, the pressure throughout a million homes in the city inexorably building as folk slept and turned and dreamed, the worn-out hose connector on Oliver's machine began to drip.

By the middle of that week the drip had become a trickle, and when his basement-dwelling neighbours returned from work after a couple of Friday evening drinks with colleagues, they found water pouring through their bedroom ceiling.

They rushed upstairs and banged on Oliver's door. They then phoned their landlord. Mr Paphides arrived in his silver Lexus within the hour, but why would he have spare keys to the flat of one of his tenants?

The three of them watched helplessly as the water ran a course along the ceiling and erratically down into the buckets and washing-up bowl that the couple had placed on the floor where their bed had, until very recently, stood.

The landlord called Oliver's mobile, but it rang unanswered. He then called a locksmith, the man he always used on his many properties in north London when there was a need to replace or repair a lock.

Stan was there in no time, and in only a few minutes had opened the door with the expertise that went some way towards warranting his £140 call-out charge. Paphides turned the water off at the stopcock beneath the sink and swore a great deal in both Greek and English. As he mopped up the water from the kitchen floor, the couple downstairs went about trying to restore order to their bedroom.

Using a sheet of paper from one of the several notepads around the writer's flat, the landlord printed in capital letters a note explaining what had happened and taped it to the outside of Oliver's front door in the hall.

He called again on the couple in the basement, opened his hands in a gesture of despair and said, 'Please, you must contact your insurers.'

'The Osman Writers' Centre. Good morning, Keira speaking.'

'Keira, hello. My name's Andrew, Andrew Hardiman. I'm Tom Oliver's agent.'

'Yes?' she said.

'The thing is, Keira – I'm sorry, did you say Keira?'

'Yes, Keira,' she repeated for the umpteenth time in her life.

'I'm trying to reach Tom, and I'm not getting any reply on his phone at home.'

'Really?' she said.

'You don't happen to know his whereabouts, I suppose?'

'Me?' she said, surprised. 'No. He was here last week, teaching,' she offered.

'Exactly,' said Hardiman. 'But he doesn't seem to have come back to London. I was wondering whether he said anything to you about going on anywhere?'

'No, nothing at all,' she said. 'I know that he does sometimes use a cottage in Wales,' she added. 'Have you tried him there?'

'No. But he usually tells me if he's going to be working

up there on account of me having to remind him to charge his phone up and switch it on.'

'Is it important?' she asked.

'Well, actually, Keira, just between ourselves, it is. I've got some interest from a TV production company in one of his books, and they want a meeting as soon as.'

'I see,' she said. 'As I say, he was here last week. He left on Saturday morning. I can't say I actually saw him go, because I had to be down in Ludlow, but he'd gone by the time I got back.'

'Right,' he said. 'Thanks for your help, anyway. I'll track him down, no doubt.'

The next day Hardiman walked from his office above a dry-cleaner's on Parkway in Camden up to Oliver's flat in Primrose Hill.

At the Gloucester Avenue house he rang Oliver's bell and then tried each of the others until he eventually got a response. An Australian girl who was working nights and renting the top-floor apartment let him in with no very good grace, having left her bed to walk down three flights of stairs to open the door to a complete stranger.

Hardiman thanked her as she sprinted back up the stairs, and then he sifted the piles of mail in the hall. There was plenty for Oliver, mostly junk, but one of the envelopes was date-stamped eight days previously.

He went along the hall and read the note taped to Oliver's door. It looked like a child might have written it, with the pen held tight, the letters in capitals, and an illegible signature at the bottom of it, the sort that pubescent kids practise to give their name a flourish. 'Mr Oliver, There Has Been Flood. The Basemant Sealing Is Ruin. Call Mr Paphides . . .'

Where the fuck was Oliver? Hardiman had represented him for the last three years. Two-page contracts with advances of a few grand, and all ancillary rights remaining with the publisher; tiny royalty payments in June and December, and foreign sales in the low hundreds. And now there was a sniff of something that might, at last, make a decent figure, the man had gone AWOL.

The following morning Hardiman called Oliver's flat half-a-dozen times and tried his mobile every couple of hours. He had no other contact numbers – no family, no friends. Why should he?

After lunch, he put his feet up on the desk and smoked a cigarette as the traffic hurried along the noisy street below. He felt like a private detective in a film noir. He read the letter from Pale Moon TV Productions again.

Tom Oliver was the wrong side of fifty and he had a reputation for being both awkward and self-regarding. But right now, he had an outside chance of earning some real money if his novel – or better still, series of novels – made it onto TV.

Worst case scenario, they'd get some decent development money to do an outline. And who knows what then? With a foot in the TV door, anything could happen. A ninety-minute pilot? A two-parter? A full-blown series using the best of Oliver's stuff until the half-dozen novels had been exhausted, and a bunch of hungry youngsters, ravenous to cut their screenwriting teeth, would bash their brains out to get their own stories made, stories merely based on Oliver's by now franchised characters. The possibilities, no matter how remote, were beguiling. It could be a gravy train as long as *Star Trek* or *Only Fools and Horses*. You just never knew with TV.

Hardiman picked up the phone, slowly dialled 999, and asked the operator what exactly the procedure was to report someone who you believed could be missing. The woman listened impassively and responded in a monotone that could have been construed as indifference.

She took Hardiman's contact details and said that she would pass the information on to someone who would look into it.

That someone would have been Detective Sergeant John Soames, but he was lying in a hospital bed in St Thomas's hospital and had rather more pressing concerns just now as the consultant sat with him and his wife and pointed out the shadow on the X-ray of his lung that represented a very bleak future indeed.

Kavanagh, marking time in the office as a ludicrous investigation into his conduct the previous weekend on Crouch End Broadway was being pursued, picked up the enquiry from Soames' desk, just as ACC Hyland had said he should and, a couple of hours later, returned Hardiman's call.

SEVENTEEN

'Salt?'

'Hi.'

'What's going on?'

'How do you mean, Frank?'

'What have you got on?'

'Jogging bottoms and a tee shirt. Why?'

'Very good. What have you got on next week, Jane?'

'Tons. Why?'

'Be a good constable, eh, and just run your diary past me.'

'Is this some new game, Frank?'

'No, not exactly,' he said, without elaboration.

'I'm in court tomorrow, and then there's a surveillance I'm involved with in Peckham where we're out to blag some Romanians who've got kids of fifteen working in the sex trade.'

'Is that it?' he said.

'No. I'm taking my mum out for supper. Why? Do you want to come?'

'Love to,' he said. It was almost worth having the odd day or two of being a little out of sorts just to feel the harmony of normal service being resumed. Almost. OK, he'd still got a bruise on his forehead and the enquiry was an irksome prospect, but if his relationship was on course, Kavanagh reckoned, he could cope with just about anything else.

'How do you fancy a few days in the country?' he said.

'Which country?' she replied.

'*The* country. Fields and all. Least it was the last time I was there. Shropshire.'

'And why would I want to be in Shropshire, Frank? Have you booked us a few days away? One of those romantic short breaks?'

'Not quite,' he said. 'We've got a misper.'

'How come? And why's it come to you?' she said.

'It's for Soames, but you know he's laid up and Hyland wanted me to pick up anything awkward on his desk so it's come across to me.'

'Right,' she said. 'So who's gone AWOL that requires DI Kavanagh on the case, then?'

'He's a writer. Apparently some people know of him. Someone called Oliver. Tom Oliver. You ever heard of him?'

'Yes,' she said.

'That's the thing about you, Jane. You're a well-read woman. And I need someone who knows what's what. The only thing I've ever seen anyone read down here at the nick is the *Da Vinci Code* and Martina Cole.'

'Yes, I'm Mastermind,' she said, fully aware and a little ashamed of the fact that she had given up her aspirational reading a long time ago now. Like a lot of thinking women, she was a member of a book club and she always had a decent book on the go, but when was the last time she had read a nineteenth-century classic, got fed and sated on rereading a Jane Austen or a Dickens doorstop?

'So what's it about? Why Shropshire?' she asked.

'Tom Oliver was at a writers' centre up there, teaching. But he hasn't come home. His agent's the one who alerted us. I think there must be money involved because he's very insistent. And he says it's completely out of character for Oliver to go off the radar like this.' There was a silence on the phone line. 'So, what do you reckon, Jane? Can you do it?' he asked.

'I can probably cover some of the other stuff, but I'll have to appear in court, unless you want me in jail for contempt. And what about my mum?'

'Can your sister not do it? Or one of your brothers?'

'You don't have a Jewish mother, Frank. You don't quite understand how these things work, do you?'

'No,' he said. 'But if you'll come up to Shropshire, I might have a Jewish mother-in-law one of these days!'

'It's her birthday,' she said, imagining the consequences of missing the promised supper.

'You can tell her that I pulled rank, and that you're in-dispensable,' he suggested.

'Alright, I'll speak to her. But you owe her, and me. When are we leaving?'

'I'm the advance party. I'm going later today. There's a couple of things I have to do first,' he said. 'You come up as soon as you can after you've done your court thing tomorrow.'

'What have we got so far?' she asked.

'Well, what do you know about Oliver?' he replied.

'He writes comedy, doesn't he? You know, campus stuff, set in a college somewhere? It's a bit out of fashion now, isn't it?'

'I've no idea,' said Kavanagh. 'You tell me.'

'I read one once,' she added. 'But I couldn't tell you anything about it now. But then again, I've read *Middlemarch* three times and I couldn't quote you a line from that either. And it was his agent who alerted us to his disappearance?'

'Yes, someone called Hardiman. Andrew Hardiman. He'd some business he needed to discuss with him. He couldn't reach him so he went to his flat, but it's obvious he hasn't been there. There's a note on the door from the landlord saying there's been a flood.'

'And you've spoken to the writing centre?'

'Yes, I've spoken to the centre director there. Apparently, he did his thing there and left.'

'Where is the place?' she asked.

'Up past Craven Arms, off the A49 from Ludlow. It's on property that belongs to Richard Osman . . .'

'Osman the playwright? I thought he was dead. I haven't heard of him for years.'

'Apparently not,' said Kavanagh. 'Just not very well.'

'He was massive in the Seventies,' she went on.

'Well, he's in a wheelchair now,' said the inspector. 'He's had a stroke. He and his missus still live on the estate, but they gave the big house over to a trust a few years ago.'

'You've been reading up?' she said.

'Wikipedia,' he answered.

'Just don't trust it,' she said.

'His wife, Margaret Osman, is the main mover now, apparently. They provide bursaries for writers, all that sort of thing,' he said.

'Anything else?' asked Salt.

'That's about it, I reckon,' said Kavanagh. 'I've spoken to the landlord of Oliver's flat in Primrose Hill and I'm going round there with one of our people later. I'll take a look around and then I'll get on the road.'

'OK,' she said. 'Take care.'

'Thanks. You too. I'll email you the details and see you up there.'

EIGHTEEN

I t was hardly necessary, but why make things difficult?
Kavanagh emailed Sergeant Jeff Earle a brief message up at the police station at Craven Arms and said he'd be there later that day. He didn't have to. He could just as easily have breezed in – the London-based copper with a Birmingham accent – and alienated the couple of constables there and the sergeant in charge. But why do that? No, he contacted them, said he'd be there about five, depending on the traffic.

Round at Oliver's flat, just as his agent Andrew Hardiman had said, there were the stacks of mail in the hall and the note from the landlord taped to the door. But there was no sign of Tom Oliver.

Kavanagh knelt down and, wearing surgical gloves, shovelled all the mail into a couple of clear plastic evidence envelopes. He slipped on his protective overshoes as one of the specialists from Scotland Yard gained entry to the flat. His job done, the locksmith went outside and sat on his toolbox on the steps and smoked a cigarette.

Kavanagh stood alone in the little interior hall, just inside the door of the flat. For the Detective Inspector, this was about as good as it got. He felt calm and tranquil. Was this what people got up to when they meditated for an hour or chanted their morning mantra, he wondered? His senses were attuned and alive, but in a peaceful, contemplative way.

He felt the atmosphere in the place, thick with another person's doings, their former presence, and took in the unremarkable scene, but with a kind of commonplace wonder as he read the picture before him.

Salt might have *Middlemarch,* but this was *his* book. There might be nothing to find, no wrongdoing or crime committed, but this was the place that would, most likely, tell him what he needed to know.

Every year in the United Kingdom, some 200,000 people go missing. About 198,000 of them turn up again within a day or two, or at least have the consideration to let family or friends know just where they are and why they've gone away. A few thousand don't. And of those few thousand, a very few come to serious harm or, even worse for their loved ones, are never ever found again. The dilemma for the police is trying to ascertain just what it is, in any one of these disappearances, that they are actually dealing with.

Is it a marriage breakdown, a domestic, perhaps, someone having an affair and running away with their new partner? Or is it the disappearance of someone with debts or enemies or a recent very large insurance policy that their nearest and dearest is about to benefit from?

Was Tom Oliver a man who'd met someone and gone to Dublin or Rio for the week without a by-your-leave? Had he checked into a hotel a mile from the centre on a whim, and even now was sitting in a chintzy lounge reading the local paper? Had he gone to visit a nephew in Milan, a long-lost friend somewhere about whom he'd never spoken to anyone?

Kavanagh savoured the moment and felt a deep yearning.

This was what they taught coppers to do at college. Read the scene; touch only with care, wear protection and move nothing, of course.

The wooden slatted blinds were half closed. The answer-phone light was blinking. He felt like a man with a stash: something good to anticipate, something to return to.

His guts moved and he would have liked nothing so much as to have gone to the loo and sat down. There were news-papers around and the TV page of an old *Sunday Times* had a couple of programmes ringed.

He walked to the window, looked down at the locksmith on the step, who himself was watching a couple of college girls in short skirts walk by on the other side of the street.

The stereo was on standby. Kavanagh picked up the CD sleeve next to it. He pressed Play and went through to the kitchen, holding the box. The chortling aquatic warbler filtered through to the next room. British Birdsong, Volume Two. Was there a better job in the entire world? You really couldn't make it up.

Oliver had washed up before he'd left, after a solitary cold meal, Kavanagh reckoned – one plate, knife, fork, spoon and bowl – and left the stuff to dry on the draining board.

He opened the washing-machine door. The stuff inside smelled rank.

In the adjoining bedroom, the pale blue duvet was turned down, the pillows plumped up.

There were several books piled up by the alarm clock radio, including an illustrated Pepys and an autobiography by someone called Sebastian Horsley. There was also an Afghan writer's novel, an anthology of poetry and a slim selection of poet Sarah Cassin's most recently published work.

He checked the track number on the CD as a flock of Berwick swans flew by. Identifying birds from their song was like any other quiz question: once you knew the answer, it was easy. Now he knew it, these squawks were obviously the huge white bird with the fearsome reputation. But was it just a countryside myth, Kavanagh wondered as he stood at the kitchen door and watched the blinking telephone light. He'd heard it often enough, but he'd never met anyone whose arm had been broken by a swan. He'd never met anyone who even knew of someone whose arm had been broken in combat with a swan. Maybe it was just propaganda. A tale put about to deter people who might wish to harm cygnets?

He sat on the sofa in front of the low table as the sound of the birds faded, and the extraordinary sound of the booming bittern began. He smiled at the noise of the thing, opened his pad, picked up the phone and tapped in 1571. There were nine messages, five of which were from Oliver's agent. They began intriguingly as Hardiman, calling several days ago and sounding quietly self-satisfied, mentioned having some good news for his client, something they should talk about, 'pronto'. They then followed an arc that went from smug composure to solicitous engagement and ended with growing irritation as his calls went unreturned. The most recent one, left only a couple of days previously, simply said: 'Tom. Call me.'

Someone called Derek had phoned suggesting they might meet for a drink but, halfway through leaving his message had remembered that Oliver had told him that he was going to be away this week, and the man said he'd call back in a few days' time.

There was a call from his building society to confirm a forthcoming appointment, and two messages from Keira at the Writers' Centre, the first confirming his visit and reminding him to bring copies of his latest book for sale, the second, a little agitated, saying there had been an 'unavoidable change of plans' and that if he picked this up before leaving for Shropshire that he should call her and she would explain, but that it was nothing serious, and 'not to worry'.

But the most intriguing message on the machine was from a woman who felt no need to say who she was. 'Tom, you must be in the shower or something. I just called to say have a good week,' and then, very quietly, 'I do miss you, you know. Take care.'

Kavanagh listed each call in his pad, and then played them all through again. He liked putting pictures to voices. He'd never know just what the man who phoned from the credit card company, or the woman who pitched him his car insurance actually looked like, but he always conjectured some image, and he was quite sure that he was invariably wrong.

He knew he must be wrong because he sometimes covered his eyes when a reporter filed a story from some godforsaken spot on the TV news, or they wheeled on a little-known politician, or the doyenne of a financial institution to talk up the economy or explain the fall in the Nikkei or Dow Jones. He'd conjure the picture of a dark man of twenty-five, only to open his eyes to see a rubicund, fair bloke of fifty filling the screen.

The woman who spoke so affectionately to Oliver's machine, he imagined, was forty, slim, dark, educated and urbane.

Back at the station, he made the enquiries necessary to trace the sources of the incoming calls on Oliver's phone and immediately dialled the woman's number in Bicester.

An answerphone cut in after the fourth ring with an automated message. After the tone, Kavanagh said breezily, 'Hello, this is Detective Inspector Kavanagh from the Metropolitan Police. This is a message for Andrea Moore. It's only a routine matter, but it is important and I'd be grateful if you could call me back as soon as possible. Many thanks.' He left both his office and mobile numbers.

NINETEEN

Shropshire

S ergeant Jeff Earle was a strong-looking man. You didn't really see people who looked like Earle in London. He belonged here, in the countryside. He would surely have played rugby when he was a young man, thought Kavanagh, and he knew he'd drink decent local beer, not gassy foreign lager.

He stood unnaturally erect as he tried to compensate for the back pain that had plagued him for the last several years. Over six-feet tall, he was broad-shouldered with a ruddy face. Housman might well have seen him on the streets of Ludlow, marching off to make the foes of England sorry they were born, a hundred-odd years ago.

Kavanagh extended his hand to the man. One of the very few things that, as an adult, he had formed any certainty about was that his own nature had been defined by the subservient role that his father had played in his parents' marriage. Frank senior had always played second fiddle in his childhood home, and Kavanagh reckoned that his absent father had left him, even now, at his middle age, looking for someone to fill that role.

His father hadn't been a bad man, not by any means. He was a kind soul who wanted nothing so much as a pint and a quiet sit with the paper in the evening. OK, he did sometimes spend a bit too much at the (illegal) bookies, and there were a couple of occasions when the men talking to him at the front door of their suburban Birmingham house in quiet, determined tones certainly didn't look particularly well-intentioned. But, really, young Frank's abiding memories of his doe-eyed father were of a tall man, whose height meant that he could bowl a decent length at Sunday afternoon cricket matches out at the sports ground of the accountancy firm for whom he worked. He was an easy-going man. Trouble was, Frank's mother, Rosemary, was anything but. She was filled with all the ambition and drive that Frank Kavanagh lacked. She didn't want to rest, it wasn't in her nature, and she didn't allow anyone close to her to rest either. She'd move the furniture around the house single-handedly, get up early to wash and clean, often had two jobs (she was a hair-dresser by trade) and sometimes three, when her husband had been particularly impecunious at the bookmakers. She was always planning and scheming and devising, and while that might well be how empires are built and tradesmen grow rich and books and symphonies get written, it isn't relaxing.

In her case, it was also true that many of her schemes were unrealistic. She nurtured a dream that they should move away from their Birmingham suburb out to the country where she would open a hairdressing salon while her husband ran the garage next door. It was a good plan in so far as it went. But it went only to show that she hadn't taken into account that there might be only a few folk in a village in need of a shampoo and set on a regular basis and, more to the point, her husband was not only uninterested in cars, he didn't even drive. He owned a 28-inch-wheel Raleigh cycle. That was all. He'd have had no more idea how to change the spark plugs on a Standard 10 than fly.

'How was your journey?' asked the sergeant.

'Not bad,' said Kavanagh. 'Not bad, considering. You used to be able to plan a journey and try and dodge the traffic a bit, but these days it never stops. I had to go down to Brighton at four in the morning a couple of weeks ago and the traffic on the M25 was ridiculous, even at that time.'

'Yes?' said Earle, at a loss to add anything. He'd never been on the M25, or to Brighton for that matter.

'Fancy a cuppa?' said the local cop.

'Sure,' said Kavanagh, being accommodating. He only drank tea when he had a blessed fry-up these days – two or three times a year at most.

Earle switched the kettle on. 'So this statue's worth a bit then?' he said.

'Sorry?' said Kavanagh, glancing around the office for a clue as to the man's meaning.

'The bronze. The one that's gone missing . . .'

'I'm sorry, Jeff, but you've lost me. What bronze is that, then?'

'Are we at cross purposes?' asked the sergeant, turning away from the kettle towards Kavanagh.

'I don't actually know what it is you're talking about,' said the inspector.

'Are you not up here about the bronze? Your email said you needed to come up to check out the Writers' Centre. I naturally thought . . .'

'I've not heard anything about a bronze,' said Kavanagh. 'You've had something stolen?'

'Yes, quite a valuable piece has gone missing from the centre. Sometime last week. I'd never seen it myself, but apparently it's always there, in the hall of the main house.'

'I see,' said the inspector.

'So?' queried the sergeant. 'Your visit?'

'Nothing to do with statues,' he smiled. 'I'm up here looking into the disappearance of a bloke called Tom Oliver, and the last sighting we've got of him was when he was tutoring at the centre here.'

'Oh, right,' said the sergeant as the kettle began to bubble and billow steam. 'Well, at least we've cleared that up.'

'What about your statue, then?' asked the inspector. 'Have you got any leads?'

'No,' said Earle without elaboration.

'Any thoughts about it?' pursued the inspector, hoping to elicit some expression of interest in the theft.

'Not really,' said the copper.

'But you've had a look around up there?'

'Not exactly,' he replied as he poured a little boiling water into the glazed brown teapot and swirled it around. 'I'd guess one of the writers on the course must have nicked it. So I'm not going to find it in a field, am I? And there's acres of land up there, as well as the lake and the woods. There's even a couple of deep mine shafts.'

'Really?' said Kavanagh. 'What were they mining for here?'

'Before they went up north, Stiperstones way, they were looking for lead I think, years ago now.' He tipped three big spoonfuls of tea into the pot and stirred it round. 'Anyway, we haven't got the men for that kind of search. We're too busy doling out ASBOs to the kids on a Friday night,' he added with just a quick crease of his lips that might have suggested a smirk.

'Yes, I suppose so,' said Kavanagh.

'Jane?'
'Frank?'

'How you doing?'

'Fine.'

'What are you up to?'

'I'm in the bath,' she said, and trickled her hand through the water. 'How's Shropshire?' she asked.

'Odd,' he said. 'A bit of a misunderstanding with the local law enforcement officers. I'll tell you about it when we meet, but it's sorted now.'

'Right,' she said.

'Did you speak to your mother yet?' he asked.

'Yes.'

'And?'

'She wasn't happy.'

'No, I bet.'

'Why do you ask?' said Salt.

Silence.

'Frank?'

'Yes, I'm here,' he said quietly.

'Is there a problem?' she asked.

'No, not exactly,' he replied.

'What do you mean, "not exactly"?'

'It's just that, I went to Oliver's flat . . .'

'Yes?'

'Nothing out of the ordinary, but there was a message on his phone from a woman, someone called Andrea Moore.'

'So?' said Salt.

'I had her number traced and called her. I left a message and asked her to call me.'

'Yes, Frank. I'm following,' she said, 'and there's nothing I can't understand yet.'

'She called me back up here and it's delicate. She's married but she's been seeing Oliver. Her husband's no idea, obviously, and she's asked for discretion . . .'

'So what's the problem?' said Salt.

'We obviously need to speak to her.'

'Of course,' she said.

'Someone's got to talk to her, and sooner rather than later. I've arranged it for tomorrow lunchtime . . .'

'You want me to postpone coming so that I can speak to her?' she said.

'Exactly,' he said.

'So I've cancelled my mother's birthday . . .' she began.

'I'm sorry, Jane. It was unavoidable. You know what the hippies say?'

'No. What do they say?'

'Things change,' he said weakly.

'I'm not a hippy, Frank.'

'Will you do it? And then come up here as soon as you've spoken to her?' he asked. There was another silence, just the sound of splashing into the bath as she ran more hot water. 'You could still make it to your mum's do, all being well.'

'Yes, except she's not actually speaking to me now.'

'I'm sorry,' he said. 'It's just that this could be important. You know that.'

'Yes, I do,' she agreed.

'Andrea Moore's a writer. It's why I need you to interview her,' he offered, placatory.

'I've heard of her,' said Salt, showing interest. 'I think she writes historical novels. I haven't read her, but I know the name.'

'She lives in Bicester, but she asked if you could meet in Birmingham. There's a French restaurant near the magistrates' court building . . .'

'A French restaurant in Birmingham?' repeated Salt. 'Things must be looking up.'

He let the slight on his home city pass. 'Right,' he said, tempted to tell her that he was sure Andrea Moore would be dark, slim and forty, but decided instead to keep quiet about his guessing games and their high failure rate for the time being.

'Let me have the details, and I'll come up as soon as I'm done.'

'Sure,' he said. 'Jane, do you think your mum might appreciate some flowers? From me, you know, for her birthday?'

'It's possible,' she said. 'But it's just as likely they'll go straight in the bin.'

'Right,' he said. 'Thanks. Find out whatever you can about Tom Oliver's relationship with Andrea Moore, see whether she's got anything useful on what might have happened to him, OK?'

'Sure,' she said.

'See you soon. Bye.'

TWENTY

Birmingham

DC Jane Salt immediately liked Andrea Moore.
There was something about some people, in spite of themselves. Folk were always turning up on *Desert Island Discs* or teatime chat shows and, although you couldn't always put your finger on it, there was just something about them that irked, something that got under your skin: a false trail, a phoney self-deprecation that was, in fact, its very opposite – a 'look at me and my engaging modesty' guise. And that was even before you heard their terrible choice of records.

Salt had always reckoned that angular John Lennon would have been a difficult bloke to rub along with – of that she was sure – but she was equally sure that, in spite of his posturing, bed peace and naked album covers, she would have infinitely preferred the difficult bespectacled Beatle to his winsome former writing partner. Lennon was a truculent curmudgeon, no doubt, but he was certainly the real deal.

Novelist Andrea Moore wasn't a singer in a mop-top band, she was a writer of historical fiction, and she too felt no need to sell herself. In fact, she gave the distinct impression that she was not bothered what Salt – or anyone else for that matter – thought of her. And this trait, of course, meant that people tended to take her at her own assessment of herself. This lack of neediness struck a particular chord with Salt, a woman who sometimes regretted her own tendency to seek approval, often from people about whose opinions she cared little.

They sat across from one another in the French restaurant just opposite the chocolate-brick magistrates' court at the very bottom of Corporation Street in Birmingham. Round tables, bentwood chairs; waiters in knee-length, starched white aprons over dark trousers.

When they'd ordered food and a bottle of wine, Salt began.

'Andrea – do you mind if I call you Andrea? What can you tell me about Tom Oliver?'

'What is it you need to know?' she said guardedly.

'Anything. Anything at all that might help us to find him. Where did you two first meet, and how long have you known one another?'

'We both do some work for a literary agency. You know, they hire writers like Tom and me to read manuscripts and write reports on them for would-be writers. It's not bad work, and most of what we see is so bad it's actually quite encouraging.'

Salt smiled.

'I shouldn't have said that. It makes me sound horrible, but it is true. Just occasionally you get to see something good though, and that makes up for all the terrible stuff.'

'I'm sure,' said Salt.

'Has Tom really gone missing?' she asked seriously.

Questions answered with questions: the procedure was familiar to Salt and every other cop in the land, and it was understandable, given people's curiosity, but it did make for slow progress.

'Yes,' she said, 'as DI Kavanagh told you on the phone, he hasn't been seen since he tutored a course in Shropshire that ended last Saturday morning.'

'How strange,' said Moore.

'You know him well, I believe?' asked Salt.

The infinitesimal flick of Andrea's eyes in the direction of the younger woman said as much as the two women might have covered in an hour of candid talk.

'Yes, we know one another well,' she said. 'I told your colleague, the inspector, but I wasn't able to speak openly, if you see what I mean.'

'Of course,' said Salt.

'I've known Tom for quite some time . . .' She paused and again gave a longer look towards Salt. Maybe the woman did sometimes seek, if not approval, then at least sanction. 'But, yes, since last year, we'd become a lot closer.'

She poured them water from the heavy jug, the lemon slices blocking the funnel, droplets of condensation trickling down the outside of the thick glass where they were absorbed by the linen tablecloth. 'This is in confidence?' she said quietly.

'Of course,' said Salt.

'You know, my husband . . .'

'I will treat everything you tell me in confidence,' she reiterated.

It was a hollow claim, really, a sign of intentions, perhaps, but not a warranty. If things changed, when they went to the next stage – as they often did – commitments such as this would be forgotten, just as the lovers' troth, plighted in passion, often becomes irrelevant history.

And Andrea wasn't a stupid woman. The contrary: she knew that this assurance, given with a sort of token sincerity, was worthless. More to the point, she also knew that if she didn't reveal certain incontrovertible facts about her relationship with Tom Oliver, the police would very easily ascertain them. Her only potential ally, the woman sitting opposite her right now might, possibly, be able to influence the shape of any events which might unfold, events which some other (anonymous) police person would have no compunction in treating with discretion. It was the lesser of two.

'You say you'd become close?' prompted Salt.

The waiter stood over them holding a bottle of wine at the same time as glancing away, reluctant to play any part in yet another diner's wine pantomime. In the effete young man's view, punters had two choices: they accepted the proffered wine because they knew no better (invariably the case), or they sniffed it – some even holding it away from them to examine the colour – and then rolled it around their mouths before swallowing it down and pronouncing it fit. Rarely someone out to impress a girlfriend or a colleague, perhaps, would send perfectly good wine back to the cellar. Salt nodded her approval to the waiter without looking up.

'Please,' she prompted Moore, 'go on.'

The writer waited as the young man filled their glasses, carefully wiped the neck of the bottle, and walked away.

'Of Tom's few friends, most are women,' she said, without apparent malice or resentment.

'Friends?' repeated Salt.

'Yes,' she said. 'Some of them have been lovers, but he seems to have a knack of remaining close to women, even when the relationship's no longer intimate.'

'Quite an achievement,' said Salt.

'He's not a "new man" or anything like that, but he knows how to listen. He pays attention to what you say – or at least he appears to, which is a reasonable second best. I think it's partly what makes him a good writer. He listens well.'

Salt gave the other woman a slightly sceptical smile.

'Forget having a sense of humour, or even being good in bed.' A man at the next table looked up. 'I reckon it's really quite simple with most women,' she continued. 'Just listen to what we've got to say, which is sometimes all we want and, well, the rest will follow.'

'And you and Tom? You were lovers?' said Salt quietly.

'Yes. Last year, in the autumn. It had been brewing for a while. We both knew that, I'm sure. Tom's not the best looking man on the bus – he's no Brad Pitt – but then I'm not Juliette Binoche, am I? He must be nearly sixty, and I'm forty-seven. Maybe we felt we weren't quite ready for a bus pass.' She didn't wait for Salt's response, just went on, 'Things haven't been particularly good with my husband for a while. I'm pretty sure he had an affair a little while ago, even though he's always denied it. In a way, I hope he did. But even suspecting he might have done gave me the freedom to . . . well, to do what I wanted, I suppose.'

The waiter brought their starters and started to step away as he uttered the platitude, 'Enjoy.'

'Excuse me,' said Salt.

'Madam?' he replied, surprised.

'Do you have a beer mat, please?'

'I beg your pardon?' he said. It was the first unanticipated question he'd heard that day.

'For the table,' said Salt. 'It's uneven.'

'I'll see to it,' he said and sauntered away.

'And?' said Salt as she parted the crab cake with her fork.

'It was last autumn. We'd eaten here, actually. It was convenient for him. He was working one day a week at the university that term, teaching a creative-writing module. I'd come up from Oxfordshire for something or other, and we met over lunch. It was September, a lovely day, warm and sunny and even Birmingham looked nice.' There was a long pause as the woman drank water. 'We had a long lunch and then walked around the art gallery. Later, I suggested we go to a hotel,' she added brazenly.

'Yes?' said Salt. The waiter returned with a beer mat, folded it in two and tucked it under one of the table legs.

'Thank you,' said Salt. 'And?' she asked Andrea.

'We took a room at the Jury's Inn on Broad Street. What is it Chaucer says?' she said without hope or expectation of any recognition. *"In wommen vinolent is no defence."'*

Salt completed the medieval couplet. *'"This knowen lecchours by experience."'*

'My God,' said Moore, 'a police person who knows *The Wife of Bath*? I'm very impressed. Let's drink to that.'

Salt sipped her water. 'I'm sorry. I have to get back to London. It's a family do.'

'Of course, but how come the Chaucer?' asked Moore, refilling her own glass.

'Sixth-form English, and a passionate teacher,' said Salt. 'Mr Wright. There must be a dozen women of my age out there somewhere who have chunks of *The Wife of Bath* off to a T. *"I have had my worlde as in my tyme, but age, allas! that al wole envenyme, Hath me biraft my beautee and my pith."'* And here they declaimed together, *'"Lat go, farewell! The devil go therwith!"'*

The women clinked their water and wine glasses and laughed at the affection they felt for the poet.

'Anyway,' said Salt, 'you were saying, you and Tom?'

'We were like a couple of kids bunking off from school and going to the afternoon flicks, except we spent the afternoon in bed,' said Moore.

'And it continued?' said Salt.

'Yes. We occasionally saw one another in London, but more often, I'd come up here. I was doing research on St Philip's. Do you know it?'

'No,' said Salt.

'Not much loss,' added Moore tartly. 'Birmingham's cathedral, and not exactly one of the crowning glories of ecclesiastical architecture.'

'And you and Tom, more recently?' prompted Salt.

'We'd spend the odd time together, but really, it had faded, to be honest. I was never going to leave Jerry and the children – that was never even a remote possibility. And anyway, it wouldn't have worked, we both knew that. I don't think Tom wants anyone to live with him, not as man and wife.' She took another sip of wine. 'Also, I'm quite sure he was seeing other women. I wasn't the only woman in his life. He never said as much and I never asked. I didn't feel I had the right to. And why shouldn't he? After all, after our times together, I went home to my family. What was he supposed to do for the next fortnight? Just wait for me? Whatever the reason, things gradually seemed to change, and our meetings became less frequent.

'We remained close, and we did spend an afternoon together a couple of weeks before he went to Shropshire. I couldn't stay the night. I think it was something to do with Harry, he's my son. He's eighteen. He was playing with his band, and Jerry and I wanted to go along and see them. Not that he'd have allowed us to had he known.'

'And did you think he was OK?'

'He was brilliant!'

'No, Tom. Did Oliver seem alright to you? Was there anything unusual? Anything at all?'

'He was fine. His usual self, a bit maudlin, a bit pre-occupied, the same as ever. We had a nice afternoon.'

Both women ate in silence for a few minutes.

'What's he like as a writer?' asked Salt.

'How do you mean?' said Andrea.

'How is he regarded, generally? What's his standing?'

'Well, some writers don't do anything particularly wonderful, but somehow they sell lots. No names, but I'm sure you know who I mean. And there are some who spend years doing good work and never seem to get the recognition that – mostly other writers – feel they should.'

'And Tom's one of these?' asked Salt.

'As a writer, he's well regarded, but to be brutally honest, he's a bit out of time. You know the kind of books he writes – those campus novels – they've really had their day. And he was a bit unlucky, I guess. You know, he didn't have the break-through book or the pot of gold that's a TV series.'

'And that's it?' queried Salt. 'Luck?'

'Well, there might be more to it than that. All these things add up, I suppose.'

'Go on,' she urged.

'As I say, I think Tom was quite good with half the population – women – just as long as they weren't any kind of threat to him. But he also fell out with a lot of people, too. Mostly men, and the thing about Tom is, if you fall out with him . . .'

'Yes?'

'He's a tough adversary,' said Moore.

'How do you mean? Violent?' suggested Salt.

'Not as far as I know,' she said. 'But you don't fall out with him and make it up with a chummy text the next day. He doesn't have skirmishes. He has real battles; feuds and bad feelings that go back years, sometimes really nasty stuff, I have to say. And always to do with the thing that's really important to him.'

'Relationships? Women?' said Salt.

'No, not women,' said Moore categorically. 'His work. His writing. That's the thing he really cares about.'

'I see,' said Salt and she brushed a few breadcrumbs into a little pile beside her side plate. 'And that was the last time you saw him, a couple of weeks before he went to Shropshire?'

'Yes.'

'There's one thing I have to ask you, Andrea.'

'Yes?' said the novelist.

'Your husband, Jerry, are you quite sure he knows nothing about your relationship with Tom?'

'I'm sure,' she said. 'Not only have we been very careful, but if Jerry knew, he's not the kind of man not to confront me, and it would be the end of our marriage, I assure you. Why do you ask?'

'If he'd found out about you two, he'd be an obvious suspect in wanting to harm Oliver,' she said.

'It's out of the question,' said Moore emphatically.

'I'll take your word for it,' said Salt. 'Can you jot down the details about where and when you spent the afternoon the last time you saw Tom?' She handed the woman her pad.

Moore put her knife and fork carefully together on her empty plate. 'We did text one another a couple of times, and I left a message on his phone the day before he was going away, but I didn't hear back from him,' she said as she wrote.

Like any good cop, prior to their meeting, Jane Salt had already been in touch with Moore's ISP to check her email and, courtesy of T Mobile, had already read every text message she'd sent and received in the previous month.

'That's really all I know,' said Moore, handing the police-woman's pad back to her. 'I just hope he's alright.'

TWENTY-ONE

Shropshire

As usual, Kavanagh had listened with less than full attention to Jeff Earle's directions to the centre from the police station at Craven Arms, and he sailed blithely past the concealed entrance on the tight bend.

Why on earth, he wondered, would writers want to come to a remote country house in a heavily wooded valley to practise their craft? If they needed stuff to write about, wouldn't they be better off spending a day or two on Camden High Street or a Hackney housing estate?

In the village, he pulled into the garage. It might be rural Shropshire, but folk still needed petrol and an MOT certificate for their cars. He bought a packet of tobacco and passed the time of day with the proprietor before driving back up the road.

Centre Director Kiera Noonan was a formidable-looking woman with the strong shoulders and upright bearing of an athlete and, with blue streaks in her dirty blonde hair, was an exotic animal to find amidst the monochrome colours of a Shropshire landscape.

The women Kavanagh had been close to, and certainly those with whom he had been romantically involved, had tended to be slight in build.

Appearance was critical to first impressions. For years now, having sat through any number of trials and committals, the cop had arrived at the entirely reactionary conclusion that justice might just as well be served (and the taxpayer very much better so) if the accused were sent down – or, just occasionally, not – simply on account of how they appeared.

In his experience, the bloke who looked as if he might lash out at the stranger in the pub if his pint were spilled was exactly the character who almost invariably did. You *could* judge a very great number of books by their covers.

Yes, Keira was every bit the macaw in this world of starlings.

'So, how long have you been at the centre, Miss Noonan?'

She spooned coffee into a cafetière as Kavanagh stood in the sunlit doorway.

'Call me Keira, if you like,' she said, smiling broadly. 'Everyone does.'

'Thanks.'

'About eighteen months. I have a contract for two years. It's what the Trust does, so that people don't get stale, you know.'

'Sure,' he acquiesced.

She carried cups through and set them down on one of the pine tables and then poured the hot water into the cafetière.

'Occasionally, they might grant an extension, but usually, it's two years and that's it.'

'You've six months to go?'

'Good maths,' she said.

He smiled and took a seat at the table. 'And then what?'

'I don't know. I'm a writer. Or trying to be. It's part of the reason I wanted the job. I'll get going on my book again, I guess. Being here seemed like a great idea, you know, and that I'd get lots of inspiration, being around writers and all that . . .' Her delivery had that rising note at the end of each sentence that made statements sound like questions.

'Not so?' he suggested as she eased the plunger down through the coffee grounds.

'There's so much to do around the place. Supervising the cleaning and cooking, organizing things for a new group of students every week. Booking the writers, sorting out travel, food deliveries, meetings, finance, the grounds, it's a lot of work.'

'Sure,' he said.

'But plenty of writers have held down a day job as well as doing their own work,' she went on.

'Yes?' he said.

'T.S. Eliot was working in a bank at the same time as he was writing *The Waste Land*.'

'Really?' said Kavanagh. He knew of Eliot, of course, but hardly knew the poem.

'I don't think he was a cashier on the counter, exactly, just

in an office somewhere.' Again the upward lilt at the sentence's
end. 'And Charles Dodgson—'

'Never heard of him,' volunteered Kavanagh playfully.

'You have,' she said. 'Lewis Carroll?'

'Oh, right,' he said.

'He was a mathematics don at Oxford when he wrote *Alice*.
I could go on,' she said.

'I bet you could,' he said, 'but I need to ask you a few
questions.'

But she'd started and was on a roll. 'Fielding was a magis-
trate; Trollope ran the post office, and Larkin was a librarian.
Good one, too, apparently.'

As she poured the coffee, through the open kitchen door
came the caw of crows in the sycamores and the muffled
whine of machinery in the woods someplace far off.

She rolled a cigarette and then went to the back door and
leaned there as she lit it. 'Bliss,' she said, inhaling the smoke
deeply and then fluming it out through her mouth in a long,
steady stream. Kavanagh never smoked before the afternoon,
and often not until the evening, but Keira made this morning
pursuit look positively beguiling and he was tempted to join
her. Instead, he took out his pad and said, 'Quite a few people
work here, then?'

'Yes,' she replied. 'Do you want me to go through them?
There's the housekeeper, Shirley; Leon, he's the handyman
and gardener, and the two part-time cleaners, the Polish
girls, Ilona and Renata. They rent a flat over at Craven
Arms.'

'And what about the owners of the place, Richard Osman
and his wife? I know he's ill.'

'Richard is incapacitated. He had a severe stroke.'

'And Mrs Osman? What about her?'

'What can I tell you? Maggie's very independent; she
doesn't like a lot of fussing over her.'

'No?' he said.

'She's getting on now. And between me and you, Inspector,
she drinks a little bit more than is good for her, but she's –
what's the phrase you use in this country? She's sharp as a
tack. She's still working, too.'

'Really? What does she do?'

'She's a sculptor. She works every day, and she doesn't

welcome interruptions, I can tell you that. We shop for her, when we get our own supplies in for the centre, and Leon or Shirley takes them down to the cottage once a week. It's part of the original agreement. She and Richard would be housed and looked after here for as long as they were alive.'

'I see,' he said.

'They've been offered a carer to come in to help get Richard up and put him to bed at night, but Maggie still does it all herself.'

'I see,' he said again. 'It must be grim.'

She pushed her cigarette butt deep into the soft earth in the old handcart outside the kitchen door and said reflectively, 'When you think of the mind that wrote those plays . . .'

'Yes,' he agreed, 'awful.'

'Locked-in syndrome. He can understand what's going on, he just can't express anything. I wasn't here then, but Shirley says that on the day that the place was handed over to the Trust there was a garden party here with lots of writers and dignitaries and politicians, and she says it was just awful, with Richard in his chair, a July afternoon, a blanket around his knees, and all these people drinking wine and champagne and coming up and taking his hand as he lay there, helplessly.'

'It sounds terrible,' said Kavanagh, and they maintained a respectful silence for a few moments. 'Do they have any children?' he eventually asked.

'Margaret is Richard's third wife. I think they were both in their forties when they met. There were no children from either of his previous marriages. I believe Maggie already had a daughter, but she was killed in a car crash when she was at university.'

'I see,' he said. He finished his coffee. 'I'd like to see the room that Oliver was staying in, just to check it over, and then I'll take a look around outside if you don't mind.'

'Be my guest,' she said. 'He had the room at the top of the stairs on the left. All the rooms are called after famous writers. Tom was in Oscar Wilde last week.'

'Really?' The inspector smirked.

She handed him a booklet of that year's courses from the pile on the table and he flipped idly through it as she cleared the coffee cups. 'And the grounds are pretty extensive, I'm told,' he said.

'Yes, you can walk for miles around the woods and fields,' she said.

'And what about Tom Oliver? Did you know him well? He'd tutored here before, I believe?'

'Yes,' she said, 'a couple of times. I believe he was a good tutor.'

'Yes?' said Kavanagh.

'It's not always the case. Sometimes, some of the more high-profile writers seem to think it's enough for them just to turn up and be here.'

'Not so?' he said.

'Being star-struck lasts for about a day. Once a student hears someone slurping their tea at breakfast or spots a bit of dandruff on their collar, they come down to earth pretty quickly. They soon forget all about reputations and just want some feedback on their own work. Yes, Tom Oliver's not as big a writer as some we have here, but he was quite popular as a tutor.'

'And who was his co-tutor, this Sarah Cassin?' he said as he looked at the booklet.

'She's a poet,' said Keira.

'A poet and a novelist?' said Kavanagh. 'Is that how it works?'

'Yes, we always have two writers, different disciplines, but generally a man and a woman. Not always, though – sexual politics . . .'

'Sorry?' he said.

'Lesbian and gay people, you know, they might prefer to work with same-sex writers. Not often, but it happens.'

'I see,' he said, and got to his feet. 'Right, I'd better get going . . .'

'Actually, Sarah didn't tutor the course in the end.'

'Really? How come?' he asked.

'She was booked, but her husband had an accident – well, actually, we didn't mention this to the students, we didn't want to say anything so upsetting, but he was mugged, the night before the course, and she had to drop out. Sarah felt she couldn't leave him on his own.'

'And?' he said, sitting down once more.

'And what?'

'What happened? What did you do?'

'I was at a loss. It was very short notice and so I checked on a couple of other writers, people I thought might be up for it, but they were either abroad or tutoring elsewhere. I don't know if you're aware, Inspector, but this kind of work is what a lot of writers do these days, just to make ends meet. It's an important part of their earnings. Eventually, Cath Wooley stepped in. She's a poet, too, and she doesn't live far away.'

'I see,' he said, and jotted her details in his notepad.

'Between ourselves,' began Kiera tentatively, 'she's not . . . what shall we say? She's not quite as well regarded, if you like, as Sarah, not quite as high profile. Catherine was a rising star and showed a lot of early promise, but it was never fully realized, and she now does more of this sort of work. I believe she also tutors at a prison in Cheshire where she teaches writing skills.'

'Really?' said Kavanagh.

'I was a bit concerned that the students would be put out by the change, but needs must.'

'And were they OK?'

'Yes, there was a little bit of muttering at first, but they went with it and it worked out fine.'

'Good,' he said. 'Thanks for the coffee. I'll take a look at Oscar Wilde's room then.'

'Sure,' she said.

As he got to his feet he said, 'You don't have any idea where Tom Oliver might have gone, I suppose?'

'Me?' she said. 'Of course not. How would I?'

'Just one more thing,' he began. 'Last week, when everyone was here, was there anything out of the ordinary? Anything unusual?'

'How do you mean?'

'Well, anything at all out of the ordinary,' he said again. 'The tutor who was booked, Sarah Cassin, for example. She couldn't come. That's unusual, you know?'

'It's a writers' centre, Inspector,' she said. 'It's not *Big Brother*. There were no fights. There never are. Nothing like that.'

He ignored the sarcasm. 'No issues between any of those present?'

'No. Not that I was aware of. Although my inviting Catherine was a bit of a faux pas.'

'Go on,' he said.

'Well, I only found out later, but she and Tom Oliver had had a bit of a fall out in the past, some literary tiff, apparently.'

'Tell me more,' he asked, leaning against the table.

'A few years ago – I was still in America – Catherine had reviewed his latest book very badly, and then, not long after, they had a stand-up row at some function or other. It got very heated.'

'Blimey,' he said.

'I'd no idea about this, obviously. I just knew them as writers.'

'But didn't she ask who the other tutor was when you phoned her?'

'Yes. I told her, and she said something like, "Oh, Tom Oliver. I know Tom. That should make for an interesting week," and that was that.'

'And what about him?' said Kavanagh. 'How did he react?'

'I tried to tell him about the change of tutor before he got here, but I couldn't reach him. Apparently, he'd already left home, and I couldn't get through on his mobile at the cottage where he was staying. We had a chat here in the kitchen and he told me what had happened between them. But I have to say, to his credit, he was professional about it and said he'd just get on with it. And they did. It was all very civil.'

'I see,' he said. 'Right, just one more thing. This statue thing that's gone missing?'

'Yes?'

'Any thoughts?'

'No.'

'Do you reckon it's been stolen?' he asked.

'I suppose so,' she replied.

'You don't think so, though?'

'I don't think the kind of people that come here steal things, Inspector. They don't even take the towels and the coat-hangers, you know. It's not a Travelodge. It's just not that sort of mindset.'

'No,' he agreed. 'Funny though, the tutor who's booked can't make it; a bronze that's been here for ever disappears, and then Tom Oliver doesn't return home.'

'It is odd, isn't it?' she agreed.

'In my work, you know,' said Kavanagh thoughtfully, 'we don't really like coincidences.'

'No?' she said. 'Well, we've something in common, then.'

'How do you mean?' he asked.

'Writers don't like them either. When people are teaching fiction here – and I've sat in on plenty of workshops – they always say: coincidences in your novel? One at most.'

'Mmm,' he said, 'that many?'

She smiled.

'Thanks for your time. I'll get out and take a look around.'

TWENTY-TWO

K avanagh tapped the door and opened it. A wardrobe, a double bed and a dressing table, inexpensive pine furniture, old stuff that looked just right in the white-painted room. And a desk by the window with a chair that you wouldn't be comfortable in for very long.

Kavanagh sat on the edge of the bed. Lovely view through the not very clean window, scudding clouds across the palest blue, almost white English sky. The sash window rattled a little as each gusty breeze blew by.

He breathed in deeply, tried to scent out the sense of the place. Eyes level with the dressing-table surface, he could see the ring where a tea cup or glass had stood and left its mark.

He got up and opened the wardrobe door: a spare blanket and an ancient-looking hot-water bottle. A few coat hangers hung forlornly from the rail and there was a good deal of dust on the glued, strengthening joints at the back of the thing, but the room offered no clues as to its previous resident's current whereabouts.

Kavanagh stood at the window and watched as the gardener went past in a Land Rover with a trailer full of wood chips.

He pushed up the bottom sash of the window and put his head out. On the gravel below were several cigarette ends, and on the air just the faintest suggestion of one of his favourite smells. Very few people used creosote these days to protect their fence posts: the coal-tar product had fallen foul of European health and safety regulations and nowadays sweet-smelling, watery liquids were used that did the job half as well.

Outside, the young man was reversing the trailer, and Kavanagh watched, impressed by his casual dexterity.

'How you doing?' he asked as the young man got out of the cab.

'Alright,' he said. 'You?'

'Alright,' said Kavanagh.

The man went round the side of the trailer.

'Not a bad day,' said the cop.

'Yes,' he said. 'Not bad.'

He slipped the bolts on either side of it and dropped the rear flap. Kavanagh would have happily swapped places with the man as he slid his spade into the pile of bark chips there. He'd had a holiday with Rachael once in Tunisia. The weather had been nice, the hotel fine. But just how many cheap novels can a man read, how many Coca Colas drink, before he yearns for a bit of something more taxing, something with a modicum of routine and a hint of meaning?

Early mornings, from the balcony of their room, he'd watch the pool attendant with his net making rhythmic sweeps across the still, blue water; later, he'd observe the gardener as he went about his slow tasks. By the third day he wanted to ask if one of them would care to lie on a sunlounger amongst the Europeans and read some paperback and let him, instead, take the big net or hoe around the geraniums and date palms.

'I used to have one of these,' he said.

The young man chucked another spadeful of bark onto the earth and glanced at the green Land Rover with its faded, canvas tilt. 'Yes?'

'It was before everybody owned a four-by-four just for going down the shops . . .'

'Right,' said the man.

'Good days,' said Kavanagh.

'Yes?' said the man.

'What year's this?' asked Kavanagh, walking to the back and reading the old-style metal embossed number plate. 'Seventy-three?'

'Seventy-four,' said the man.

'Yes?' said Kavanagh, coming back to the front and shading his eyes as he peered in through the window to read the odometer. 'It'll go on for ever.'

'MOT'd last week,' volunteered the gardener.

Kavanagh tapped the vehicle's determinedly non-aero-dynamic front wing. 'You work here, then?' said the inspector, stating the obvious.

The man turned the earth mulch with his fork. 'Yes.'

'And are you a writer?' asked the policeman.

'No, not me. I'm not a writer,' he said.

'I'm Kavanagh,' said the cop. 'Detective Inspector

Kavanagh.' he extended his hand. The gardener wiped his palm on the thigh of his combat trousers and shook the policeman's hand.

'Leon,' he said. 'Is there something up?'

'Probably nothing,' ventured Kavanagh, 'but someone might have gone missing. We're just checking it out. Routine enquiry.'

'Might have?' queried the gardener.

'Yes, we can't be sure at the moment.'

'Who's that, then?' he asked.

'One of the tutors. From last week. A man called Tom Oliver. Did you meet him at all?'

'Not really,' he said. 'Well, I went in on the last night, listened to him and the other woman read some of their stuff, then we all went to the pub. It's what usually happens on the last night.'

'Yes?' said Kavanagh. 'Was that the last time you saw him?'

'Yes, I think so. There's always people wandering about, you know.'

'Sure. How long you been working here, then?' he asked.

'Over a year,' he said.

'But you're not a writer, you say?'

'No,' he said again.

'Are you local?' The man's accent was no more Shropshire than Kavanagh's was.

'No. I'm from up Manchester way,' said the gardener.

'What brought you down here?' asked Kavanagh.

'How do you mean?' he said.

'Well, you're not a writer, so how come you're working here? It's a bit off the beaten track, I'd have thought.'

'I was doing a crap job in Manchester, working for the parks department, so I saw this and thought, why not have a go somewhere different, away from the city?'

'Fair enough,' said Kavanagh. 'But they didn't want a writer?'

'Have you met Keira?' he asked.

'Yes, just now,' said Kavanagh. 'Why?'

'She told me that the last thing they wanted was a writer. They've had writers working here before and they'd always be nipping off into the woods to write their poems and stuff. They just wanted someone reliable. Someone to go to the village, pick people up from the station and look after the grounds, that's all.'

'I see,' said the inspector.

The two men stood there awkwardly for a moment, Leon unsure whether he should continue with his work.

'What's in the drums?' asked the policeman, gesturing to a couple of big plastic containers lashed in the back of the vehicle.

'Oil,' said the gardener.

'Oil?' repeated Kavanagh, no wiser. 'How do you mean?'

'They were on about converting this. To run on chip fat, bio-fuel, you know what I mean?'

'Oh, yes, I'm with you,' said the cop.

'Recycling and all that,' he added.

'Course,' agreed Kavanagh. Eventually, he said, 'And the other tutor who was here last week, a woman called Catherine Wooley?'

'What about her?' asked Leon.

'You met her, too?'

'Like I say, she was reading her poems on the last night. I didn't understand a word myself, and then she was down the pub with everyone else.'

'You talk to her at all?' asked Kavanagh.

'Not really. Just hello, that sort of thing. She was here last year, too,' Leon volunteered. 'Some old guy was teaching here and he fell down the stairs, bit pissed I think, and broke his wrist. Keira needed to get someone in for the last couple of days, so she got her.'

'Right,' said Kavanagh. 'Thanks a lot.' He turned to leave. 'Incidentally, Leon, has anyone spoken to you about the statue that's been nicked from the house?'

'Yes, the sergeant from Craven Arms.'

'And?

'And what?'

'You got any idea what might have happened to it?'

'Been nicked, I s'pose,' he concurred.

'Yes,' said the inspector. 'I suppose so. Right, I'd better take a look around.' He gestured to the lake. 'Who looks after the sluice gate?'

'How do you mean?' said the gardener.

'You know, the sluice that controls the water, who looks after it?'

'No idea. Why?'

'We might have to drain it. You know, like on the telly. It's the first place people hide things.'

'What, you're gonna drain all that just to look for a statue?' he said.

'What else?' said Kavanagh, and walked away as the man returned to his work.

TWENTY-THREE

The building on the other side of the lake that American Keira Noonan had quaintly referred to as a cottage turned out to be nothing of the sort.

It was a red-brick estate house, a modest example of the arts and crafts period, with tall chimneys, a precipitous apex roof and an ornate porch with a solid, dark-stained and planked front door. It had probably been built to house the estate manager and his family at the same time as the main house, barn and surrounding outbuildings.

Kavanagh pulled at the bell on the front door and waited. Nothing. He edged along the gravel path and, shading his eyes against the reflection in the glass, looked in through the front window. A man with a blanket over his legs languished in a wheelchair there. He was unshaven, his eyes closed and his head lolled to one side.

A small television in the corner of the room was on. A couple of youngsters appeared to be hosting some kind of games between teams of ten-year-old children, one group decked in blue tunics, the other in red.

Kavanagh continued round the side of the building, past the frosted-glass window pane of a downstairs loo, and then a slim pantry window.

At the back of the house the kitchen was deserted, as was the dining room with its golden parquet floor. He could hear orchestral music; it was not coming from the house, but from a single-storey adjacent building, the side door of which was ajar. 'Hello,' he said, knocking.

'Yes, yes, what is it?' called a woman's voice irascibly.

'Sorry,' said the inspector. 'Mrs Osman?'

'Yes,' she said, glancing up at the man and immediately returning to her welding torch and the metalwork that was clamped to a heavy vice in front of her.

'Mrs Osman, I'm Inspector Kavanagh,' he called above the hiss and sparks of the flame. 'Do you think we might have a word?'

She removed her goggles, adjusted the flame to a limp yellow and placed the torch on its stand. She then switched off the battered-looking tape player that was perched on a shelf above one of the workbenches in the place. 'What is it?' she said again. 'What do you want?'

'I'm sorry to disturb you, but it's about the missing man, Tom Oliver.'

'Tom who?' she said, her exasperation with the interruption only too clear.

'Tom Oliver. The writer? He was tutoring here last week, but he hasn't returned home, and we're at a loss to know just where he's got to.'

'I'm afraid I can't help you,' she said. 'I have nothing to do with the centre. What goes on up there is nothing to do with me. Everything's in the hands of the trustees. Now, if you don't mind, I'm extremely busy.'

'Mrs Osman, I'm sorry, but I really will have to ask for a few minutes of your time. We're concerned about Mr Oliver's whereabouts . . .'

She turned off the gas bottle and took another long look at the piece held in the vice before turning to the inspector. She cut an odd figure in her dark-blue overalls, which were a couple of sizes too big for her, the sleeves rolled up to the elbow of her wiry arms – arms that were dotted with liver spots.

'Perhaps we could go into the house? It shouldn't take long,' said Kavanagh. 'I need to speak to everyone on the estate.'

She put her goggles aside and led them out of the converted garage and into the kitchen where she stood with her back to the sink unit. Kavanagh remained standing just inside the open back door.

'Your husband?' he ventured, feeling he simply had to acknowledge the presence of the other person in the room next door.

'Yes?' she said. 'What about him?'

'Is he . . . is he alright? Would you like to go and . . .?'

'Is my husband something to do with your enquiries?'

'No, of course not. It's just that, he's obviously alone . . .'

'Yes, he is,' she said without further elaboration and inclined her head as she encouraged him to continue.

'You didn't know Mr Oliver, then?' he asked.

'No.'

'And you say you don't have anything to do with the centre?'

'Nothing,' she said. 'They bring down my shopping once a week. That's all.'

'I see,' he said. 'And no contact with the tutors or the students?'

'I occasionally see them in the grounds.'

'Last week?' he prompted.

'Last week I had to speak to someone about leaving the path.'

'Do you have any idea who that was?' he asked.

'No. Why? He told me his name, but I've forgotten it. Does it matter?'

'It's not possible to say what might matter at the moment, Mrs Osman, which is exactly why I'm here.'

'I don't see how I can help you. I work here and, as you seem to know, my husband is incapacitated.'

'Yes,' said the inspector. 'How long has . . . how long has he been . . .?'

'Several years now.'

'I'm sorry,' said Kavanagh. 'And he set up the centre?'

'No,' she said.

'No?' asked Kavanagh.

'It was my doing.'

'Yours?' he said.

'I had power of attorney,' she said wearily.

'And you wanted to help other writers?'

'Yes, of course.'

'To perpetuate your husband's name?'

'In a sense.'

'In a sense?' he repeated, tiring of the ping-pong rally involved in eliciting anything at all from the woman.

'Do you know my husband's work, Mr . . .?' she asked.

'Kavanagh. Inspector Frank Kavanagh,' he replied. 'A little,' he went on. 'I know of some of his plays, from the Seventies.'

'He was a very radical playwright.'

'Yes, I believe so,' he agreed.

'But like many writers, he struggled at first and he had little or no support from anyone. It was several years before his work was staged.'

'I see,' said the inspector, wondering exactly where this history lesson was leading.

'It taught him a lesson that he never forgot, or tired of repeating.'

'Yes?' said Kavanagh. 'What was that?'

'That writers should not be cosseted.'

'Really?' said Kavanagh, smiling, but failing to see the connection.

'Really,' she repeated. 'Like a lot of writers, Richard has a special gene.'

'Yes?' he asked.

'It's the hate gene.'

'And what is that?' he asked, intrigued.

'Richard hated everyone: critics, directors, actors, members of the audience, people who coughed over a line, or laughed too long, or not at all. But what he really hated most of all, with an almost messianic zeal, was . . .'

'Yes?' he urged.

'Other writers,' she said.

'Is that so?' asked Kavanagh, shocked by the strength of the woman's feeling and expression.

'He felt contempt for them if he disliked their work, and an even greater loathing if they had the temerity to produce anything which he thought any good.'

'Blimey,' said the inspector, shocked by the force of this declaration. 'Would you care to elaborate?' he asked tentatively.

'Our marriage, Inspector, was difficult. It was not a happy relationship,' she added.

'No?' he said.

'Richard had been married twice before.' The use of her husband's name seemed to force her into an intimacy that was unwelcome, the very word distasteful on her lips. 'He had a reputation – I knew all about that before we married, of course.'

'Yes?' he said.

'But, like many women, I thought our life together could be different, and that he would change. We were both artists, after all, and we had our individual lives.'

'Yes,' he said.

'But that wasn't to be. He didn't for a moment see us as equals. In fact, the contrary: he constantly undermined me and my work. He drank heavily and, of course, he continued to sleep with other women whenever they made themselves available to him, which was painfully often. By this time, the Eighties and Nineties, his creative fire had died and he was writing very little; he was a spent force. And the less he wrote, the more embittered he became. Anything he did produce, the critics savaged. Everyone knew the work was poor, and it would have been a mercy simply to ignore these attempts at seeking to find his former voice. But they were like jackals closing in on a dying animal.'

'I'm so sorry,' said Kavanagh. 'It must have been dreadful.'

She ignored the policeman's sympathy and continued. 'And then one afternoon, completely out of the blue – for I thought his rage and bitterness would drive him on for ever – he had a massive stroke.'

'I see,' said Kavanagh.

'And I was in a position to . . .' She thought for a moment, recollecting exactly that time.

'Yes?' he prompted.

'I was in a position to repay all of his "kindness" of the previous years.'

'Go on,' he said, bracing himself for what was to follow.

'A centre for writers. In his house. A place where others might flourish and find support for their work, something which he would have found absolute anathema. It was so apt, somehow, such a wonderful idea, that I immediately put it in motion,' she concluded.

The inspector was at a complete loss as to what to say. Could the woman really be serious about inflicting this pain upon another? 'I suppose I'm surprised that you're choosing to tell me this, Mrs Osman.'

'Yes,' she said. 'I'm sure you are, but then no-one is witness to what takes place in someone else's marriage. You know those people who kill themselves, and sometimes their own children, to hurt an unfaithful husband or wife? Only they know just how strong those feelings are. And fortunately, Mr Kavanagh, your understanding is not what I am seeking – nor anyone else's for that matter.'

Kavanagh was silent. The woman's revelation was made even more grotesque by the knowledge of her husband lying next door slumped in his chair.

'Your husband, he has no speech? No . . . volition?' he asked, seeking the best word.

'None,' she said.

'His mind, though?' he asked, afraid of what he might hear in answer.

'Oh, yes, he knows what's happening. All this in his name.'

'My God,' said Kavanagh.

'God?' she repeated. 'I never had any truck with that "what goes round, comes round" nonsense,' she said. 'I never flirted with eastern religion, karma and all that stuff. But I have to say, it did cross my mind on the day that I handed the place over to the trust, and the string quartet played on the lawn, with Richard lying there in his chair, that maybe there is something in all that philosophy . . .'

Kavanagh walked away from the house. He had known unhappiness: his marriage to Rachael had been a troubled union and even now he could summon bitter memories of the pain that her infidelity had inflicted on him. Yes, he'd often wished her dead; it would have freed him from the misery of the thought of her being with one or another of the men with whom she'd had affairs. But wishing her dead was as nothing: would he have chosen, ever, even at his most distraught, to torture her in this fashion? Is this really what people were capable of doing to one another? The final redress of the balance of hurts done?

He began the climb up the track, into the woods beyond the bracken-covered hillsides.

Forty minutes later, he looked down on the roof of the centre half a mile away, and through the tree tops in the autumn quiet, glimpsed the mercury surface of the lake.

He sat on his haunches, rolled a cigarette and leaned against the trunk of a giant beech as he inhaled the smoke. In the distance, a red delivery van drove up towards the house. It stopped halfway up the track and the driver exchanged a few words with the driver of the Land Rover.

A few minutes later, Kavanagh ground the cigarette butt into the sandy earth and called Salt.

'Hello?' she said.

'Jane?'

'Frank? How you doing?'

'Not so good,' he said.

'What's going on?'

'I've just spoken to Margaret Osman. I'll tell you all about it when I see you. But it's a very gloomy tale.'

'You sound upset,' she said considerately.

'I'll be OK,' he said. 'The thing is, Jane, I'm just not sure what we've got here. Oliver's missing, that much we know, and there's a couple of things that might tie in, but they might be absolutely nothing to do with anything.'

'What things?' she asked.

'Well, there's a little statue, a figure of Richard Osman, that's gone missing. Then Oliver's co-tutor didn't show up because her husband was mugged the night before she was due here, and the woman who did get to work with him, a poet called Catherine Wooley – it turns out that she'd had a big fallout with Oliver a while ago. You know, is it something, or is it nothing? Is it a crime scene I've got here? Should I close the place down and fence it off, or is Oliver just going to turn up tomorrow?'

'Yes,' she said. 'I suppose if the attack on that other tutor's husband is in any way connected, it's a question of looking at who was to benefit from her not being able to come.'

'Sure,' he agreed. 'The obvious person was Catherine Wooley, who came in her stead. But that's crazy. I don't know how much they get paid for doing this kind of thing, but she's not going to get someone mugged just for a week's work, no matter how skint she might be, surely?'

'Folk. Nowt so queer as,' said Salt.

'Mmm,' said Kavanagh, unconvinced. 'More to the point, right now, there's a dozen folk descending on the place from all over the country for a two-day songwriting course that's due to start in a couple of hours' time.'

'Perhaps just have a word and restrict their movements until you've had a look around. You'll obviously need to keep everyone out of what was Oliver's room until it's been checked over properly.'

'Of course,' he agreed.

'So, what do you think?' she asked.

'What I think is, I just don't know. I'm going to get a couple of local lads to dig out the CCTV. There are only two obvious routes going south, and my trusty sergeant up here – OK, he's not exactly Columbo, but he says there's cameras on a traffic island on the one road and a garage that's got a decent system on the other. It shouldn't take them long to pick up Oliver's car, given we know roughly when he left. And then at least we'll know exactly what time he was on the road and which way he was going . . .'

'If he left at all,' she said.

'If he left at all,' he agreed.

'Where does the woman whose husband was mugged live?' she asked.

'Hereford,' he said. 'I'm planning on going down there as soon as I can, see if there's anything more to the attack on her husband than meets the eye.'

'Sure,' said Salt. There was a pause and then she asked, 'Incidentally, any developments on the Crouch End have-a-go-hero copper enquiry?'

'Haven't heard anything,' he said. 'It only needs one witness to come forward, some public-spirited citizen, and it'd be sorted. But you know what people are like these days: no-one wants to get involved, especially where we're concerned.'

'I'm sure it'll be OK,' she offered reassuringly.

'You reckon?' he said cynically. 'Last time I was down there, all they'd got was one of those yellow boards asking if anyone saw anything, blah blah blah. The best they can hope for that is that some youngster doesn't take it home for his bedroom to show his mates.'

'What's your hotel like?' she said, keen to change the subject.

'It's a room in the local pub. The floorboards are at a crazy angle, the window doesn't open and the bed's going to creak every time I move. Apart from that, it's fine.'

'Why don't we try and get over to Birmingham some time?' she said. 'We haven't seen one another properly for days. What do you think?'

'I think it's the best thing I've heard today. You take care, and I'll see you soon.'

'You too,' she said, and hung up.

TWENTY-FOUR

Hereford

'Good fences make good neighbours,' poet Robert Frost had once suggested, but six feet of larch-lap hadn't been enough to keep Sarah Cassin and her husband Will on friendly terms with the folk next door.

'Mrs Cassin?' said Kavanagh as the woman opened her front door to him.

'Sarah,' said the woman. 'Please, call me Sarah.'

'Of course,' said the inspector. 'Sarah, I'm DI Frank Kavanagh, we spoke on the phone.'

'Excuse these, please,' she said as they negotiated their way past several stout cardboard boxes stacked in the hallway of the Victorian house.

'It's the new book,' she said. 'I like to have a few copies.'

'Yes, of course,' he said. There must have been a good couple of hundred, he reckoned.

'Come through.' She gestured and he followed her into the front sitting room with its big bay window and two comfy sofas. 'Will,' she called up the stairs, 'the policeman is here. Would you like some coffee, Inspector?'

'That would be nice,' he said. Like social workers, cops very quickly learned in which houses they were safe to accept a drink. Some of the people they visited would be as likely to put bleach in your tea as see you off the premises refreshed.

She disappeared and he stood at the window and watched the traffic. 'Hello,' said the man who had appeared silently at the doorway. 'I'm Will. Will Cassin.'

'I'm pleased to meet you, Will,' said the inspector, taking a few steps towards him and extending his hand.

Few people realize the repercussions of being the victim of crime. These days, the perpetrators of some violent deed are less likely to show contrition or shame than to be seen leaving court giving the finger to the local TV news crew who are on the building's steps to cover the story.

Cassin still had the blacked eyes and broken nose of a boxer who'd fought several brutal rounds; he was heavily swollen around his forehead and cheeks where he had been kicked, and his left arm was in plaster from the elbow to the wrist. And for this, the shambling, traumatized man would merit an entry – just one more statistic – in the following year's figures for recorded crime.

Kavanagh saw all too clearly that there was more in the man's eyes than just the physical pain inflicted by kicks and punches. Although his GP had prescribed heavy doses of tranquillizers and sleeping pills, the geography lecturer now looked like the shell of a man, timorous and afraid.

'How are you feeling now?' asked the inspector considerately, but rather fatuously.

'Terrible,' said Cassin unequivocally.

'Of course,' he said. 'I know the local police have spoken to you, but do you mind if I ask you again – do you have any idea at all who might have done this?'

Cassin lowered himself onto a straight-backed chair, wincing as he did so. 'No,' he murmured.

'None?'

'Not really.'

'Not really?' repeated the inspector.

'None of it makes any sense,' added Cassin.

'But I believe you said something to the local officer about a dispute with a neighbour?'

Sarah Cassin carried in a tray of coffee and biscuits and looked at her husband with the sadness that's usually the preserve of a parent for an injured child.

'Are you OK, Will?' she said quietly.

'Yes,' he said, 'I'm alright.'

She poured the coffee.

'Could you tell me about this business with your neighbour?' Kavanagh continued.

'It didn't involve me. Well, not directly,' started the man. 'I cycle most places. Well, I used to,' he said, 'but Sarah . . . she parks the car on the road just round the corner.' He gestured with a half-raised arm.

'We have done for years,' she continued, 'because it's a

quieter road. The traffic's got heavier and heavier here.' And, as if to emphasize the point, a turquoise Argos delivery truck thundered past the window.

'There were fewer cars on the road then,' he said. 'When we first came here, several of the local houses were occupied by elderly folk, people who didn't own cars themselves, and so there was never any problem about parking.'

Sarah passed Kavanagh his coffee and pushed the little plate of biscuits towards him. 'We've never had a crossed word with any of the neighbours. And then these people moved in,' she said.

'Yes. Go on,' encouraged the inspector.

'They were never particularly friendly. That's up to them, but it did feel different. The area immediately felt changed by their being here.

'They've several cars in the family, there's a couple of grown-up boys, one's a trainee chef and one's at college doing some sort of sports course, and so immediately, the parking situation became a bit of an issue.'

'Is it difficult right outside your own house, here?' asked the inspector reasonably, gesturing through the window.

'I left the car there overnight a few months ago and the wing mirror was knocked off by a passing vehicle,' she said. 'It cost a hundred pounds.'

'I see,' he said.

'I went back to trying to park around the corner, but always considerately,' she went on. 'One or other of their sons might be away, or even . . .' It was clear that she didn't want to use his name.

'Fraser?' offered Kavanagh, looking at his notebook.

'Yes, that's right,' she concurred. 'It seemed so silly to park a hundred yards away when there were sometimes spaces right there.'

'Yes, quite,' he said supportively.

Her husband continued. 'One morning, there was a note on the car. Very aggressive. Frankly, if the man had just had a polite word, we'd have done as he wanted. He's no right, of course; it's a public road, but it is outside their house, and we'd have cooperated.'

'Yes,' agreed Kavanagh. 'So he put a note on your car?'

'Yes,' she said, 'and for a while I parked way up the road,

and then I just got to thinking, this is ridiculous. One week – I think the son had gone on holiday with some of his mates, and so there was plenty of space – I parked there again. The next morning there was a huge gouge down the side of the car.'

'Did you say anything?' asked the inspector.

'What could we do? There was no proof. And anyway, who knows, maybe it was just some yob. Not them at all. But I had to report it to the police to put in an insurance claim. The policeman came and I didn't say anything about the dispute with the Frasers for fear of escalating things, but this young officer was clearly very diligent and he called on everybody in the street to see if anyone had seen or heard anything.'

'Next time I saw Fraser,' continued her husband, 'he gave me that friendly hand gesture,' and the man mimicked the familiar masturbatory abuse.

'What's he do, this neighbour of yours?' asked the inspector.

'Works for PC World,' said Sarah. 'He's a warehouseman or something like that on the retail park on the edge of town.'

Kavanagh drank his coffee. 'As you say, there's nothing specific, and it'd never hold up, but between ourselves, if you had to guess . . . you think what happened to you that Sunday night would be down to him?'

The man shrugged his shoulders. 'How can I think anything else?'

'It was a serious assault,' said Kavanagh. 'I think that forensics might have been able to do something had his clothing been examined at the time.'

'I would have had to accuse him, and then what? The police in their house, examining everything? What then? What if he's innocent? It's going to ruin all of our lives here for ever . . .'

'Yes,' said Kavanagh. 'I do see, but really, things couldn't get much worse than they are now.'

The man sighed his agreement with a shallow gasp, all that his fractured ribs allowed.

'There was one thing I didn't understand,' said the inspector. 'Reading the notes on the crime report, when you were found and helped by a passer-by, when the police arrived they found a copy of a DVD near where you'd been attacked. Is that right?'

'Apparently,' said Cassin, without any interest whatsoever.

'Any thoughts?' pressed Kavanagh. 'A copy of *Falling Down* in a box. It wasn't new, but there were no fingerprints on it. It had been wiped clean and then presumably only handled with gloves. Why would someone do that?'

'I've no idea,' said the man. 'They don't even know whether it belonged to the thug who attacked me.'

'Did you hear him drop it?' probed Kavanagh.

'I don't know,' said Cassin. 'I wasn't listening for anything. All I wanted was for him to stop beating me.'

'Of course,' said the inspector. 'I'm sorry. Of course you did.'

'Will,' said his wife considerately, 'why don't you go back and lie down? I can tell the inspector anything he needs to know.'

'Yes, I think I will,' he said. 'I'm sorry.'

'Please,' said Kavanagh, and got to his feet as the man shuffled out of the room. They listened as he made a slow progress up the stairs.

'You said on the phone that Tom's missing?' she began.

'That's right,' said Kavanagh. 'He taught the course but has now disappeared, and one of our lines of enquiry has to focus on the circumstances of your not coming.'

'How do you mean?' she said.

'There's always a motive, even if they are sometimes a bit convoluted, so one of our lines of enquiry is to see if anyone was to benefit from your husband being beaten, which effectively then prevented you from coming.'

'And who did benefit?' she asked.

'Well, I imagine you know that Catherine Wooley came instead of you?' he said.

'Yes, of course,' she said. 'Keira at the centre phoned to tell me.'

'Do you know her?' he asked.

'No. I know her work, that's all. But we've never met,' she said.

'So she benefited,' said the inspector.

'I don't know her, Inspector, but I hardly think Catherine Wooley's likely to have been involved in the business of attacking my husband. Do you?'

'I'm sure not,' he said. 'There are a couple of other things, though,' he went on. 'As well as Tom Oliver being missing and the attack on your husband, that same week, a bronze figurine of Richard Osman was stolen from the centre.'

'Really?' she said.

'It's the sort of thing where we need to examine whether there could be any connection between the events.'

'Of course,' she agreed.

'Having said that, I'm not a conspiracy theorist. I find it's the apparently obvious explanation for events that turns out to be what's usually happened.'

'Yes?' she said.

'The problem with conspiracies is that, apart from anything else, history suggests that if two people conspire, one of them will eventually talk. People who believe that the Princess of Wales was killed by the authorities would have us believe that half the secret services around the world were involved. Are all these people going to maintain silence for twenty years? Isn't one of them going to sell their story to the press for the biggest payday in history? No, in my experience, the most likely explanation is the most likely explanation. I can't go and arrest your neighbour, but strictly off the record and between ourselves, if I'd got to bet my mortgage on who attacked your husband, it would be someone pretty close to home.'

'And how would that relate to Tom's disappearance?' she asked.

'I've no idea. But like I say, there's always a motive, and it's often a question of finding out just what that motive is, which is why we have to look at everything. Right now, we're checking CCTV and following all the usual procedures for a missing person. He might turn up, but it's been a bit too long now and I'd be lying if I said that we aren't increasingly concerned.' He finished his coffee and got to his feet. 'Right, thank you for your time, Sarah,' he said. 'I'd best be off. I do hope your husband feels better soon. It's a real ordeal he's been through.'

'Thank you,' said the woman.

In the hall, Kavanagh asked her, 'May I take one of these, please?'

'Of course,' she said. 'Are you a poetry reader, Inspector?

'Not really,' he said. 'But I have a close friend who is.' She took a copy of her work out of the box. 'Would you sign it for her, please? To Jane, if you would?'

She wrote in the flyleaf of the book.

'How much do I owe you?' he asked.

'Please, it's my pleasure,' she said, handing him the book.

'I insist,' he said. 'It's your living, and anyway, we're not allowed to accept gifts. I could find myself on a corruption charge and lose that pension I've been working all these years for.'

'Are you sure?' she smiled.

'Absolutely.'

'Cost price, then,' she said. 'Seven pounds.' He gave her the cash, and they shook hands.

There was no scratch or broken mirror on his BMW, but as he sat there and wrote up his notes, he was aware of the heavy figure standing beside the curtains in the house next door, watching him.

TWENTY-FIVE

Birmingham

K avanagh and Salt had arranged to meet in Waterstone's just outside Birmingham's New Street station, a place so grim that from there, for any visitor to the city, things can only ever get better.

The inspector had an awkward relationship with his former home. Even after spending so long in the seething mass that was London, there was no gainsaying the fact that, just as Wordsworth had asserted, earth really did not have 'anything to show more fair.'

Birmingham, by contrast, and for all his filial connection with the place, was clearly in a woeful state. Every third shop along Corporation Street, a bustling Mecca of retailing when he was a child, was now empty. Many of those that were trading sold cheap tat that spilled out onto the pavements and would have shamed even Oxford Street traders.

Whether it was the container-loads of Chinese imports that had flooded the market since that country's emergence in its new, capitalist garb, or the convenience of Internet shopping that was the cause, the high streets of most cities had now become blighted places, occupied only by franchise coffee shops and charity outlets, travel agents and ubiquitous building societies.

And in Birmingham, like everywhere else today, every hundred yards or so there was a fast-food restaurant or a barn-sized chain pub, home to forlorn-looking drinkers, people who sat behind the plate-glass windows cradling pints of lager at ten o'clock in the morning.

Yes, visiting the place had, these days, become a lowering experience for Frank Kavanagh. But nostalgia was a powerful drug, and as he walked out of the multi-storey car park behind Hill Street, the policeman recalled clearly the excitement of trips to Dolcis as a teenager – the very name beguiling, so unexplained and exotic – to buy Italian shoes at an incredibly expensive 59/11d.

With the exception of the newly restored neoclassical town hall and Victorian edifices like the council offices on Chamberlain Square, Birmingham city centre was not favoured with architectural gems. But Waterstone's bookstore, converted a dozen years ago from the defunct Midland Bank, and right next door to the former Midland Hotel, retained a certain stolid probity that made even hardback book buying seem frivolous.

And Kavanagh liked bookstores. They were invariably sanctuaries of peace in an increasingly frantic world. And for some reason, generally speaking, even indigent people, folk who might well have been expected to gravitate to their warmth and use their hygienic toilets, tended to avoid them. OK, the staff often looked bored and, with their stringy bodies and dark clothes, perhaps their sex lives would not bear too much scrutiny, but Kavanagh invariably felt at home amongst the shelves there.

He also felt a queasy personal connection with this particular place.

A few years ago now, one early evening, his mother, reminiscing about her marriage to his late father was, as was her custom, rewriting history.

By the time of Kavanagh's childhood, their marriage was an acrimonious affair. Perhaps there had been a time when the pretty hairdresser and the tall young man from East Grinstead had been in love. Certainly Kavanagh's father had shocked him one day as, walking to the Sunday lunchtime pub, he told Frank that during the war, at their 'dinner' break from the munitions factory where he was working – which would have been in the middle of the night – he'd cycle home to their first flat, in Edgbaston.

'Why?' asked Kavanagh, having witnessed only years of skirmishes and terrible atmospheres in his parents' home.

'Why do you think?' smirked his father. The knowing comment made the forty-year-old detective, a man with a mortgage and a dozen successful murder prosecutions behind him, feel like a gauche twelve-year-old.

These warring people, then, before he was born, had actually had a life of love? His mother, that contrary, abrasive woman, had once been desired by his father so much that he would cycle home through the blackout darkness so that they could make love for half an hour?

But it had got worse that evening as she had continued to airbrush the picture of their married life. Increasingly lost in her reverie, she went on, 'I know your father wasn't a bad man, but he didn't really know how to make a woman *feel* like a woman . . .'

'Mum,' said Kavanagh quietly. These confidences – his mother some sort of sex object; his father a humiliated man – were not things that he wished to hear.

'I liked sex, but your father, he didn't understand love-making, not really . . .'

'Mum,' he said again, counselling her to stop.

'And when I left him for those few weeks – you must remember, Frank, you'd have been about fourteen . . .'

Kavanagh remembered those 'few weeks' only too well: the chaotic house; school work not done; sandwiches not made nor shopping bought, where a sort of insanity descended and no-one, not his mother nor his father, had taken him aside and made any attempt whatsoever to explain just what was happening.

'I had become involved with Derek. Derek Parlane.'

Young Kavanagh had only ever once glimpsed this supplier of lotions and shampoos to his mother's suburban hairdressing salon.

'Derek was never going to leave his wife, but at least we had some time together. And Derek was a man who *did* know how to treat a woman . . .'

'Mum,' said Kavanagh sternly, 'I don't want to hear this. Really, please.' He lowered his head into his hands as his mother's milky eyes filled with tears.

Kavanagh was no Doctor Johnson, but he was an interested reader and he sauntered along the shelves in the fiction section where he looked in vain for anything by Tom Oliver. He examined a couple of Andrea Moore's historical novels, and then climbed the central staircase to the poetry section and picked up a copy of Sarah Cassin's earlier collection.

'How you doing, Inspector?' said the familiar voice behind him.

'Not bad,' he said and, without turning, he replaced the slim volume on the shelf and reached behind him, putting both his arms around Salt's waist and pulling her gently towards him.

'It's good to feel you,' he said.

'You, too,' said Salt, as she snuggled into his back.

'I got a couple of books, but there's nothing here by Oliver,' he said.

'You know why?' she said.

'Go on?'

'There was a piece in the *Times* yesterday. "Missing author climbs the charts." Oliver's last book has gone from nowhere to number eighteen in the paperback best-seller list, and all on the strength of a couple of newspaper stories about his possible disappearance.'

'He's obviously staged it himself to boost his sales,' said the inspector.

'Maybe,' said Salt. 'Stranger things have happened.'

TWENTY-SIX

S alt liked sex and Kavanagh liked sex and Salt liked Kavanagh and the inspector liked Salt.

But they were both adults and they'd both had decent sex before.

What they hadn't had, and what they liked very much indeed, was this closeness that they felt afterwards.

They had been hungry for one another and he'd pushed slowly to be long inside her. He'd cupped her buttocks as she held him to her again and again, and he'd watched her eyes and she'd watched his face as he called, 'Oh, God, Jane,' as he came. And, moments later, still murmuring, 'Oh, God, Jane. Oh, God,' and kissing her neck and breast as he made his final thrusts, she, too, finally released by these words of his, just as much as by his hands and lips on her, also came.

Ten minutes later, propped up on the pillows, she lay crooked in his arm. It was dusk and there was only a murmur of traffic outside the window of the second-floor room in the Grand Hotel on Birmingham's Colmore Row.

'That was nice,' she said and laid her hand on his thigh. He pushed her hair away and kissed her forehead.

'It was,' he said. 'Very.'

Lots of couples whose relationships are strong work together. Cops, teachers, people in medicine, even writers, sometimes. It can be good to share with your partner stuff that only that partner would fully understand. The insolent child who makes the teacher want to kill him is largely beyond the comprehension of anyone who has not also been subjected to that contemptuous sneer. The doctor telling a patient: 'Yes, the results are back, but I'm afraid things don't look very good.' People outside medicine won't fully understand how that GP can do these things, see his next patient twenty minutes later, and still play golf that afternoon. Comprehension's easier if your wife's the practice sister, or your husband the locum in a surgery down the road.

Kavanagh had spent entire evenings in the pub with other

cops, and even though a train had plunged into a gorge in India, a typhoon struck the Philippines, and a madman shot six people dead on the subway in New York, the officers there would often speak of nothing but the murder case that they were dealing with that week.

A few minutes before nine, Salt turned on the TV as the credits for yet another cookery show rolled.

Although Sergeant Jeff Earle had confidently assured house-keeper Shirley that the missing figurine of Richard Osman would not be making it onto BBC TV's *Crimewatch*, in fact, the quirky story was exactly what the producer was looking for in that week's show as a late filler.

OK, in strictly media terms the whole thing was borderline naff, and perhaps a little Agatha Christie-ish to make the cut at that week's production meeting, but now that, as well as the missing bronze, there was the unexplained disappearance of mid-list writer Tom Oliver, the item began to look a bit more of a prospect.

A package was rapidly put together, an end-of-show tail-piece to lighten the tone of the customary bleak fare of rape and murder and the almost bloke-ish jollity of the 'most wanted' picture gallery. Looking at those horrible faces and dead eyes staring back at you, you didn't need to be a profes-sional to surmise that you'd best close the shop or cross the street if one of these characters approached.

Five minutes before the end, they featured the Osman item. The presenter adduced one 'fact' and posited a single query to the five million viewers of the voyeuristic show: 'The bronze figurine of the distinguished playwright has been estimated to be worth at least £1,000 . . .'

'Really?' queried Salt.

'No idea,' whispered Kavanagh. 'They've probably made it up.'

The TV presenter went on: 'Whoever stole the piece can hardly sell it, so distinctive it is, which leaves the prospect of its being melted down and sold for a fraction of its real value as scrap metal. Did some overzealous fan want it? And has he or she arranged for it to be stolen? Its whereabouts remain a mystery, but the estate and Richard Osman – who is sadly no longer in very good health – and Margaret, his elderly wife, would obviously like to have it returned.' And then, turning direct to the camera, the presenter continued: 'But, just as intriguing, and possibly much more seriously, at about the same time as the statuette went missing, so did this man, the novelist Tom Oliver.' They cut to a book jacket photograph of the writer. 'Since tutoring a course at the centre more than a week ago, Mr Oliver has not returned to his London home, and whilst it's not unknown for him to go off alone – sometimes to fairly isolated places when he's working on a book, for example – it's completely out of character for him not to have told either his friends or his agent of his intentions.

'Has anyone seen him? Does anyone know where he is? The police are in the process of speaking to all of the people who were on that course, but is there anyone out there who has any knowledge of Mr Oliver's affairs that could lead the police to ascertain his whereabouts? Does anyone have any idea why he might possibly be in someone's bad books? Sorry about that awful pun. I didn't write it; blame my producer. Can you help with either the location of the missing bronze or the disappearance of Tom Oliver? If so, please contact either the incident room at Craven Arms, or the *Crimewatch* freephone number. Lines are open until midnight.'

'Not bad, Inspector,' said Salt as Kavanagh switched off the TV. 'So, let's have a look at what we've got. What about the man who was beaten up, Sarah Cassin's husband, Will?'

'He's in a bad way,' said Kavanagh. 'If it was just a random assault, or some cock-up of mistaken identity, the poor guy was very badly beaten. I'm sure the neighbour's done it – a bloke called Fraser. It was probably just a stupid parking dispute that got out of hand. And Fraser's got a bit of previous. OK, it was a football-related attack, and it was way back in the Eighties, but it shows he's capable of violence. The Cassins didn't want to accuse him for fear of the situation getting even worse.'

'Worse?' she said. 'What's he going to do next? Kill him?'

'Quite. Anyway, Will Cassin didn't want to pursue it.'

'What about the DVD you say they found?' she asked. 'What was it again?'

'*Falling Down*,' he said. 'Do you know it?'

'Remind me,' she said.

'It's a Michael Douglas movie. I can't stand him personally,' he volunteered. 'It's a sort of odd, mish-mash film. The
Douglas character's driving home and he gets stuck in traffic,
and basically he falls apart.'

'Is that it?' she said.

'Well, he's on the edge, and then he runs into all sorts of
grief. Bad guys, people who want to rob him or turn him over.
It's a heavy-handed parable: dystopian society falling apart
kind of thing.'

'Right,' she said. 'And how does it tie in with what happened
to Will Cassin?'

'Probably not at all,' he said. 'Maybe the assailant just had
it with him and dropped it, maybe it was already lying there
and it's got nothing whatever to do with the attack. The local
cops just picked it up from the ground when they went to the
scene that night, but they didn't connect it in any way to
the assault.'

'And should we?' she asked.

'I don't suppose so. Except for one thing: why does an old
DVD have no fingerprints on it from the user? Someone has
wiped it so clean there's not a mark or a smudge on it? That
is odd.'

'Sure,' she agreed. 'Right, anything else? How did you get
on this morning?'

Kavanagh had spent half the morning on the third floor at
the West Midlands Police Headquarters standing beside a
young PC and her colleague as they trawled the CCTV footage
that had been sent down from Shropshire the previous afternoon. The tapes from these two cameras covered the only
feasible routes south that Oliver would have taken when he
left the centre over a week ago.

But it had been a fruitless task. The quality of the images
from the cameras was pretty good, much improved from
the grainy stuff that the detective inspector had sometimes
examined when he had found himself doing similar work
twenty years ago, times when it was often difficult to tell
from the murky videotapes of that time a Renault Five from
a Mercedes estate. These days, the images were so clear that
you could discern a driver's broken tooth or smudged lipstick.

What they couldn't see this morning, though, was a 1997
slate-grey Saab 900. What was going on? Had Oliver gone

down some godforsaken Shropshire lane rather than headed for the A49, and south to London? Had he not gone south at all, but travelled north or east or west to do something entirely different? Something which he had not mentioned to his agent, Andrew Hardiman; to his sometime lover, Andrea Moore, or to anyone else for that matter?

'Nothing,' he said. 'Checked all the stuff we've got and he's not there. No car. No Tom Oliver.'

'He's gone somewhere else?' she said.

'Must have done. But who goes off to the seaside or wherever and doesn't tell anyone? Not even his agent or the woman he's seeing? It doesn't add up,' he said.

'What about the staff?' asked Salt. 'Are they all kosher? The centre director, Keira – you say she invited Catherine Wooley as substitute when Sarah was effectively taken out of the equation?'

'Yes, and there was a bit of previous between Wooley and Oliver — something about which Keira says she knew nothing. She also says she tried to reach a couple of other writers first.'

'Yes? How come?' asked Salt.

'Wooley wasn't her first choice on account of her not really being a Premier League poet any more, apparently. She's slipped a bit in the ratings. But the other writers she tried to get weren't available. Wooley was, and she's local, so she ended up stepping in. One other thing about her is that she does some work at a local nick, helping the inmates to write, a bit of basic skills and a bit of getting them to write poetry, for therapy, you know. "I killed a man but I'm not all bad" sort of thing, I suppose.'

'So what?' said Salt.

'Well, she's going to at least have come into contact with some dodgy characters, isn't she?'

'I guess,' agreed Salt. 'Anyway, that just leaves us with Tom Oliver and Andrea Moore,' she said.

'The oldest story,' he agreed. 'Maybe Andrea's old man rumbled his missus having an affair with Oliver and has taken matters into his own hands?'

'It's possible,' said Salt, 'but she's absolutely certain that he doesn't know about it. In any event, we'd better get down there and speak to him. What about the other centre staff?'

'There's a couple of Polish girls who do the cleaning. Their

English is actually pretty good, but we've got a translator coming up just to make sure we don't miss anything. The gardener's a young bloke called Leon something or other. He doesn't have much to do with the writers or students, just sits in on the last evening sessions when the tutors do a bit of a reading and then joins them when everyone goes down the pub.'

'What about the housekeeper?' she said.

'No, there's nothing there,' he said conclusively. 'She's in her fifties and has worked at the house since before it was a writers' place. She's worked for the Osmans for years.'

'And the Osmans themselves? What about them?' she asked.

'Like I said — if you can believe it — Margaret Osman set up the centre simply to torture her husband. Her malice is almost beyond belief, but I'm sure she hasn't got anything to do with Oliver's disappearance. She has nothing to do with the place. And also, even though she's as tough as an old walnut, she must be nearly seventy years old.'

'Fair enough,' said Salt. 'I think we've got to dig a bit more on the Cassins' neighbour, and we'd better also see if there's CCTV on any other routes.'

'Yes,' he agreed. 'I'll get back up to the centre and have the local lads root out any traffic tapes. And can you get across and interview Catherine Wooley?'

'Sure,' she said. 'And what then?'

'Then we'll have covered every other option and we'll have no choice but to instigate a full search to make sure that Oliver's not still up there somewhere.'

TWENTY-SEVEN

Shropshire

The next morning, Kavanagh drove the thirty-odd miles from Birmingham, through Kidderminster and Ludlow, back up to the centre, whilst Salt was en route to see poet Catherine Wooley in Snailbeach, just south of Shrewsbury.

There would come a day, of course, when everyone would be on the bus or train or tram, or even back up on horseback for all he knew, as people struggled to put right the damage wrought on a fragile earth. But for the time being, at least, people seemed to be pretty attached to the idea of sitting inside cars at sixty, seventy or eighty miles an hour, alone and at peace with their thoughts, and apparently inviolate. Well, just so long as you didn't meet the lunatic coming the other way who was straddling the white line and took you out of this or any other future equation.

At ten thirty, the inspector turned off the road and bumped along the track up to the centre. There was now a black and yellow crime tape strung around the car park and a PC was standing idly by to make sure that the course's songwriters didn't transgress. Oliver's room was sealed, of course, and the bearded tutor who would have used it was installed in another room in the main house.

Kavanagh sat in his car, the door ajar, and listened to the folksy sound of a female voice accompanied by a strumming guitar coming from the open door of the adjacent barn.

In his young teens, like every other kid in Birmingham at that time, Kavanagh had been in thrall to the Everly Brothers, Buddy Holly and Elvis Presley. These men (they were all men) were purveyors of a powerful stimulant, a drug so potent that the opening words of 'Hound Dog' gave you the rush of a visceral thrill even before the first chords had ceased.

But then, in his mid-teens, Kavanagh had heard the new man on the block, one Robert Zimmerman, and after only one play of the seminal *Freewheelin'*, Elvis now sounded about as relevant as Doris Day. In the hour or so that it took Dylan to go through those thirteen songs, for Kavanagh, the world had changed for ever, and it was surely on account of that man's songs that, right now, a voice like this was emanating from a Shropshire barn.

The woman's clunky strumming ceased and there was polite applause. Kavanagh got out of the car and said hello to the young PC.

He sat on the boot, pulled on his wellington boots and strolled down towards the lake. Water is a magnet, its very otherness suggesting the possibility that at any moment at all, something unexpected might happen. A fish might break the surface, a rat, perhaps, slip into the lapping water from the quiet bank.

There were a few ripples and a rowing boat gently bumped the side of the substantial wooden jetty, one plank of which, at the water's edge, was broken.

In such a picturesque place, the dinghy should have been a traditional, timber-planked little boat; in fact, it was a modern, white-hulled fibreglass thing with a tide mark around the water line like a badly cleaned bath. He was almost tempted to step into it and row out, like the delinquent Wordsworth's scary bit in *The Prelude*.

He could row about as well as any other man brought up in Birmingham. Hardly at all. He'd gone up and down the river at Stratford upon Avon with Salt a couple of times when they'd been to see something at the theatre, each of them taking turns and laughing a lot as they gradually tried to get the hang of it, but that was all.

But here, apart from anything else, there were no oars shipped in the little craft, just a foot of water that would have to be baled out the next time someone took it out. He looked across the lake's surface to the sluice gate in the distance and turned back towards his car.

From the estate garage came the noise of someone at work.

'Hi,' said the inspector.

'Alright?' said Leon as he lifted the bonnet of the Land Rover.

The policeman sunk his hands into his pockets and walked

around the vehicle as Leon checked the oil. 'You still thinking you might convert it?'

'Might do,' said Leon.

'You know what I don't understand?' said Kavanagh.

'What's that?' said the young man as he ran the dipstick through a bit of rag and then held it away from him to check the level.

'What I don't understand is,' said Kavanagh pointing to the big drums that were still lashed onto the back of the vehicle, 'before people were putting this stuff into their fuel tanks, where did the chippies get rid of it all?'

'No idea,' said Leon.

'And how much do you need to run a car anyway?' the inspector went on. 'I mean, all the chip shops in the country, are they really getting through enough of this stuff to run that many cars?'

'I don't know,' said the young man. He unscrewed the cap and poured water from a two-litre plastic bottle into the radiator, his hand steady to the task.

'But you've got enough?' said the cop.

'Yes,' he said, screwed the cap down and dropped the heavy green bonnet with a resounding crash.

'Do you mind if I . . .?' asked the inspector, nodding towards the cab. Leon shrugged. 'Like I said, I used to have one. It takes me back,' he said, and climbed up into the upright driver's seat. He watched in the driving mirror as Leon put down the water bottle and picked up something from the workbench.

The young man came around the back of the vehicle as Kavanagh moved in the seat. 'Heater was knackered on mine,' he said as Leon wiped his hands on the cloth he held there.

'I tell you another thing,' volunteered Kavanagh, still trying to watch the younger man as he stood there, just out of sight. 'You take a potato, right . . .'

'A potato?' repeated Leon.

'Well, not me. Mr Walker. Mr Smith. They take a potato. Big King Edward. Costs what?' he asked rhetorically. 'How much?'

'A King Edward potato?' said Leon, a little incredulous.

'Five pence. Let's call it five pence,' said Kavanagh as he depressed the clutch and moved the gear shift back and forth like a child at play, all the time watching for the young man in the mirror.

'Cut it in half, slice it thin, fry it and stick it in a bag and they charge . . . how much do they charge, Leon? I haven't bought a bag of crisps for a long time.'

'Nor me,' said Leon. 'I don't eat them.'

'That's what I call business,' said the policeman with a flourish. 'A five pence potato becomes a fifty-pence bag of crisps. Maybe a quid. I've no idea. Good, eh?'

'I'd better get on,' said Leon, not quite as impressed with the inspector's grasp of economic profitability theory as he appeared to be himself.

'Sure,' said Kavanagh. 'Me, too. We've got a man to find and people to see. We're giving all the rooms a quick once over and if nothing turns up, we'll have a full search to organize.'

'Yes?' said Leon.

'What else?' said the inspector. 'I don't want to do it unless it's absolutely necessary, of course. Helicopters, dogs, lots of officers, you've no idea. It costs an absolute fortune.' He glanced again at the basic instruments of the old vehicle as he stepped down from the cab.

'Right, I'll be seeing you,' he said and walked away towards the car park.

TWENTY-EIGHT

Snailbeach

Whilst Kavanagh was mulling over the relative merits of Mississipi's Elvis Presley and his Minnesota-born compatriot, Robert Zimmerman, Jane Salt was snaking up past the old lead mine workings in the village of Snailbeach, just a few miles south of Shrewsbury.

She parked outside the Stiperstones Inn, poured herself a cup of coffee from her flask and looked across the vacant miles of the Shropshire plain below.

Ten minutes later, she got out of the car and walked back down the road to the site of the remaining mineshafts and pit buildings.

The landscape was barren, the surrounding earth poisoned by the spoil from the toxic metal's workings of a century ago. Here and there, a solitary birch sapling that had found a few feet of uncorrupted earth was asserting itself but, apart from these few white-barked spindly things, nothing was growing here now, nor probably ever would again.

She stood in the wind in front of the information board, identified the buildings, shafts and pit cranes before her, the little bit of rail track upon which the wagons had been driven to the smelting house a mile away. A hundred years ago this place had employed five hundred men. Five hundred employees would have meant almost five hundred families, and those families would have needed schools and pubs and churches and bread and meat and candles and boots. It was hard to imagine, standing here now in the silence and the breeze.

She walked back up to the inn with the Devil's Chair, the highest of the Stiperstone hills, towering above her behind it.

Salt was a city cop who'd taken down many a drunk with his arm up his back and even kneed the occasional particularly lairy one in the groin when the need had been great and her patience short, but she still felt awkward and self-conscious about walking into the tight-knit community of a village pub alone.

There was a shop door adjacent to the pub with a dozen plastic dustbins outside, each one filled with different leisure items: balls, rackets, kites and frisbees, and a white Fiat van that stood just in front of the doorway itself had its sliding door wide open to reveal hundreds more domestic items inside. Quite a big selection of goods for sale, she thought, given that hers was one of only three cars in the car park, and one of those was up on bricks and hadn't been anywhere for many years.

But there was a tourist information sign hanging outside the shop and she reckoned that in return for the stipend awarded the shopkeeper for this service, she was entitled to ask for directions to Catherine Wooley's home.

Inside the labyrinthine place, where things were stacked on precipitous shelves and even hung from hooks in the ceiling, she picked up a carton of orange juice and took it to the man who was sitting in an angler's chair way below the polished timber counter. He barely looked up as she counted out the correct change, just sat there reading the local newspaper. She put the coins on the counter and asked, 'Do you happen to know where Catherine Wooley lives?'

'Past the village hall, through the ford and turn left,' he said, glancing up briefly, in much the same way as he might have directed a customer to the mustard or camping gas in his shop. 'Keep going along the lane and you'll get there. It's no more than a mile.'

'Thank you,' she said.

The man's inept retailing clearly told its own story and Salt contented herself with a friendly parting enquiry to the inexperienced shopkeeper. 'Have you been here long?' she asked as she picked up the carton of juice.

'Forty years,' he said.

She followed the man's instructions as the lane got narrower and narrower until it eventually became a rutted tarmac track the width of a single vehicle. Her Honda lurched in and out of the puddles left by a recent heavy shower and she fully lowered the driver's side window. The breeze brought into the car the woody smell of autumn's decay from the hedgerow.

At the end of the lane she drove through a five-bar gate at the hand-painted sign for Henlle Cottage. An ancient weather-bleached Renault Four with its tailgate open to the elements was serving as an improvised greenhouse, the yellowing leaves and ripe fruit of a couple of tomato plants in a growbag flourishing in the warmth there.

Several wind chimes were suspended from branches of the damson and apple trees in the garden, and an industrial-size bamboo model hung from a bracket just outside the cottage. Uniquely, perhaps, Salt found these things irritating. Rather than their presumed soothing qualities, they merely made her want to shout: 'Shut *up*!'

She stood in the porch of the stone cottage amongst the boots and wellies, thick socks and walking sticks. Every shelf was covered with geraniums, the pungent smell of which filled the warm, airless place. She rang the hanging bell a couple of times as the wind chimes plinked and plonked their melancholy sound.

'Hello, coming,' called a sing-song voice as a dog gave a couple of half-hearted barks.

'Hi, come in, come in,' said the woman. 'You must be Constable Salt? I'm Catherine.'

'Hello,' said Salt. 'Pleased to meet you,' and she followed the woman into the low-ceilinged room that ran the length of the two former quarrymen's cottages that had been converted into one dwelling. An elderly Jack Russell waddled up to her, head down, but then returned to its basket in the corner, little interested in the policewoman.

'You found us alright, then?' asked the woman.

'Satellite navigation,' said Salt, a woman with the view that life was not so short that there wasn't time to name things properly. She even wrote text messages in full with appropriate punctuation. 'And a little help from the village shop,' she added.

'It's quite something, isn't it?' said Wooley. 'Please, have a seat.' She moved a couple of books and her spectacles from the sofa. 'Would you like some tea or something? I was just going to have a cup.'

'A glass of water would be fine, thanks,' said Salt.

The woman went through to the kitchen, filled the kettle and returned with water for Salt. She sat opposite her. 'I've never been interviewed by the police before. I was quite excited when you phoned.'

Salt smiled. 'As I said on the phone, it's about Tom Oliver.'

'Yes?' said Wooley, leaning forward a little. 'I heard about the appeal on the television.'

'You didn't see it?' asked Salt.

'We don't have one,' she said. 'Never have had.'

'Right. Well, Tom Oliver appears to be missing.'

'When you say "missing", what exactly do you mean?' she asked.

'Just that,' said Salt. 'Since he left the centre – assuming that he did leave – he's not been seen. His agent got in touch with us, but we've drawn a blank on his movements. It looks as if you could be one of the last people actually to have seen him.'

'Gosh,' she said as the kettle boiled. 'Excuse me a moment,' and she went through to the kitchen. 'Would you like some shortbread?' she called.

'No, thanks,' said the policewoman. 'Did you actually see Mr Oliver leave on the Saturday morning?' she asked as the woman brought in the tea tray.

'No, I don't think I did. People tend to get away in their own time. The proper goodbyes are said the night before, generally.'

'I see,' said Salt. 'And he said goodbye to you?'

She thought for a moment. 'I don't remember him actually saying goodbye. He was pretty quiet that night, and we'd all been to the pub. People came back in dribs and drabs, you know.'

'What about his car? Did you notice whether it was still there in the morning?'

'I'm afraid not. It's not the kind of thing I would notice. I don't even know what kind of car he has.'

'I see,' said Salt, and opened her notepad. 'Am I right in saying that there had once been a falling out between you and Tom?'

'Yes, that is right,' she agreed. 'It was a misunderstanding, that's all. He is a very prickly man, not at all the easiest person to get on with, and I'd reviewed one of his books—'

'Badly, I believe,' said Salt.

'Well, it wasn't really that bad,' she said, 'but he took offence at some phrase I'd used.'

'And there was a follow-up?'

'Yes, he attacked me in public. He was drunk.'

'I see,' said the policewoman. 'You must have been angry?'

'I was hurt. I try not to get angry about people's behaviour. We're not always in control of our emotions, are we?' she said defensively. 'I practise yoga as a way of dealing with negative feelings.'

'Really?' said Salt as the wind chimes clinked and she tried to cope with her own negative feelings.

'Did you think it was at all odd that Keira should invite you to co-tutor, given your history with Tom Oliver?'

'Yes, in a way. But apparently she didn't know, and when I said as much to her, she said that they were really stuck for someone at short notice. Anyway, I'm not someone to hold a grudge. And I assumed that she must have sorted it out with Tom. He must have decided that he'd been in the wrong, and let the whole thing go.'

'And you got along OK that week?' asked Salt.

'It was alright. We worked separately, did our workshops and tutorials and we didn't mention the past. The week was reasonably successful, I think. Certainly on the teaching side.'

'And other things?' queried Salt.

'Is this conversation confidential?' asked Wooley.

'Of course,' said Salt.

'There are always little things going on . . .'

'Go on,' urged the policewoman.

'Tom has a reputation, you know?'

'Reputation for what?' asked Salt.

'With women.'

'Yes?' said the constable.

'I think it was obvious to everyone that he was very taken with a woman on the course, a youngster called Romilly. She was extremely talented, and very attractive, too.'

'Go on,' said Salt.

'Romilly is only about twenty-five, and Tom must be well over fifty but, you know, stranger things have happened. He was clearly smitten and, in truth, it did look at first as though she was responding to his attention.'

'Yes?' said Salt.

'The thing is, on these courses, it's quite a hothouse sort of atmosphere.'

'Go on,' Salt said again.

'There aren't orgies or anything like that, but you have to remember that people are there for all sorts of reasons. There may well be a desire to find oneself; but all the better if you happen to find someone else, too,' she said. 'Actually, it's the heterosexuals I feel sorry for,' she mused.

'Really?' said the constable.

'Yes. I mean, every other person, quite literally, is a member of the opposite sex. The choices are huge. So much better to be gay. There's only a very limited pool to fish in. Not that I would, of course. We're very happy, Celine and myself. We've been together for seven years now'

'So what happened, between Oliver and this girl?' asked Salt.

'Romilly seemed to be responding to him, but then, unless I'm mistaken, she got involved with a man much closer to her own age, one of the other students, a man called Malcolm. He seemed nice enough but it was obvious he wasn't half the writer she was. By the last night, after a few drinks, they made no secret of their feelings for one another.'

'And how did Oliver react? To being usurped in this way?' pressed Salt.

'He was very quiet but, as I just said to you, he's often difficult and moody anyway. I think he was much more put out by being usurped by the guest reader who came in midweek.'

'Guest reader?' asked Salt.

'Yes, the centre always has a guest reader on Wednesday evenings. It breaks up the teaching pattern. A writer called Simon Jackson came to read and he was a great success with everyone. Except Tom. Oliver was really irked by him, it was obvious.'

'I see,' said Salt. 'And what about the person who was due to tutor until you were called in – Sarah Cassin, I believe?'

'Yes?' said Wooley.

'Do you know her?'

'No, not directly. We've never met. I know of her work.'

'Are you aware of what happened that prevented her coming?'

'Of course. Keira told me. Her husband was mugged. He was badly hurt, I believe.'

'Yes, that's right,' said Salt. 'So, just to recap, Sarah can't come, and then Tom Oliver goes missing?'

'Apparently,' said Wooley, not acknowledging any connection between the two events.

'I believe you also do some work with prisoners?' said Salt.

'That's right,' said Wooley. 'Very rewarding it is, too,' she said brightly.

'I'm sure,' said Salt. 'You must meet all sorts of people there?'

'Of course,' she said. 'But they're no different from any of us, really.'

'Is that so?' said Salt with a measure of cynicism.

'I don't think so,' she said. 'What is it Housman says?'

'I don't know, what does Housman say?' asked the constable. Salt had always found the man's quatrains and rhyming couplets on the trite side.

'"*There sleeps in Shrewsbury jail tonight / Or wakes as may betide / A better lad, if things went right / Than most that sleep outside . . ."*'

'Mmm,' said Salt, not entirely convinced by Housman's notion of Shropshire felons.

'So, you're in contact with criminals on a regular basis?' said Salt.

'Of course,' agreed Wooley. 'You're not really about to suggest that I could be involved with Oliver's disappearance, just on account of my working with men that I've met in prison? The idea's quite ridiculous,' she said. 'We're vetted by the Home Office, the prison governor and the trustees, and there's no contact whatsoever on a personal level. We never give contact details and are forbidden from keeping in touch with prisoners after they are released, except at official meeting places such as the probation office.'

Salt listened to Wooley's affronted plea for reason, and then reached into her bag, pulled out a sheet of A4 and passed it to her.

'What's this?' asked the woman, reaching for her glasses, the atmosphere markedly changed in the room.

She looked at the copy of the email that she had sent to her partner a week or so previously, a message which had been for Celine's eyes only. She flushed as she glanced at the familiar words there. 'Where did you get this?' she asked, aggrieved.

'We have to check things,' said Salt. 'This could be a very serious enquiry. I accessed it from your ISP.'

'It's an email, that's all,' said Wooley defensively.

'It is an email,' concurred Salt. 'But it's quite a vindictive one, I'd say,' she added.

'It's just a few words to my partner. Anyone could have written this,' she replied.

Salt extended her hand and Wooley handed back the sheet. The policewoman read: '"... *and Oliver's being as objectionable as ever. He's been making a fool of himself over some youngster. Tonight he read a chunk of what he calls his 'relationship book'. It was fantastic ... ally cringe-making. The Old Man and the Semen might be a good title! They all saw the funny side: they laughed ... at him! Ho Ho Ho. It's late. Longing to see you tomorrow. Catherine xxx*" Is there anything else you'd like to tell me?' asked Salt.

'It's an email,' said Wooley. 'A bit of drunken talk. It means nothing.'

'No?'

'No. Of course not. Tom Oliver is well known for his self-regarding unpleasantness,' she said categorically. 'He's his own worst enemy. He made a fool of himself that night, and he'd made a fool of himself lusting after the young girl earlier in the week. If something's happened to him, I'm sorry. But to be honest, there'll be few tears shed for him, and one thing's for certain: I've done nothing wrong.'

TWENTY-NINE

I f your wife is having an affair and you find out about it, you have several options: you can kill her; you can kill yourself; you can kill her lover, or you can pack a bag and quietly leave home.

The most common approach is to kill your spouse, rather than her lover. In a way, this figures. Why should you go and kill a man you've never met, just because he's cuckolded you? If your wife hadn't acquiesced, it wouldn't have happened. And you don't know this man from Adam; it's your wife – whom you know well – who has betrayed you, not a man you've never met and could pass on the street or stand next to at the football or in the pub without realizing.

And anyway, unless you're a hypocrite and a liar, you have to acknowledge that you – and almost every other bloke you know – would just as likely jump in the sack with someone else's attractive missus if you had half a chance. You shouldn't blame men; it's just the way they are. Remember, most people don't help themselves in the supermarket not because they're upstanding citizens; they don't steal because the consequences of getting caught are more unpleasant than paying for their steak and pasta.

So, you kill your wife. If you get caught – and you almost certainly will – you will go to prison. Contemporary policing methods, advances in forensic science and DNA testing have made the business of murder a wholly unequal contest, particularly, as is invariably the case, when victim and assailant are known to one another. Frankly, these days, it's a bit like fielding a team of Sunday morning pub amateurs against the first-team players of Manchester United: the killer has about as much chance of escaping detection as the Three Pigeons do of holding off Tevez, Berbatov and Ronaldo for ninety minutes.

The only way of getting away with a capital crime, really, is to deny the police any opportunity to contradict what both you and they know is a barefaced lie. They know you've killed her; you know you've killed her, but no scrap of evidence can be evinced. And this is very easily achieved. You walk to the top of a cliff or quarry or very high building (rural outdoors is obviously best, given the preponderance of CCTV in every urban area) and you give your spouse a decent shove in the back. He or she falls to their death and there's not a scrap of evidence to show that they didn't simply lose their footing. OK, the three-month old, £500,000 insurance policy on a life might be one of a dozen reasons that the diligent cops don't believe your version of events for a minute.

'But, hey, Mr Policeman,' you say, 'go on, prove it. You might be having an affair with your colleague from work or the teenage sweetheart who's only recently got in touch through Friends Reunited; you might have debts of thousands on your Visa card, and the neighbours might well have heard your midnight rows but, come on, copper, prove it.'

Without the need for over-elaborate plots (always full of dangers and opportunities for this, that and the other to go wrong); with no difficult-to-acquire poisons, complex weapons, staged car crashes with brake hoses severed, nor feckless hit-men in tow, the thing should be a breeze.

Don't write up your plans in a diary; don't call a mate or lover on your BT line, or tap them a hubristic text on your mobile ('You should have seen him fall') or in any other way commit thoughts of your dark deeds to paper or electronics, and you should be fine.

You'll not be popular with her family, her friends, or the constabulary, maybe – *The police said after the inquest that although their enquiries are continuing, they are not looking for anyone else in connection with the tragic death of Mr Smith* – but you will have got away with murder.

Tom Oliver's lover, Andrea Moore, was extremely loath to have the police interview her husband. And the police, at least in the shape of DC Jane Salt, were almost as loath to do it. *Almost*. The fact was that the cops were running out of options. They'd spoken to almost all of the people they could trace who would want to do the missing author harm (a decent number, by any reckoning) and they'd drawn blanks, or at least they'd not come up with anything substantive.

However, if Andrea Moore's husband, chiropodist Jerry, had somehow found out about his wife's trysts with misanthropic

Tom Oliver, although he might have lacked the wherewithal to take his bunion scalpel to his cheating wife or her lover, perhaps he could have been involved in facilitating harm to his rival for her affections.

Would he have known how to go about contracting some delinquent from the badlands of Liverpool 8 to dispose of the man at his behest – a stratagem always doomed to failure given the kind of feckless people who make themselves known as being available for this kind of work, and whose capacity to embrace the essential values of discretion and loyalty are always in short supply?

It seemed unlikely, perhaps. But then again, Jerry was a chiropodist, and chiropodists probably don't think like other men, or for that matter, like other people at all.

These were the questions that Salt felt she had to address. And soon.

But Andrea Moore was altogether less sanguine. She had more or less accepted the policewoman's tacit assurances that, having eulogized mediaeval poet Geoffrey Chaucer together over a bottle of wine in the Birmingham restaurant, there was little likelihood that Salt would ever need to interview her husband about Tom Oliver's disappearance. Andrea was quite certain that her husband knew nothing of her extra-marital activities with the writer. And anyway, even if he did, she pleaded with the policewoman down the phone as she stood at the bottom of her Oxfordshire garden, it was inconceivable that he could have sought out Oliver and done him harm. 'He's a chiropodist, Jane,' she pleaded quietly and in desperation.

Salt was apologetic, but resolute. This interview was going to happen. Her mind was made up. If they were lucky, perhaps her husband would not learn that his wife had been having an affair.

She explained to the historical novelist that, as a friend of the missing writer, an enquiry of this sort was routine as the police spread their net ever wider in their search for answers, a net which was now cast to embrace even quite distant colleagues and acquaintances of the man.

How many people, after all, she asked Moore, knew about how the police really worked? They watched *The Bill* and *CSI*, and that was it. But the stuff that really happened in any police enquiry was far too tedious to make television. Who was going to tune in to watch hundreds of interviews being conducted, and boxes full of witness statements being collated as they were cross-checked for times and places, facts and alibis? Simple stuff like the same name coming up a couple of times were what resulted in the second knock at the door. And it was humdrum things like this that led to someone appearing in the dock twelve months down the line, not the plucky hunches or cranky insights of criminal 'profilers', those ubiquitous folk beloved of TV writers, who were universally ridiculed by police officers themselves. Unlike the diligent, plodding cops, these people had never caught a single felon yet. Arch TV, a run out for some well-known actor, perhaps, but a criminal catcher? *Please.* Forget it.

'But, Jane, you promised me it wouldn't be necessary,' pleaded Moore, the red cherry-tree leaves lying about her on the dew-covered grass of her autumn garden.

'No, I didn't say that,' said Salt gently but emphatically. 'I said I'd do everything I could to avoid disclosing your relationship with Oliver. And I will do, but I need to ascertain just what your husband knows – if anything – and to do that, I simply have to speak to him.'

'I feel cheated,' said Moore despondently, without recognizing the irony of her own words.

'I'm sorry,' said Salt, but offered nothing to ameliorate the woman's grave concerns. 'It has to be done. To be frank, we're running out of options. If your husband has an alibi, and he's clearly not involved, we'll simply move on.'

'Jerry's not a fool; he'll know there's something up.'

'I'm sorry, Mrs Moore.' The formality of the mode of address signalled to the woman that any further protest would be in vain.

'So when are you coming?' she asked, reluctantly accepting the inevitability of the situation.

'Tomorrow afternoon. But I'll phone him first and arrange to see him at his surgery. I need to speak to him alone.'

'Why?' asked Moore immediately.

'It's just the way we do these things,' said Salt. 'Believe me, I'll do my best to maintain your confidence, I really will. Goodbye.'

THIRTY

Shropshire

K avanagh reckoned TV had a lot to answer for, and he wasn't thinking only of the conglomerate media thieves who'd somehow nicked all the decent football matches and put them on pay TV. He was thinking about cop shows, 'reality' TV, and even the news.

To organize a search, especially when the search area was many acres of hilly, wooded, inaccessible land in rural Shropshire, was no mean feat. On television, all that viewers saw were a few PCs picking their way in a line across a field as they went about their patient task. The worst thing that was likely to happen was one of them being glimpsed on camera with a grin on his face as he shared a joke with a colleague, rather than manifesting a demeanour that would, more properly, suit the gravity of the task as they searched for a weapon, an infant's body or a missing gangster's dismembered limb.

But the fact was, with the best will in the world, Kavanagh was in a cul-de-sac. They'd spoken to any number of people close to the missing writer. Salt was about to speak to Andrea Moore's husband, Jerry, and an interview with Sarah and Will Cassin's one-time football hooligan neighbour, Ray Fraser, was imminent.

According to Romilly Thorne, her relationship with neo-pornographer Malcolm Carter had not endured beyond the few days following their time at the Writing Centre.

Kavanagh caught up with her on a poor line in the corridor of some Brussels' European Union building where her editor had sent her to file a piece on textile quotas.

'You spent time with a man called Malcolm Carter, apparently?' ventured the inspector.

'Who on earth told you that?' she responded tartly, turning to the wall and speaking barely audibly.

'Well, with respect, Ms Thorne, that's not exactly the point here. We have a serious enquiry underway and we need to establish facts. Is it not the case that you became friendly with Mr Carter?'

'We spent a little time together,' she said defensively.

'And since the course finished?' he asked. 'Have you seen one another?'

'Why?' she asked, affronted.

'Please,' said Kavanagh. 'Believe me, I wouldn't be asking you these things if it weren't important.'

'No,' said Romilly. 'I haven't seen him at all. Look, Inspector, it's really awkward for me speaking to you from here, but the thing is, up in Shropshire, it was really quite difficult.'

'Go on?' he said,

'Tom Oliver, he became quite attentive, and whilst at first it was not unflattering – you know, he was once a fairly well-regarded novelist – after a couple of days, I began to feel uncomfortable with the situation.'

'Sure,' said the inspector, 'I understand. Go on.'

'He was a lot older than me, but more to the point, I wasn't there looking for a relationship; I was there to try and improve my writing, that was all.'

'Of course,' said Kavanagh. 'But is it the case that you then became involved with Malcolm Carter?'

'I did, yes, but all this makes me sound like some kind of loose woman,' she said, offended. 'Malcolm and I, we had a drink together, a little tipsy kiss, maybe, but that's all.'

'Enough to put Tom Oliver's nose out of joint?' asked the inspector.

'How should I know what was going to upset him?' she rejoined. 'I barely knew him.'

'Did he seem alright, though?'

'No, in honesty, he didn't. He seemed very quiet that last day or two, but there was a general feeling that he'd been put out on account of another writer, Simon Jackson, coming in and stealing the limelight. If he was a bit low, I think it was because of that, and nothing to do with any feelings that he can only have imagined that he might have for me. He really hardly knew me, after all.'

'And you're sure you haven't seen Carter since the course ended? I must tell you we haven't been able to speak to him yet, but we certainly will be doing so shortly.'

'No,' she said firmly, 'of course not. We exchanged a couple of emails, and then we had a phone call, but with me back in London, him up there in the Midlands, it just didn't feel right.'

'I see,' he said.

'Look, Inspector, you'll have to excuse me, my meeting's about to start and if I don't get these figures, my editor will kill me. I really have to go now.'

'Right,' he said. 'I'll be in touch if we need to speak again.'

An hour later, the entire enquiry team were wedged into the incident room at the police station in Craven Arms.

Salt had confronted Catherine Wooley with the intemperate email that she had sent to her partner, Celine. The contents of that message were distinctly unfriendly, but did it mean anything more than that? Could she really have done Oliver harm?

Salt was an experienced cop whose instincts were informed by a perceptive intelligence. 'If Catherine Wooley is involved in anything sinister or violent,' she told the briefing, 'we'd better embark on a big prison-building programme right away, because half the country is going to have to be locked up. She's gay, she's a not very good poet – according to her peers – and she's certainly no fan of Tom Oliver, but involved with his disappearance? I don't think so. OK, she does do some work with cons in the local nick and so has some dealings with iffy punters, but the woman's no motive beyond a little literary fall-out several years ago. And anyway, she's got a garden full of bloody wind chimes,' she concluded, as if this fact alone, whilst it might cast aspersions on her nature, naturally acquitted her of malfeasance.

Kavanagh got to his feet, stood in front of the white-boards, flip-charts and PowerPoint screen, the information on dates, times, places and personnel all displayed there. 'This guy, Malcolm Carter,' and he pointed to the tall man's photo and biography amongst the list of the centre's other tutees for that week, 'has obviously got to be interviewed. For the time being, he's safely ensconced at a writers' retreat in the Scottish Highlands where he's working on his novel. I've spoken to him on the phone and he's not going anywhere. I've sent someone over from Inverness nick to

speak to him with a list of questions, and he'll be back
down south in a couple of days' time if anything looks amiss
and we need to interview him further. I've got a call booked
with ACC Hyland immediately after this meeting to get
authorization for a search team, and I've arranged to have
the dogs brought across from Shrewsbury and Telford. We've
got to seriously consider the possibility that Oliver could
still be up there somewhere. But if he is, apart from anything
else, where did his car get to?'

Kavanagh knew that a full search of the area surrounding the
centre would mean some forty officers being taken away from
their normal duties for as long as it took. Resources were not
infinite and the daily grind of rounding up drug dealers,
extortionists, people traffickers, car thieves, burglars and every
other mountebank and ne'er-do-well on the streets of West
Mercia would inevitably be put on hold for God knows how
long.

And this redeployment of personnel would have a direct
and immediate effect on the public's cherished notion of officer
'visibility' on the streets, notwithstanding that every shred of
evidence showed that this presence made no significant impact
upon crime whatsoever. The contrary: the fact that a copper
was seen on the high street in the middle of the afternoon
meant that he wasn't out in a car with his expensive and very
efficient ANPR kit, reading the cloned number-plates of blag-
gers who would doubtless, at that very moment, be driving
stolen cars on their way to Post Office heists somewhere. Oh,
well. Needs must. Either way, the consequences of this
redeployment would be serious.

Assistant Chief Constable Hyland was not familiar with
novelist Tom Oliver, nor his lightweight campus capers; he
personally preferred books about Second World War military
strategy, a subject upon which he had become something of
an authority. All he did know was that DI Kavanagh, who
was, anyway, under investigation following a complaint of
assault from a member of the public, was now asking for
authority to deploy forty officers, a scuba unit, a thermal
imaging helicopter and several dogs in a search of some very
extensive and difficult terrain.

Seeing his budget for the year escalating enormously on

account of this one case, Hyland said, 'Incidentally, Inspector, are you aware of the latest figures for analysis of just one item at the Forensic Science labs?'

'No, I'm not, sir,' said Kavanagh, used as he was to the ACC's rather oblique approach to difficult policy decisions.

'I've got the revised figures here. They came in last week,' he said and Kavanagh listened as the man tapped away at his keyboard.

'Here we are,' he said, and read from the screen. 'For each item, one hundred and sixty pounds. For each *item*, Frank. Can you believe that?'

'No, sir. It is very expensive,' agreed Kavanagh. What exactly was he supposed to suggest, he wondered? A January sale, perhaps, when the mass of evidence from any major enquiry might be presented in job lots to the lab? Or that they offer a two-for-one sale now and again?

'What I'm saying is, just remember the budget, Frank,' he said. 'Results are vital, of course, but we've got to make the money go round, too, eh?'

'Of course, sir,' said Kavanagh. 'Of course.'

The squad was to assemble at Craven Arms at seven the following morning for an initial local briefing, followed by a thorough search of the countryside immediately surrounding the centre and an examination of the lake.

Statistically, the likelihood was that if they were to find Oliver – and his death had involved foul play – the missing man would be found not far from a path. Evidence showed that corpses were very rarely carried more than a few yards from a road or track: killers might well employ extreme violence in pursuit of their murderous ends, but they invariably baulked at then transporting a lifeless body more than a few yards before its perfunctory incarceration in a shallow grave, babbling stream or brackish culvert.

The police were by no means stupid, and they often knew criminals' likely behaviour rather better than the criminals knew that behaviour themselves. After all, it was they who had the benefit of huge experience, whereas most murderers were inexperienced, embarking, as they were, upon their gruesome tasks for the first and only time.

*   *   *

After the briefing and his telephone call with ACC Hyland, one of the team contacted the local waterways authority and requested that an engineer open the sluice gate so that the water might be drained from the lake.

Forensics officers, meanwhile, would undertake a thorough examination of Oliver's room. But events in Bordesley Green in Birmingham meant that for the time being, at least, even the ACC was in no position to facilitate the sniffer dogs being transported from their urban kennels to rural Shropshire in the search for a missing writer: right now, every available dog was deployed in the homes and offices, workplaces and lock-up garages of half a dozen men whose behaviour was of rather more pressing concern to the Home Office, MI5 and the counter terrorist squads of the West Midlands force. With luck, the dogs would be free from their current tasks in only a day or two.

But Kavanagh did not have the luxury of further delay, and he ordered the manpower, at least, to travel to Shropshire the following morning. The helicopter was already committed for the first part of the day but would fly up to the scene by noon.

The songwriters on their two-day midweek course were apprised of the developing situation by Kiera, the centre director, and offered either a full refund or the opportunity to enrol on a similar course the following spring.

Within the hour, having amended their travel plans and arrangements, they were escorted from the premises, song lyrics folded in their document bags, guitars, flutes, tin whistles, kazoos and even a mandolin stowed safely in their music cases.

THIRTY-ONE

Bicester

If you are a rookie cop policing the rowdy centre of a small English town this Friday night, your greatest friend is not your extending baton, the burly colleague by your side, your handcuffs or even your pepper spray. Your best friend is plain old wet rain, and the heavier it falls, the better.

Even shaven-headed boys and strapless, half-naked girls move pretty quickly through rain. And a damp uniform is a price that most cops – excepting the odd psychopath who actually looks forward to manhandling a few yobs, just as much as the yobs relish fighting the figure in blue – will gladly pay to end their late shift without having been spat at, kicked or punched by members of a drunken, menacing crowd.

But for the cop who's charged with investigating a kidnapping, an abduction or a killing, his best friend is as unlikely a candidate as the beat copper's rain: T Mobile and Virgin, O2 and Orange.

Jerry Moore looked quite dinky in his white tunic with its fetching round collar, Salt thought, not unlike a slightly overweight, pink-cheeked priest. His surgery was a high-tech, minimalist place just off Bicester's main street, and the clinic had a not unpleasing scent of very faint antiseptic that matched perfectly the stainless-steel fittings, bare surfaces and bright lights of the place. Bunion consultations might be unsexy, but getting them treated here wouldn't come cheap, Salt imagined.

The man loosened his collar and sat opposite her on his treatment stool, but not quite so close as he would have done for a consultation. He was closely shaven and well groomed in the way that people who are working up close and personal are well advised to be. One iffy scent or bit of unsightly neck stubble, Moore knew very well, and you could easily lose a patient.

'Tell me again, Miss Salt,' he said, 'I'm not at all clear just what it is you wanted to speak to me about.'

'Of course,' said Salt, as she sat forward in the treatment chair, trying to assume the persona of a policewoman rather than a patient in need of corn plasters. 'We're looking into the possible, or at least apparent disappearance of someone your wife knows,' she went on.

'Andrea knows?' he repeated. 'So why do you need to speak to me, exactly?'

'The missing man, Tom Oliver, and your wife once shared a publisher,' she said vaguely. 'And we know that they've done work for a literary agency . . .'

'Yes?' he said. 'So what has Andrea's knowing the man got to do with your enquiry?'

'Quite possibly nothing,' she said, 'but we're scrabbling about a bit, and we're having to cast the net of our enquiries wider and wider. We're checking all of his acquaintances, business colleagues and old friends . . .'

'But haven't you spoken to her already?' he pursued. 'I understood that you had.'

'Yes,' said the policewoman inconclusively, and quickly moved on. 'Did you ever meet Mr Oliver yourself?'

'How would I?' he asked.

'A social event, perhaps? A literary function?'

'I've barely heard of the man. I've never read anything of his and I've certainly not met him,' he said, making no attempt to disguise his growing incomprehension at the apparent pointlessness of the questions.

'I see,' she said. 'But just to tick the boxes, as it were, I'd like to ascertain your whereabouts on a couple of recent occasions . . .'

'*My* whereabouts?' he said, by now clearly irritated. 'Why on earth would you need to check my whereabouts?'

'It's procedure,' she lied. 'It saves us duplicating our work. One interview and it's done. There'll be no need for any further questioning if we can just clarify a couple of things now.'

'This is bizarre,' he said. 'It's truly absurd. But go on, if it's necessary, let's deal with it and get it over with and I can get on.'

'Last weekend, beginning last Friday evening, that's the last time that Tom Oliver was definitely seen by anyone that we know of . . .'

'Yes?' he said.

'Could you possibly tell me where you were on that Friday?'

'Are you serious?' he asked.

'I'm afraid so,' she said. 'I am.'

He got up, reached into a drawer and took out an A6 business diary. 'I had appointments that morning. I worked through lunch seeing a couple of extra patients, and then left for the day.'

'You took the afternoon off?' she said.

'Yes.'

'Do you often take Friday afternoons off?' she asked.

'Occasionally, if I can arrange it,' he said.

'And what did you do?' she asked.

'I went walking.'

'Yes?' she said. 'Where?'

'On Muswell Hill.'

'Muswell Hill?' she said, surprised. 'In London?'

'No, not in London. Muswell Hill in Oxfordshire. It's a local feature, about ten miles south of here.'

'I don't know it,' she said, jotting the name in her pad. 'Is it nice?'

'It's one of my favourite spots,' he volunteered.

'You often walk there?'

'Sometimes,' he replied.

'How often?' she probed.

'Every couple of weeks, perhaps,' he said.

'You take Friday afternoons off from the practice whenever you can,' she clarified, 'and sometimes walk on Muswell Hill?'

'I'm not aware there's anything particularly extraordinary about that,' he said.

'Of course not,' agreed Salt. 'And your wife, Andrea, does she go with you?'

'No,' he said.

'A friend, perhaps?' she asked, her pen poised.

'I walk alone.'

'I see,' said Salt. 'Would there be anyone who could verify your account of your afternoon walk, in particular, last Friday? Did you meet anyone? Chat with anyone, or even say hello?'

'I can't recall,' he said.

'Do you think you could try, Mr Moore?' she asked, leaning back in the chair. 'It's important.'

'The reason I walk is that I spend most of my working day with people. I talk to patients a good deal – they expect it, of course – and so it's good to be alone for a few hours.'

'Yes, I can imagine,' she said. 'You drove down there?'

'Yes,' he said, slightly hesitantly.

'Good,' she said.

'Why "good"?' he asked.

'Cameras. You know, there are thousands of them.'

'You actually intend to look for me on CCTV?' he said, incredulous.

'It's routine,' she said. 'It's very straightforward these days and, should we need to, it'll provide easy verification.'

'I'm sure,' he said quietly.

'Just one other thing,' she said. 'Do you have a phone, Mr Moore?'

'Of course,' he said.

'Would it be possible for me to borrow it for a short time?'

'Why do want my phone?' he asked, exasperated.

'Corroboration. There's absolutely no need to be concerned. The contrary: it will verify fully your account of things.'

'How will my phone help?' he asked dispiritedly.

'The average person sends two texts and makes three mobile phone calls every day,' she said smiling. 'I don't know what your usage is, of course, but if you made any calls that afternoon – something I'm sure you won't be able to remember – we can use what they call triangulation to help pinpoint your exact whereabouts. We find it incredibly useful.'

'This is absurd,' he said. 'I've never met this man in my life, and yet you want to ascertain my movements? It makes no sense.'

'You know, Mr Moore, people who come to any kind of harm have often fallen foul of people they know, no matter how tenuous the connection. Obviously, we both know that's not the case here, but we are duty-bound to examine all of the missing person's contacts. It would be a dereliction of duty not to consider every avenue of enquiry. A quick check of your phone by the electronics and communications people will verify everything you have just told me, and then we can leave it at that and move on.'

The man looked forlorn, like a child who has been disappointed to be shown just how a magician has made a rabbit appear from his hat. He handed the policewoman his phone. 'Will that be all?' he asked.

'I think so,' she said. 'Thank you very much for your time.' She got to her feet.

He walked her to the door, just as he did with every patient. 'Ms Salt . . .' he began.

'Yes?' she said.

He looked down at his brogues.

'Was there something?' she asked considerately.

They stood there at the door, his hand on the handle. Experience had taught her that there were times when silence was the most incisive form of enquiry.

'Will you have a seat for a moment?' he said and went to the cooler and poured himself a cup of water. 'Does my wife have to know about this conversation?' he asked.

'It depends, of course,' said Salt, sitting back down. 'Perhaps if you tell me what's on your mind and we can take things from there. Whatever it is, I'm sure you'll feel better for telling me.'

'I doubt that,' he said, and then went on with his story. 'Nearly two years ago, a young man came to see me, here in the surgery. He was experiencing a lot of pain walking – it was to do with his having flat feet, it transpired, you know . . .'

Salt barely contained a giggle. Young men? Flat feet? It didn't compute, somehow.

The chiropodist recognized her amusement. 'Yes, it sounds absurd of course. Anyway, I treated him, recommended bare-foot walking, foot gymnastics for his fallen arches, all the usual approaches to the problem. I asked him what he did and, after some beating around the bush, he told me he did some modelling and also that he worked for an escort agency. He was a very personable, intelligent young man, and yes, very attractive. It was easy to imagine some businessman with a secret life in a strange city taking this handsome young man out for dinner.'

'Yes?' said Salt.

'Two weeks later, he came for a further consultation and we chatted some more. We talked about the school he had been to and how he had discovered his own sexual orien-tation. I found myself telling him about my own very limited experiences at the minor public school that I had attended. I'd never told anyone about the things that happened there, not even Andrea. It was nothing sinister, just a couple of teenage crushes and a bit of naked flirting with an older boy.

'When I left school and went to university in Edinburgh, I left that life behind me. It's where I met Andrea, in fact.

'We have two children together and have had a normal heterosexual life. I've looked at the odd magazine and exchanged glances with men here and there, but I'd never done anything about those latent feelings except to deny them in myself. I kept telling myself that I was a father and husband, a man whose only place was in an affectionate relationship with his wife.

'But of course, there was something missing, and when Nathaniel came to my clinic that first day, and on his subsequent visits, he powerfully awakened those unresolved feelings in me.'

'I see,' said Salt, intrigued.

'Also, I suppose I'd always assumed that a man who was paid for his company would be manipulative and exploitative. Nat was neither of these things. He was clearly very bright, but he was also understanding and thoughtful. We simply enjoyed one another's company in a way that I haven't enjoyed another human being's warmth for a very long time. And before you jump to the obvious conclusion, Ms Salt, no, Nat didn't want anything from me. OK, I did pay for our hotels and meals and things like that, but he was spending time with me when he could have been working and earning, so that was only fair.

'Like a lot of couples who have been married as long as we have, Andrea and I rarely have sex these days, and to be honest, she didn't seem any more interested than I was. I even wondered at one point whether she might be seeing someone herself, but it was just reflected guilt at my own conduct, I'm sure.'

'Yes,' said Salt. 'I'm sure.'

'We first consummated our relationship when my wife was away at a book festival in Leeds, and thereafter I began to live for our meetings. In fact, anytime that Andrea was away – and she had a period when she had to be in Birmingham one night a week – Nat and I would meet to spend time together, sometimes the night, sometimes just a few hours.'

'Will he verify all this?' asked Salt.

'I imagine so,' he said. 'But does Andrea have to know? It would be the end of us, of course, and I don't want that. Nat knows, and I know, we don't have a future together as a couple. It's a lovely relationship with a beautiful young man, but if I were ill, or in need, it's Andrea and my children who would be there, I don't have any illusions about that.'

'There should be no need for her to know unless you choose to tell her,' said Salt. 'Would you write down Nathaniel's contact details, please? I'll need to speak to him, of course.'

He jotted down the man's numbers on a sheet from a pharmaceutical supplier's pad.

'I'll still need to take your phone, just to verify things, but I shouldn't need it for long,' said Salt.

'Of course,' he said. 'But you'll find that what I've just told you now is true. I wasn't at Muswell Hill last Friday. Nat and I were together in a room at the Queen's Hotel in Cheltenham Spa.'

He saw her to the door once more. 'I'm not sure exactly what to say,' she began. 'I hope things work out for you.'

'For my marriage?' he said wistfully.

'For your marriage, yes, if that's what you both want. For you and the young man, perhaps? I don't know. Relationships can sometimes be very difficult.'

'Thank you, Constable,' he said. 'You've really been very understanding.'

THIRTY-TWO

Shropshire

Kavanagh felt omnipotent as he stood on a ridge amidst the trees and watched the level of the lake inch away. Of course, he couldn't actually see the water level falling, but with the sluice gate fully open, he could see the water fluming through it over the ledge in a strong and even curtain as the normally shallow stream below swelled with the torrent.

The centre was no longer a place for songwriters, poets and novelists to hone their craft, but a designated crime scene with a PC stationed at the bottom of the lane who was now barring entry to all but vehicles on police business.

The staff had been sent home – Keira and Leon to a bed-and-breakfast place in the village – as white-suited forensics officers examined the accommodation and dusted and scraped and taped for signs of blood or any unduly excessive cleaning.

And, out of sight of the inspector, a line of cops were at this very moment picking their way through the undergrowth. Armed with threshing poles and rakes, the men and women inched forward through the terrain, teasing every root and branch and thistle and clump of bracken as they looked for any clue to Oliver's whereabouts.

More used to working in parks and scrubland frequented by urban criminals in the West Midlands and West Mercia, this was pleasant work indeed.

And anyway, there wasn't a copper amongst them who was in any way fearful of finding a body, no matter how badly decomposed that corpse might be. That was not only part of the job; it was a result. What they didn't find here was the stuff that other searches invariably yielded: syringes, condoms, human excrement, stained tissues, dog dirt, underwear, sanitary towels, sweet wrappers and every cigarette packet and fag end known to man.

Here, in this green and pleasant, little-frequented-by-any-human-being-land, was merely nature's work: mole hills and badger setts, rabbit warrens, worm-casts and leaf mould, the imperceptibly decomposing foliage of myriad previous seasons.

Watching all that he could see, and merely sensing the rest, Kavanagh might well be omnipotent up on his ridge, but it was a power with which he was not at all at ease: everything that was happening here was happening at his behest. And whilst the senior policeman wasn't keen to find a corpse, and didn't wish Tom Oliver – a man he'd never even met – any harm, if all of this was some pointless exercise and for some reason the man announced his whereabouts to agent, lover or friend tomorrow afternoon, the inspector would have some very awkward questions to answer, and some serious explaining to do to his Assistant Chief Constable.

The sun was a hazy disc whose light fell across the surface of the lake as Kavanagh scanned the water with his binoculars. The distant sound of the church bells in the village made their way through the still morning air and up to where he stood, watching.

The level of the lake had fallen in the hour that he had been there, the 'painter' tethering the little dinghy aside the jetty grown taut as the slack on the rope was taken up and the prow of the boat rose very slightly out of the water.

At noon he walked down the hill and joined the line of searching officers for half an hour and tramped alongside them through the undergrowth fifty or sixty yards from the house and barn.

At 12.45, they broke for lunch and collected food and hot drinks from the catering truck parked on the drive in front of the big house.

Kavanagh took a burger, put a lid on a cup of coffee and made his way back up the hill to his former vantage point. He sat on his haunches and continued to watch as he ate and sipped the lukewarm coffee in its polystyrene cup.

Just after two o'clock in the afternoon, his eye was drawn to the water as it appeared to be parting and covering, parting and covering a slab of something just beyond the jetty.

He put his coffee on the ground, focussed his binoculars

on the place and watched as the slab tantalizingly revealed itself again, before the water rippled over it once more.

He continued to watch and his eyes ached with the effort until, eventually, as the water level fell another inch or two, it closed over the slab no more. The metal shining in the sunlight a few feet from the jetty's edge was the roof of a car.

He dropped the remains of his burger and coffee in the grass and lumbered as quickly as he could through the bracken-covered slope back down the hill.

There was no time to await the arrival of a crane and hoist from Telford, and anyway, the men from the UWSU, the under-water search unit, were already on site standing by in their big Mercedes van – an inflatable dinghy strapped to the roof – and more than ready to go. All this hanging around was part of the job, of course, but it was like being on a film set: interminable waiting, a brief scene, and then hours more ennui.

A scuba diver was immediately suited up and tethered to a safety rope, even though the water was now no more than a few feet deep.

Kavanagh and Salt stood there as the man slipped gently from the jetty into the water and onto the lake bed.

So, contrary Tom Oliver had, even in death, put them to some wholly unnecessary trouble by driving into the lake and drowning. What a strange way to kill yourself though, thought Kavanagh. Of all the relatively painless ways to go about it, why do this? The inspector's imagination baulked at the notion. Gasping for breath, as first your mouth and throat, and then your nose fill with suffocating water? Taking a gulp in the swimming pool was bad enough, but to gasp out your last in this way, trapped inside your car with no escape? How horrible was *that*? A few pills and half a bottle of Scotch, OK. A hosepipe from the exhaust into your car, a treasured CD on the player, maybe. But this? *I don't think so*, thought the inspector.

The diver part waded, part trod water the few yards out to the vehicle, struggling to free his feet from the enveloping mud of the lake's bottom, a little rope paid out to him by his colleague with every careful step.

The roof of the Saab was now several inches above the water line, a mere twelve or fifteen feet from the jetty. The diver held onto the roof line of the vehicle and then breasted himself down to the driver's side window. He stayed there for nearly half a minute, bubbles breaking the surface every few seconds. Eventually, he surfaced and moved slowly around the front of the car to the passenger side. Then, taking the door handles in his grip, he eased himself to the back of the vehicle. A few minutes later, he waded back to the jetty as his colleague drew in the safety rope. Assisted out of the lake, he removed his mask and breathing tube, took a deep breath and said to Kavanagh, even before the inspector could frame a question, 'There's no one in the car.'

'Are you certain?' asked Kavanagh.

'The car's empty,' he said without emotion. 'Just what looks like some of his gear in the boot, a couple of bags and some clothes.'

The sluice remained open and the water ebbed away as the hoist and rig made its way down the B4368 from Telford.

Salt and Kavanagh remained on the jetty as more and more of the car emerged from its watery grave. 'Well, at least no supermarket trolleys,' said Kavanagh, standing there.

'But no Tom Oliver, either,' said Salt.

'No. No Tom Oliver,' said Kavanagh. 'Where the hell's he got to?'

THIRTY-THREE

I t was very unusual indeed to see a uniformed policeman running in the countryside, and it was even more unusual if that copper had discarded his jacket, was wearing only shirt and trousers and was calling something at the top of his voice. It was just a bit too theatrical for reality.

Salt and Kavanagh, still standing on the jetty as the water level in the lake continued to fall, watched as the young PC shouted, 'Inspector! Inspector!' and all the time took huge, loping strides towards them.

'What's up?' said Kavanagh. 'What the fuck's going on?'

The man spluttered, entirely out of breath, sweat pouring down his face. 'Sergeant Earle, Sir. He sent me to tell you. He says get up there quick. They've found a body. Up on the hill, sir . . .'

'What's this?' asked Kavanagh as they stood over the woman lying in the grass, her face and neck and ankles horribly torn and disfigured.

'She's been attacked,' said Jeff Earle soberly.

'Attacked?' said Salt. 'By what?'

'Animals, I suppose,' said the sergeant. 'Fox? Badger, maybe? The local wildlife.'

'God,' said Salt, her face grimacing at the thought of what had befallen the woman. In all the years that Kavanagh had been a policeman he'd never once seen a cop throw up at the sight of a corpse, no matter how grotesquely it was mutilated or how far decomposed.

Cops were people, and they were troubled, and sometimes even traumatized, of course, and every one of them had seen things they'd rather not have seen. But even when faced with the most horrific sights, their reaction tended to be morbid fascination rather than the scene beloved of TV drama, as the inexperienced cop turns away and throws up in the bushes at the sight of his first cadaver. It just didn't happen.

Margaret Osman's malevolent strength had certainly

deserted her in death and she looked a forlorn sight, her erstwhile wiry body, abject and distorted as she appeared, still, to be reaching out in vain across the un-crossable terrain.

'Get on the phone and get the pathologist up here straight away. And the photographer,' said Kavanagh to Salt. 'And tell them to get a move on,' he added.

Salt was already dialling headquarters.

'Jesus!' he suddenly exclaimed.

'What is it?' asked Salt.

'Her old man,' he said. 'What's happened to him? You stay here. We'll go and check him out. Come on, Jeff.' The two men immediately sprinted away through the thicket.

The border collie was waiting patiently at the closed back door to the Osmans' house and wagged its tail, apparently pleased to see the two officers.

The TV was on in the corner of the room, the afflicted playwright lying slumped low in his wheelchair. Saliva dribbled down his chin, the front of his trousers was sodden and a terrible smell of his own waste filled the airless room. Earle dialled an ambulance as Kavanagh put his fingers to the man's neck and felt for any sign of life there. He earnestly hoped that he wouldn't detect any. But alas, the tiniest pulse still registered there.

He closed the man's nostrils, inhaled the fetid air of the room into his own lungs, and exhaled into the man's foul-smelling mouth. In resuscitation training, you started with a dummy, and then practised on your partner, but nothing could ever prepare you for the actual people – the drug addicts and alcoholics, the beggars and the elderly – who were the ones most likely to need your intimate attention.

Kavanagh retched as he turned away, tried to gather breath and filled the man's lungs again. 'Door,' he gasped to Earle. 'Get some air in here. Open the door, for fuck's sake.' He took a deep breath and filled Osman's lungs once more.

In the mortuary in Telford, Salt and Kavanagh watched as the pathologist went about his work. He was certain there was no foul play, just a foul death. Yes, Margaret Osman had most likely tripped and turned her ankle. It wasn't broken, just a sprain. Her stick had been found twenty yards from where she, herself, had been found. She'd managed to untie her boot in an attempt to alleviate the pain she must have felt, but she'd lacked the strength or the wherewithal to remove it from the swelling limb.

Back at the scene, the marks of her passing were clear to see. She'd dragged herself through the undergrowth for twenty yards or so, her fingernails were full of earth and grass, her palms scratched and the skin broken.

'She must have called out, used all her strength, but her cries went unheeded, I guess,' said the pathologist matter-of-factly.

'The dog probably stayed with her for a bit, and then wandered off. Maybe she shooed him off to try and raise help. Or perhaps the vermin scared it away. Who knows? Anyway, she will have used what little strength she had struggling to get back, calling out in vain, and then the darkness . . . It hasn't been particularly cold the last couple of nights, but you wouldn't want to be lying out on damp grass all night with a bad ankle sprain. They can be more painful than a break. I've see grown men cry until they get some medication,' he added.

'How long?' said Kavanagh.

'What? Before she died? It really is impossible to say. She might have survived a night. Possibly the next day if she's got a good heart. Her stomach will have the answers, except of course we don't know when she had her last meal. I don't think she'll have lived for more than forty-eight hours, though,' he said.

'Plenty long enough,' said Salt.

'Yes,' said the doctor. 'Quite long enough, I'm sure.'

'How's the old man?' asked Salt later that evening as she and Kavanagh sat in his car outside the hotel in the village.

'Well, he's still alive,' said the inspector. 'God knows if he even knows what's happening. He really is a case of better off dead, I'd have thought,' he added bleakly.

'Yes,' she said. 'Maybe. Anyway, you did well, Frank. It must have been horrible . . . doing what you did.'

'It most certainly was,' he agreed. 'Ironic, or what? The man's half dead. He's had a stroke years ago, and then he lies alone in his wheelchair for two days. His catheter bag's burst and the poor man's pressure sores are bleeding, but he somehow survives. Margaret Osman's out for her afternoon ramble, same as every day; she trips, breaks an ankle, and dies of exposure not a mile from the house.'

'It is ironic,' agreed Salt.

'So, what now?' he said.

'Well, there'll be no kissing me for a while,' she said.

He smiled. 'Fair enough. How about a drink, then?' he asked.

'Two?' she suggested.

THIRTY-FOUR

Hereford

Chiropodist Jerry Moore's admission that, whilst his wife was – wholly unknown to him – spending her Wednesday afternoons with Tom Oliver in a hotel in Birmingham he, rather than tramping the Oxfordshire countryside, was spending every free afternoon he had with former patient Nathaniel Henderson, unfortunately threw no light whatsoever on Oliver's subsequent disappearance.

'So, he was at it with a male hooker?' said Kavanagh.

'I think "escort" is the term you're looking for,' interrupted Salt.

'While his missus was having it off with Oliver?'

Kavanagh and Salt's relationship was based on trust, as well as mutual affection, and the idea of them cheating on one another was about as likely as Kavanagh taking up hanggliding or Salt wearing a cravat in bed. He had never before known just how freeing it was to be in a relationship where these were the values that obtained. Growing up in the Sixties and marrying in the Seventies, Kavanagh's notion of relationships had assumed an entirely different set of values: personal freedom and individual fulfilment were key. One followed one's own agenda, and if one 'needed' to have a relationship with someone else, then so be it. He would no more have told Rachael that she couldn't have an affair with another man than she would have censured her husband for the same thing. 'Told?' Just when did anyone who grew up during this time think that they could *tell* anyone anything when it came to these matters? Of course he and Rachael had cared for one another, and of course it was never their intention to hurt one another with their serial infidelities, but they were cast from a mould that decreed that these were the freedoms to be valued above all others, even when those freedoms were bought at a searing price.

Since he and Salt had been together, the unremarkable daily

knowledge that her fidelity to him, and his to her, was beyond question had given him an altogether different perspective on life. No, he didn't walk the streets and drive his car and attend meetings and briefings with some sort of inane smile on his face. In fact, the light on their relationship was more all-pervading than that: it was a state of quiet and unremarkable grace. The world still turned, bad things happened – both to them and to others; they faced problems and they didn't always get on. But Kavanagh knew, and Jane Salt knew, too, that no matter what the disagreement or argument or row, she wouldn't be turning to another man to punish Kavanagh for some harsh word or deed, any more than he would ever consider hurting her in a similar way.

Yes, very early on in their relationship, before it was properly a relationship at all, and when he had still been more involved with losing Rachael than he would have cared to admit, he had spent one reckless night with his former wife. He knew that he had to do it to put their years of relationship unhappiness finally behind him, and of course, Salt had discovered his treachery and he'd very nearly lost her. But even that stain was not something that she was one day going to punish him for with some deceit of her own.

'Yes,' said Salt, 'Jerry Moore's in a relationship with a male escort, and his wife was having an affair with Oliver, each of them unaware of the other's secret life. And there's probably no reason why either of them will find out.'

'Except that with every day that passes, it's looking more and more likely that Andrea Moore has lost her lover,' said Kavanagh.

'Yes,' said Salt. 'But at least her husband's alibi's stacking up, via his escort man and a detailed set of mobile phone traces.'

'So Moore's not an aggrieved husband who's knocked off his love rival, then?' said Kavanagh.

'And another line of enquiry bites the dust,' she added.

'Which brings us back to here,' said Kavanagh as they negotiated the traffic through Leominster and up towards Hereford.

'Ray Fraser,' she said as she pulled up once more the name and information they had obtained about Will and Sarah Cassin's neighbour on her Apple notepad.

'If he *was* responsible for the attack on Will Cassin, then

Cassin's wife not making it to the centre was no more or less than it seems. But if he didn't do it . . .'

'If he didn't do it,' agreed Kavanagh, 'then someone was prepared to go to extreme lengths to put obstacles in her way to prevent her being there.'

Just as Sarah Cassin had told them, Ray Fraser was a warehouseman at a computer store on a retail park on the outskirts of Hereford, his adopted home city. He'd come from the Scottish Borders originally, moved to Glasgow as a youngster and had spent his adult life there until moving to Hereford after meeting his wife, Carol, through an Internet dating site. Divorcee Carol's sons both still lived at home, and she had made it clear to Fraser early on that, no matter what their future together might hold, she had no intention of moving away from her children and the area to the frozen north.

Fraser's first, childless marriage had ended several years previously and he was perfectly happy to leave Scotland just as soon as possible.

Kavanagh and Salt had arranged to speak to him after work. It was always preferable to speak to couples separately. No matter how carefully any two people concocted a story together, cracks always appeared if there were inconsistencies to be exposed. And if partners didn't sit in on one another's interviews, it was so much easier to prise open those cracks.

They met him in the near-deserted car park at eight fifteen, just after the store had closed. 'Doesn't PC World have policies on weight?' Kavanagh murmured to Salt as the man waddled towards the inspector's BMW.

'Discrimination,' said Salt, 'and too many deep-fried Mars Bars.'

'And what about the customers?' said Kavanagh. 'Don't they have any rights?' The policeman stepped out of the car. 'Mr Fraser? DI Frank Kavanagh. Pleased to meet you.' He took the man's podgy hand in his own. 'This is my colleague, DC Salt,' he said, gesturing to the rear seat of the vehicle. 'Let's chat in the car.' He opened the front passenger door and as the man got in, the BMW sank a little under his weight.

'Mr Fraser,' Kavanagh began, 'we'd like to ask you about an incident that took place recently involving your neighbour, Will Cassin.'

Fraser said nothing, just looked at Kavanagh, his dark eyes set deep in the sockets of his emotionless face.

'You know that he was attacked?' prompted Salt.

'Of course. It was nothing to do with me. Have they been stirring things up?' he asked.

'He was badly beaten up,' said Kavanagh.

'Yes,' said the man, 'I know.'

'And there's a history of disputes between you and the Cassins, I believe?' said Kavanagh.

'There was a problem with them parking outside our house,' said the man. A smell of sweat and old deodorant had started to pervade the car. Kavanagh turned on the ignition and touched the button to lower the window a few inches.

'Problem in what sense?' Salt asked.

'It's our place,' he said as he looked at her in the driving mirror.

'Sorry?' she asked, meeting his eyes there. 'Your place?'

'It's our house,' he said in his thick accent.

'That doesn't make it yours, I don't think,' said Kavanagh. 'It is a public road, I imagine. But that's not why we're here, obviously.'

'It's outside our house,' he reiterated. 'Why don't they park outside their own place?'

'Look,' said the inspector, 'Mr Cassin was assaulted, and that assault could be related to a much more serious enquiry. It's why we need to establish the facts and any involvement that you might have had—'

'Are you accusing me?' he said. 'You must be joking. They're just trying to make trouble for us.'

'I doubt that,' said Salt. 'Although I'm sure they'd like to see whoever committed the assault brought to justice.'

'I'm telling you, it was nothing to do with me,' said Fraser again.

'Can you account for your movements the night your neighbour was attacked?' asked Kavanagh.

'I've already been asked,' he said.

'Yes, I'm sure,' said Kavanagh. 'But we need to confirm things now.'

'I was at home,' he said. 'I told the police.'

'Your wife? She was with you?'

'Look, I've already told them. We we're watching TV. It's

a Sunday night and then Carol goes up to bed. A bit before me. I stayed down for a while.'

'Watching TV?' said Salt.

'Yes.'

'You didn't go out?' asked Kavanagh.

'I'd know if I went out,' he said. 'This is Hereford. People don't go out at ten o'clock on a Sunday night.'

'But you've nothing to prove that. And there is a history of antagonism. There was the damage to the Cassins' car, something about which the police interviewed you. You're not telling me you didn't feel a little aggrieved.'

'I didn't feel "aggrieved",' he spat out. 'I felt fucking pissed off with the cops coming round and virtually accusing me.'

'I see you're still angry about it?' said Salt.

'Yes, course I am,' he said. 'Wouldn't you be?'

'Which is why, with respect, we're wondering about the attack?' she said.

'I didn't attack him. He and his missus, they're a pair of fuckin' do-gooders and I haven't got any time for them, but I didn't attack him.'

'But no alibi,' said Kavanagh.

'How am I gonna have an alibi sitting in me own front room watching the telly on a Sunday night?' he asked.

'What were you watching?' asked Salt.

He glanced at Salt in the mirror but said nothing.

'On TV?' she said again. 'What were you watching, Mr Fraser?'

'I can't remember,' he said.

'I'd like you to try,' she said quietly. 'It wasn't that long ago.'

'Football, maybe? Sunday night. Match of the Day Two?'

'You like football?' said Kavanagh.

'I like Rangers. I like watching proper football. Not the fairies you get down here,' he said scathingly.

'Well, you're not going to see them,' suggested Kavanagh.

'No, worst luck,' he agreed. 'I think I watched United,' said the Scotsman.

'I don't think so,' said Kavanagh categorically. 'United weren't on that Sunday.'

'Weren't they?' he said.

'They played on the Monday. At Portsmouth. I watched most of it down the pub. You must remember?'

'Yes, you're right,' he agreed.

'I am right,' said the cop. 'So have a bit of a think about it, eh. What were you watching?'

'I can't remember now. A bit of this, a bit of that, maybe a bit of a movie. I don't know, and what's it matter? I'd had a drink and I was watching TV, that's all. One Sunday night's like another. Who cares?'

'We do,' said Salt. 'It's important.'

'You know,' said Kavanagh, thoughtfully, 'I don't want to rake up the past . . .'

'No?' said the man. 'Then don't bother, eh.'

'But you know, your background, it's not been without its . . . difficulties?'

'Like you say, it's the past,' said Fraser.

'Of course,' said Kavanagh. 'And you paid your debt.'

'Yes, I did,' he said.

'Does your wife know about your time inside?' he asked.

'No. There was no need to tell her; it was a long time ago. It's history.'

'And there's probably no need for her to know now, if we can just straighten this out,' said the inspector.

'Typical,' he said, sneering.

'We've got an important enquiry, and we need to close the door on this part of it. If needs must, yes, it might be necessary to speak to your wife. And if we do that, of course things might have to come out.'

'You're a . . .'

'Yes?' said Kavanagh. 'Go on. I'm a what?'

'I was done for GBH, which you obviously know. It's years ago. And I did my time.'

'Yes,' said Kavanagh. 'You did. But who's to say you've not still got something inside you so that, when you're confronted – not with a Celtic fan in a kebab shop, but with a neighbour who you think has told the cops that you've gouged his car – you won't kick off again?'

'I've told you, I didn't touch Cassin. But I don't want Carol knowing about that stuff. It's not fair.'

'She hasn't got to,' said Salt. 'And you could start by convincing us that you weren't up the road that night doing your neighbour some harm.'

The man was silent, just breathing deeply and noisily. 'OK,' he began, 'I did damage her car. I'd had a few drinks and I just saw the thing outside our window and I lost it. It was late, there was nobody around and I went out with a six-inch nail and scratched it. I know I shouldn't have done it. I didn't even tell Carol it was me. I said some kid must have done it, but I think she knew, just the way she looked at me.'

'I see,' said Kavanagh. 'And what about the attack on Cassin? The truth, this time.'

'It wasn't me,' he said categorically. 'I was at home.'

'Go on,' said Salt.

'I was on the 'net.'

'EBay?' she said innocently.

'Yes. Right,' he said. 'I was on a site . . . you know.'

'A site?' repeated Kavanagh.

'For fuck's sake, have I got to spell it out for you? A bit of before-bedtime stuff. Nothing wrong in it. No kiddie porn or anything like that. Just a bit of something . . . you know. It's all legal and no harm.'

'I see,' said the inspector. 'And we can confirm that?'

'It'll be on the hard drive. I was on for about an hour. Half-ten, half-eleven, maybe.'

'And you know that was the time Cassin was attacked?' said Salt.

'The local cop said it was about eleven. That'll be when I was online.'

'How do we know you didn't log on and then go up the road and attack your neighbour, just leaving the connection open?' asked the inspector.

'Because it'll be on my card,' he said. 'It was a pay site.'

'Really? Not exactly family viewing, then?' said Kavanagh.

'Nothing illegal,' he said again.

'Right, we'll need to take your card for a day or two,' said Kavanagh. 'Check the debits and come back to you.'

Fraser leaned forward and reached into his back pocket for his wallet. He handed the inspector his credit card. 'So, can I go now?'

'Yes,' said the inspector.

'And the car? What about the damage?' he said.

'It's history,' said Salt. 'There's no point raking all that up again now. If your alibi holds up about the time Cassin was attacked, we won't be looking into the car vandalism.'

'But just a word of advice,' interrupted Kavanagh. 'Be a good neighbour. We've all got to live together, you know?'

The man grunted an acknowledgement.

'You can go for now, but don't let anything happen to your computer. It's part of your alibi, and it's possible we'll need to check it.'

Fraser walked away from the car without looking back.

'You coming up front, Constable?' said Kavanagh to Salt.

'Do you mind if I leave it for a few minutes?' she said. 'Let the atmosphere clear a bit. You know what I mean?'

'Sure,' he said, opening the window fully and chauffeuring them out of the car park into the night.

THIRTY-FIVE

Shropshire

'Keira,' said Salt as Kavanagh sat there quietly. It was the first time the two women had spoken. They were on neutral territory in the Bed and Breakfast accommodation down in the village that the police had undertaken to pay for. They didn't want Leon the gardener disappearing off to Manchester or, potentially much more problematic, Keira taking the next United Airlines back to Boston.

The centre employees should, perhaps, have been in one of the charming bow-fronted B & B cottages on Mill Street, places with squat, white-painted front doors, or one of the substantial old merchants' houses on the High Street. Alas, it was neither.

Keira and Leon had a room each in a dour-looking rendered bungalow a couple of streets back from the main thoroughfares, a sort of 1930s' buffer zone between the older, elegant properties with their deep sash windows and boot scrapers – places where lamps cast a soft light on polished tables all day long even in the brightest days of summer – and the dozen council houses that had been built in the Fifties a discreet distance above the village. This crescent was home to the only residents who didn't actually commute away from the area to earn their salaries: a bin man and his family; a council worker who cut the hedges on the surrounding lanes; a mechanic at the garage; an unmarried mother and her toddlers, and an elderly couple or two.

Many of the prosperous residents who had retired here now spent their mornings reading the *Telegraph* or the *Daily Mail* and perhaps a couple of afternoons each week put in a shift at the local charity shop in Craven Arms half an hour away, spent an hour or two in the makeshift Citizens Advice Bureau office in the village hall or did an afternoon at the local primary school helping a slow child with his faltering reading.

Keira, Salt and Kavanagh sat in the conservatory of the bed and breakfast house and drank tea.

'You heard about Margaret Osman, of course?' said Salt.

'Of course,' she repeated. 'What a tragedy. What a way for anyone to die.'

'Yes, it was terrible,' agreed Salt.

'And Richard? How is he?' asked the young American.

'He's in good hands now after his ordeal. Still in hospital, and being monitored, but he's being well looked after,' said the DC.

'We're here to ask you a few questions about Leon,' said Kavanagh.

'Yes?' said Keira, a little surprised. 'What about him?'

'You've known him long?' asked the inspector.

'Since he started at the centre,' she said.

'And when was that?'

'Over a year ago.'

'And how do you find him?' he asked.

'How do you mean, "find him"?' she replied.

'We're trying to sketch in people's backgrounds, you know,' offered Salt vaguely.

'Mine?' said Keira defensively.

'Everyone's,' said Kavanagh.

'I see,' said the young woman.

'So, what about Leon?' asked Salt.

'What about him?' she said.

'How well do you know him?'

'Somewhat.'

'"Somewhat"?' repeated Salt. 'What's that mean? You like him?' she asked.

'He's OK,' she said.

'We need a bit more than that, Keira,' said the constable sternly. 'Tom Oliver's car was in the lake, but he wasn't in it. We need to find out where he is and just what's happened to him.'

'Of course,' she said, chastened by Salt's admonitory tone.

'Just how well do you know him? Are you and he close?'

'We were for a little while, once,' she said.

'Once?' said Salt.

'Yes.'

'Not any more?' said Kavanagh.

'No,' said Keira.

'Are you sure?'

'I think I'd know,' she said.

'Why have you kept this from us?' he asked.

'I haven't kept it from you. You've never asked me anything about Leon and myself.'

'We're asking you now, Keira,' he said. 'Why don't you just put us in the picture?'

'Because we're not involved with one another. Not any more.'

'Go on,' said Salt.

'We were together for a bit. When he first arrived, you know, we did spend time. He's not really my type. He's not a reader, and I don't think he's ever been to the theatre in his life. But I was free. I didn't have a boyfriend over here, and he didn't seem to be with anyone, and we got close . . .'

'But there was something wrong?' suggested Salt.

'He never really seemed that bothered. Don't get me wrong,' she added hastily, 'I wasn't looking to have his babies or anything but, you know, he always seemed to keep me at arm's length. Am I an unattractive woman?' she said. 'And he's a nice-looking guy.'

'Sure,' agreed Salt.

'So we're both free. What's the problem?'

'And? What was the problem?' asked the policewoman.

'I've no idea,' she said. 'I wondered whether I was imagining it, or maybe it was that English reserve I'd read about in novels. It's not like that in the States, that's for sure. We went out a few times, had a drink and all, but he always kept a bit of himself back. I even started to wonder whether he was gay and he just wanted us to be friends, you know? Fair enough, I have several gay friends. But he wasn't gay, I know that. But whatever it is people do, he didn't do it. He just didn't come across. I never felt as if I had him for myself, and that he was there for me. Do you understand what I'm saying?'

'Of course,' said Salt.

'It was always me who made the moves; he just went along with things.'

'You were intimate?' said the policewoman.

'Yes, of course we slept together,' she said.

'And?' prompted Salt.

'And what? What am I supposed to tell you? It was alright,

but even then there was always that distance. I thought maybe he'd been hurt or something. Perhaps some woman had broken his heart. But he isn't a man who talks about his feelings.'

'You asked him?' she said.

'Yes, I asked him. "What's wrong?" I said. "Don't you like me? Is there still some other woman in your life someplace? Or have I just got spinach in my teeth or something?" He said there was nothing wrong. But it made me feel odd, being with a man like that, a part of him not there at all . . . so remote sometimes. The only thing he ever said was that his family situation was difficult. "Yes?" I said, "So what's new?" Who doesn't have family stuff going on? The whole world's got that. But he didn't want to go there. He wasn't going to tell me anything.'

'So, what happened?' asked Salt, intrigued. 'Between you two?'

'We let it drift, I suppose. We hung out, but just as friends, not lovers any more.'

'And now?' said Salt.

'Still friends. Actually, I still quite fancy him. You know how it is with men. If there's that bit that you can't reach, or you can't have, it's a strong lure. But we haven't been close – not in that way – for months. He's my English enigma is that man.'

The three of them sat there in silence for a minute. Eventually Kavanagh said, 'You know with Sarah Cassin not being able to come to tutor?'

'Of course,' said Keira.

'Did Leon know her at all?'

'Sarah? Yes, a bit. She tutored here last year, not long after he had started to work here. He and I were sort of getting, you know, like I said, getting to know one another.'

'Yes?' said Salt.

'And he and Sarah, they got quite friendly . . .'

'Go on,' said the cop.

'I suppose, because I was getting involved with him, my antennae were twitching. You know, another woman on the block, even though she's much older than me.'

'Sure,' smiled Salt.

'The two of them, they'd have a drink together, sit on the bench out the front where we smokers go. It was her first time here, and he hadn't long started the job, so they had that being-new thing in common. They just got a bit friendly, I think.'

'Anything else?' asked the policewoman.

'I don't think so. I remember she gave a reading on the last night, like the tutors always do, and I asked Leon if he'd like to come in and hear her. He wasn't keen – like I say, he's not really interested in writing.'

'But he sat in?' asked Kavanagh.

'Yes, I persuaded him. It was a bit of a sly move on my part, really.'

'How so?' asked Salt.

'Well, a lot of Sarah's poetry is about loss and longing, the usual stuff,' she laughed. 'What's new? And I thought it might loosen him up a bit. He seemed so knotted up. It was part of my plan to get him to open up.'

'And?' said Salt. 'Did it work?'

'No, I don't think so. He listened, of course, but he didn't take me out in the moonlight afterwards to make love down by the lake!'

'No?' said the policewoman.

'I'm afraid not,' she said.

'And was that it?' asked Kavanagh. 'Was there anything else? Anything at all?'

'No, not really.'

'Are you sure?' said Salt.

'Well, I just recall this one really odd thing she said. I remember all the other writers on the course being struck by it.'

'Yes?' urged Kavanagh. 'What was that?'

'At the end there were the usual questions, about how disciplined do you have to be, and where do you get your ideas from, all the usual, and I remember the last question Sarah was asked was what was the one thing that she needed above all others in her work as a poet.'

'And?' said Salt. 'What was it?'

'Do you want to guess?' Keira asked the two cops.

'Time to write?' said Kavanagh gamely.

Keira nodded her head and looked to Salt.

'I don't know,' she said. 'Inspiration, I suppose?'

'Routine,' said Keira.

'Yes?' said Salt.

'It was what was so odd. It wasn't anything writerly, like this or that pen or desk or anything aesthetic at all. She said that routine is what gave her the necessary calm which she found essential to write. And she said that to this end she was blessed with an absolutely perfect husband, a man who always put his watch on the bedside table, just so,' and Keira mimicked the careful action. 'Someone who always separated his newspaper before he began to read it, and put the bits he wasn't going to read into the recycling box.

'For the last ten years he'd always had a drink with the same two friends on a Sunday evening where they did the crossword in the pub together.'

Kavanagh and Salt exchanged quick glances at the apparently hum-drum revelation.

'I remember it well because it all seemed so crazy.'

'I bet,' said Salt.

'Especially to someone like me who never does the same thing twice and has no routine whatsoever. I don't even wear a watch and I never know what time it is!'

'And Leon was there for all that, too?'

'Sure. Why?'

'Did you two discuss what Sarah Cassin had said at all?' asked the policewoman.

'No,' she said. 'Never. Why would we?'

Salt picked up her tea. It was cold and she replaced it on the little glass-topped table as Keira sipped water from a bottle. 'It's nothing, she said, 'just part of the picture.'

'Thanks for your time, Keira,' said Kavanagh, getting to his feet. 'And, for the time being, would you keep this conversation strictly between ourselves?'

'Of course,' she said.

It was like any twenty-six-year-old's room, Kavanagh imagined. Ipod docking station and laptop, CDs and DVDs, micro stereo and a mess of clothes on the floor. Stella cans, mugs with half-drunk coffee in them and an ash tray, even though there was a big No Smoking sign on the back of the door and an alarm and sprinkler system installed.

Actually, Keira wasn't quite right: Leon Bell *did* read, but it wasn't Tolstoy. There were a couple of Andy McNab *Bravo*

Two-Zero derring-do type things and some paperback thrillers, books by people Kavanagh had only vaguely heard of and seen in the supermarkets and WH Smith's.

He liked movies, though. Most people get by on a *Time Out* or a *Halliwell's*, but this guy had both, as well as the *Empire Film Guide* for the previous year.

There were a couple of girly magazines in his sock drawer. 'I don't think we're gonna find the answer to things here,' said Kavanagh as he took one out. Salt pulled on her gloves and riffled through the young man's underwear.

Kavanagh sat on the edge of the bed and flipped through the adult magazine, stopping at the centre-spread of a nicely bosomed woman pleasuring herself. He revolved the picture.

'Was it something, Frank?' said Salt.

'Research,' he said.

She left him to it and worked her way through a pile of discarded newspapers at the bottom of the fitted wardrobe.

'Why'd he want this?' she said to Kavanagh.

'What is it?' he asked, a little distracted by his own 'reading'.

'A writers' magazine,' she said.

'So?' he said, replacing the magazine in the drawer and joining her where she was kneeling on the floor.

'Don't know,' said Salt. 'I think they said one of the reasons they hired Leon was because he isn't a writer and wouldn't be wandering off into the woods all the time to work on his novel.'

'Yes?'

'So what's he doing with an old copy of *Writing Today*?'

'Why not bring it along?' said Kavanagh.

THIRTY-SIX

'Leon . . .'

'Yes?'

Kavanagh looked at the young man and inclined his head slightly, gave him a searching look.

'What?' he said. It was the affronted question that a thousand school teachers would hear this day throughout the land. It said, 'Yes, go on then, challenge me, but whatever it is, I'm going to deny it, or even justify it with nothing more than my temerity. '

The interview was informal. Kavanagh had little enough to go on and he certainly didn't want the young man bringing in a solicitor to inhibit their chat. He'd invited him up for 'just a little help with our enquiries', the old familiar line.

An officer had gone down to the village where he was staying and driven him up to the centre and now the two men stood in the estate garage, facing one another.

'What?' he said again.

The cop opened his hands in a gesture that simply said, 'Please, come on.'

Leon felt awkward here, even though it was his own place, his own work environment to which, really, he had title, not this slightly unpredictable policeman. He leaned against the workbench, the big vice to his left, several tools lying there, some huge spanners and wrenches just out of reach, but he still said nothing.

'The thing about Tom Oliver, Leon, is that no fucker liked him,' said the inspector.

'Is that right?' said the young man.

'Well, no, it's not right, not strictly,' Kavanagh continued. 'He was having an affair with a woman, and she must have liked him . . .'

'Yes?' he said.

'And there'd been plenty of others.'

'Lucky man,' said Leon, as he picked up a jack handle and idly ran a rag along its length as the policeman spoke.

'But lots of people are tossers, aren't they?' he said jovially. 'You know, I drive past them every day, sit next to them in the restaurant and have to listen to them eating popcorn and sucking Coke in the flicks. The difference is, they're still here next week; still a pain in the arse, but still here. Not like our Mr Oliver, eh?'

'If you say so,' said the young man.

'So, where do you reckon he's gone, Leon?'

'How would I know?' he said, chucking the rag on the bench and patting the foot-long iron bar in the palm of his hand.

Kavanagh glanced across to the local PC who had driven Leon up here. He was leaning against the patrol car fifty yards away, his hands deep in his pockets, his thoughts clearly elsewhere.

'How indeed?' said Kavanagh, and took a couple of steps to the front of the building. 'So, where were you Sunday night, over a week ago, Leon?'

'Why, what happened?' Leon smirked.

'Very funny,' said the cop. 'What happened is that Sarah Cassin – well, her husband, a decent sort of bloke, a Friends of the Earth sort of fella, you know, goes to work on his bike, all that kind of thing, he gets whacked on the way home from the pub. Nobody else involved, just a totally unprovoked attack in a little market town.'

'Sign of the crap times, I suppose,' said Leon.

'Yes,' agreed the inspector, turning to face him. 'I'm afraid so. Cassin got a real beating. So bad – as I'm sure you know – that his missus couldn't come here; she had to stay home and look after him.'

'How would I know?' said Leon. Kavanagh ignored him.

'Sarah Cassin can't come, so what does Keira do? She calls the first substitute off the bench, Catherine Wooley. Now, here's a thing, Leon: who's the only person who knows all these things? Who can put 'em all together and make any kind of sense of them?'

'What things?' he said.

'Who knows that if Sarah can't make it down here, the most likely person to be called in is Catherine? Who knows this because the last time something similar happened, when a tutor broke his wrist – you told me about it yourself – it was Catherine that was called in. She only lives an hour away, after all. You're one of the only people who knows all this.'

'So what?' he said.

'And what's the significance of knowing who the sub might be?'

'Tell me,' he said. 'I reckon you're going to, anyway.'

'The significance, Leon, is that Catherine Wooley and Tom Oliver have got a fair old bit of previous – and to be honest, I'm not even sure how you could know such a thing, but you did – and if anything were to happen to Mr Unpopular, Tom Oliver, if he goes missing, for example, who's the first person we're going to take a good look at on account of their history?'

'So you're telling me Catherine Wooley's involved?'

Now it was Kavanagh's turn to smirk. 'Yes, course she is,' he said. 'I tell you what, Leon, DC Jane Salt's been a cop for a good few years, and she reckons if Catherine Wooley in her long skirt and clumpy sandals is someone who can – what? Kill another person? – then I'm a fuckin' salsa queen. But here's what I think you thought. I think you thought that if she was here, and you did Tom Oliver some mischief, it's gotta be her we'll be looking at, and not you. Trouble is, my old mate, it doesn't add up. We have looked at her, we've looked at her good and close, and she's no more involved with this than I am. Just 'cause she's a dyke with a bit of previous with Oliver – I see your thinking – that doesn't make her Lady Macbeth.

'Yes, and if you happened to know she does a bit of work at her local nick, that's even better. Maybe she's got one of them dodgy geezers when he's released to put a bit of grief Oliver's way. It all adds up to her being well in the frame, doesn't it?'

'So what's your point?' said Leon. 'What's any of this got to do with me?'

'Here's that thing again,' said Kavanagh. 'Where were you last Sunday evening?'

'You tell me,' he said. 'You'll have checked.'

'You're a canny operator, Leon. The fact is, I don't know what it is you're up to, and I've no idea why you took against this bloke, tosser though he was – I'm using the right tense there, I imagine – but what I am pretty sure of is that you went down to Hereford and gave Will Cassin a beating—'

'Bollocks,' he said.

'Yes? I think you took a drive down there and made sure that Sarah was indisposed for the next few days looking after her injured husband. I've checked your phone. Like I say, you're a thoughtful man. You didn't take it with you, did you? You didn't take it with you in case someone called you. One of your mates or something, and that one call would have given us a trace on your whereabouts. You certainly made sure you didn't call anyone yourself.'

'You watch a lot of TV?' said Leon.

Kavanagh ignored the facetious comment and continued. 'You left your phone here, but you weren't here. And, as it happens, someone did phone you, someone who doesn't know there's no signal here.'

'I didn't take my phone with me 'cause I wasn't in Hereford,' he said defiantly. 'If I don't answer it sometimes, maybe it's just like everybody else and I don't hear it ring? Maybe I'm out of signal up here, or I'm out for a fag or a walk in the grounds? Maybe it's just turned off or I've got my music on and I don't hear it.'

'Yes, maybe,' said Kavanagh. 'I wasn't expecting you to hold your hands up, say "fair cop and bang to rights," or anything.'

'Anyway, why don't you check the CCTV if you think I've been to Hereford?' he said, sounding almost smug.

'Because you knew that was a possibility, just the same as you knew we might check your mobile. You went to Hereford on B roads, all the way there and back without a camera to clock you once. I've checked it, and it's easy. Yes, we've got people looking at it, but we won't find anything, will we?'

'You won't find anything, 'cause I wasn't there,' he said.

'I know what I know,' said the inspector, 'but I don't know two things: I don't know why you're involved in this and I don't know what you've done with Tom Oliver. But we'll find out, no doubt. We almost always do.'

'Fair enough,' said the young man, and he lay the jack handle carefully back down on the workbench.

There was a long silence between the two men, neither of them apparently quite sure whether their exchange was over. The PC got into his patrol car and sat there with the door wide open, his feet on the gravel.

Kavanagh approached Leon. 'I've got a little something for you to have a look at here,' he said, and he pulled a folded sheet of paper from his pocket.

'What's this?' said Leon taking the document.

'Have a look at it,' said the inspector.

Leon unfolded a photocopy of the MOT certificate for the Land Rover that stood beside them. 'So what?' he queried. 'I had it done a couple of weeks ago.'

'I know you did,' said Kavanagh. 'I stopped in at the garage to get some tobacco, and the bloke there asks me what I'm doing down here. I told him I'd got a bit of an enquiry at the centre. "Oh yes," he says. "We do all their work, MOT'd the Land Rover for them only last week."'

'What's your point?' said Leon. 'What's the matter with this?'

'There's nothing the matter with it,' said the policeman. 'What's the mileage say?'

Leon looked at the document. 'Forty-two thousand, seven hundred and eighty-five,' he said. 'So?'

'What she's done now?' said Kavanagh. 'Go on, have a look. Believe me, I have.'

Leon opened the driver's door carefully and peered in at the odometer.

'What's it done, Leon?'

'Forty-two, nine-hundred and twelve. Why?'

'How's your maths?'

'Alright.'

'Do the sums,' said the inspector. 'It's done well over a hundred miles in the few days since it was tested. You told me the first time we spoke this thing only goes down to the village a couple of times a week and most of the time, she just tootles around the estate. So how come it's suddenly done this much?'

'Been busy,' he said.

'Yes,' said Kavanagh. 'I bet you have.'

'This doesn't prove a thing,' he said defiantly.

'No, it doesn't, does it?' agreed Kavanagh. 'But it's not bad for a first course, is it? Anyway, I reckon we're done for now. You can go. Just don't go too far, alright, and don't leave the village without contacting me.'

Leon walked off towards the police car. Twenty yards away, Kavanagh called after him. 'Leon?'

'What?' he said, turning.

'What do you think of Michael Douglas?'

'What do I think of Michael Douglas?' he repeated. 'Crap. I can't stand him. Why?'

'Don't go far,' said Kavanagh.

*   *   *

'Hello, *Writing Today*, Emily speaking, how can I help you?'

'Hello, this is Detective Constable Jane Salt. I emailed you my security details for confirmation checks an hour ago. As I said, we need some information about a subscriber.'

'Yes, of course,' she said. 'I'll put you through.'

'Good morning, Subscriptions.'

'This is DC Jane Salt. Could you check your list of subscribers for me please? I need to check the status of someone called Leon Bell.'

'One moment please,' she said.

Salt stood at one of the desks in the incident room headquarters in Craven Arms police station and waited. A few minutes later the woman came back on the line. 'We don't seem to have anyone of that name on our list,' she said. 'I'm sorry.'

'Are you sure?' asked Salt. 'Would you look again, please?'

'I have checked,' said the woman.

'But I have a magazine here that I think must have come to him,' said Salt. 'Your magazine is subscription only?' she asked.

'Yes, subscription only,' said the woman. 'Which issue is it?'

'Spring, last year,' said Salt.

'Perhaps he's no longer a subscriber?' suggested the woman.

'Would you check your backlist for me?' asked Salt. 'It's important.'

'One moment, please,' and she was gone again.

A couple of minutes later, she was back. 'I'm afraid there's no-one of that name,' she said.

'You're sure?' said Salt again.

'I'm quite sure,' said the woman a little tetchily.

'Thank you, anyway,' said Salt, but before she could replace the phone the woman added, 'We did have an Aaron Bell. I don't suppose that's any good to you?'

'Aaron Bell?' said Salt, intrigued.

'Yes, but his subscription lapsed. When it was due last year the usual reminders were sent out, but we obviously heard nothing more, and his direct debit seems to have been cancelled.'

'Do you have an address for him?' asked the DC.

'24 Cato Road, Fallowfield, Manchester,' she said.

'Thank you so much,' said Salt and replaced the receiver.

THIRTY-SEVEN

At lunchtime, Kavanagh picked up a sandwich and a carton of smoothie from Tesco Express and then, a hundred yards down the road, read the ads for reiki and aromatherapy treatments in the window whilst Salt waited to be served in Real Tucker, the local wholefood store.

Whenever Kavanagh went into this kind of shop and saw the range of individually priced goods, and stood in a queue where he waited patiently to be served as the person in front of him added brown rice, wholemeal flour and rice cakes to the little pile of carefully selected products before them, at those times, Kavanagh most earnestly thanked God for super-markets, with their much-maligned cornucopia of out-of-season goods; for polished, white, basmati rice and added-to and enhanced and flavour-enriched foods – all the things, in fact which not only made them look very good, but which also ensured that they tasted wonderful. Yes, if you wanted social interaction, wrinkled fruit and worse vegetables, then this was the place for you. It was the difference between fruit and chocolate: apples were a lottery of taste and consistency, and sometimes, it's true, you did have a good result; but a Mars bar was always a Mars bar.

Ten minutes later, back on overcast Craven Arms High Street, Salt's vegetable samosas wrapped in brown paper, the writers' magazine from Leon Bell's room tucked under her arm in a plastic bag, Kavanagh said, 'So, Leon Bell's got a brother who *is* a writer?'

'Apparently,' said Salt as they hurried along and the first few raindrops began to fall. 'And he had the same address as Leon had a while ago in Manchester.'

'And you reckon Leon saw the job at the centre advertised in his brother's magazine?' said the inspector.

'Looks like it,' said Salt. 'Shall we get out of this?' she said as the rain began to fall more heavily, and they turned into the foyer of the town's main hotel.

They weren't alone. The poster on a sandwich board

advertised that day's property auction and there was already a small crowd milling around the place.

They sat at the back of the room amongst the folk there, two cops surreptitiously eating samosa and tuna and sweet-corn on white bread.

The main lot, reading between the lines of the agent's colourful details, was a single-storey cottage on a couple of acres of stony pasture and a few gnarled fruit trees. The auctioneer, a tall man with a shining head, surveyed the folk in front of him seated on gilt-painted dining chairs.

Kavanagh reckoned there was a smallholder or two, possibly with land adjacent to the plot; a builder looking for a standby project, maybe, something to work on during a quiet time when his blokes could demolish the cottage and dig out the drains and foundations, rather than hang about the yard and be paid for doing very little.

A couple in their early thirties sat nervously near the aisle as if they might wish to leave quickly. And then there were the locals, folk with bags and shopping who were as relaxed as the man who comes to fix the telephone in the doctor's surgery whilst someone else sits there anxiously awaiting the results of his biopsy.

'So, what's the brotherly Aaron and Leon Bell connection?' queried Kavanagh.

'You've got me,' said Salt.

'Good,' he said, 'at least that's something,' and he rested his hand on her thigh.

'But I do know where Leon could have sussed that there was animosity between Catherine Wooley and Tom Oliver,' she said.

'Really?' said Kavanagh.

The auctioneer tapped the water glass on his table with a spoon. 'Take a look at this,' whispered Salt and passed him the magazine. 'Page twenty-eight.'

Kavanagh brushed the crumbs from his lap onto the floor and opened the magazine. Page twenty-eight featured something called Spiked, a snide diary column with an insider's knowing tone. That month's item was a supercilious account of some of the more infamous literary feuds of recent years. The diarist had wrapped up his sour piece with his favourite 'top ten' of the things, and sure enough there, at number seven,

was novelist Tom Oliver's drunken abuse of poet Catherine
Wooley after she had dissed his novel *College Affairs* in an
injudicious review.

'Good afternoon, ladies and gentlemen,' began the
auctioneer. 'We're here today to sell just the one lot: Orchard
Cottage and two acres of pasture. And there's only one thing
I want to say before bidding begins: what's being offered
today is simply not being made any more. It's a pretty cottage
and it's in a nice spot, but it comes with just over two acres
of lush meadow and productive orchard. There's apple and
pear and damson trees, and even a Victoria plum, I believe.
Do you want to keep a couple of ponies for the youngsters?
Breed some pigs? Or even graze a few sheep? You could be
self-sufficient from the garden and still sell produce in the
market here in Craven Arms. Or you could just sit back and
watch your grass grow.'

'And you think Leon read this?' Kavanagh asked Salt quietly.

'It's the same edition as the one that's advertising the job
at the centre. I reckon he looked through it and happened to
read about Oliver and Wooley. Later on, when he knows that
Oliver is coming to teach here, he remembered what he'd read
and thought that he might be able to get Wooley here and
thereby line her up as the main suspect.

'OK, it's bit of a long shot. She might be otherwise engaged,
she might refuse to come if she knows it's Oliver she'll be
teaching with, but it's worth a shot to deflect any attention
from himself and, as it happened, it worked out.'

'Yes,' said Kavanagh, 'but what's Leon got against Oliver
anyway? There's plenty that doesn't sit right about him, that
much I'll grant you, but what's his motive in wanting to harm
him?'

'I have absolutely no idea,' conceded Salt in a whisper and
with a shake of the head.

'Whatever figure you have in mind today,' continued the
auctioneer, raising his voice, and even getting Kavanagh and
Salt's attention, 'just remember, we live on a small island,
and there's only one thing they're not making any more of:
land.'

Kavanagh wasn't so sure. As a youngster in school, it had
been an article of faith that there were, in this world, five
continents.

Now, a police inspector in his fifties, there were, apparently, *seven*.

Just where the other two had come from, he had no idea at all. But when he was stuck in traffic on the M6, this awareness of an expanding earth at least offered some little comfort.

'Right, who'll start me at a hundred thousand?' asked the auctioneer.

No-one did start him at a hundred thousand, but within only two minutes, the bids had easily exceeded that figure anyway.

'A hundred and eighty, then. One hundred and eighty thousand pounds . . . One hundred and ninety thousand . . . And five, at the back of the room. One hundred and ninety-five thousand pounds . . . I'll take another five . . .'

A man with a tweed jacket and frayed jumper who looked as if he wouldn't have fifty pounds in the bank had bid up to the £190,000, but it was the builder at the back of the room who secured the lot, his solicitor sitting at his side having done his bidding, literally.

The anxious-looking young couple slipped quietly out of the room feeling foolish as their dreams of a country life fell apart.

Salt and Kavanagh followed shortly after them.

THIRTY-EIGHT

'Hello. DC Salt speaking.'

'My name's Penny Cleaton . . .'

'Yes,' said Salt. 'What can I do for you?'

'It's about the *Crimewatch* programme. Last week.'

'Yes?' said Salt, moving to the window as she sought some refuge in the busy incident room. 'Sorry, that's better, it's pretty noisy in here. What can I do for you, Mrs . . .?'

'Cleaton. Penny Cleaton,' the woman said again. 'I saw the end of the programme the other evening. It was pure luck, but we'd got the TV on for the ten o'clock news, and when I saw a picture of Tom Oliver on the screen I asked Theo – he's my husband – I asked him to turn it up and we saw the end of the item about his going missing.'

'I see,' interrupted Salt, wondering just where the woman's breathless narrative was going. 'So, do you know where Tom Oliver is?' she asked hopefully.

'No, I've no idea,' she said.

'So, what was it you . . .?' asked Salt.

'There was a joke, we . . . Well, I suppose it was a joke. About Tom Oliver being in someone's "bad books", I think they called it. I thought it was in poor taste. It's not a comedy programme, after all, is it?'

'No, it's not,' agreed Salt. 'But of course, that's not the sort of thing that the police have control over; that would be the producer. Anyway, what was your information, Mrs Cleaton?'

'I was on a course with Tom Oliver a few years ago.'

Yes,' said Salt dispiritedly. The problem with appeals to the public was that they invariably generated responses from people who had no idea just what sort of information might be useful, as opposed to inconsequential stuff that was obviously already in the public domain and of no interest whatsoever. Several people had already phoned in merely to say that they knew Tom Oliver. One man had actually called to say he'd read some of Oliver's campus novels and thought them at least as good as Malcolm Bradbury's, and rather better than Tom Sharpe's.

'Please, go on,' said Salt wearily.

'When I was on that course, I hate to say this, especially if he's come to harm, but Mr Oliver was very unpleasant to a young writer.'

'Yes?' said the DC.

'This is very personal . . .'

'It will go no further,' Salt assured her.

'He was a nice young man, quiet and introspective and clearly very committed to his work . . .'

'Go on,' said Salt.

'To be honest, although we were there for the writing, most of us had also come for some fun and a bit of sun. Maybe we'd get started on the novel we'd always told ourselves we'd write, but heavens, we weren't tortured souls, we were mostly middle-aged folk here to have a go at this thing, and when the week was over we'd go back with a bit of a tan and the opening chapter of a book that we'd almost certainly never finish.'

'But the young man?' enquired Salt, sensing the drift. 'He was different?'

'He was dedicated. He was thoughtful and serious and he wanted Tom Oliver's advice. He obviously admired him very much.'

'I see. And did he help him?' said Salt.

'Not really, no. It was so clear that the boy was talented. I don't write much, and I don't write that well. Whatever it is you have to have, I just don't have it. But I am a member of a book club, and I've always read a lot. I believe I know good writing when I see it. And Aaron was clearly a gifted—'

'Aaron?' interrupted Salt.

'Aaron,' repeated the woman. 'Why? Do you know him?'

'No, not at all,' said Salt. 'It's just that that name has cropped up. Please, go on.'

'It was clear to me – maybe others, too, I don't know, we couldn't really discuss it, obviously – but I think that instead of encouraging him, Tom Oliver actually undermined him.'

'How, exactly?' asked the policewoman.

'Well, we'd read work out loud, some exercise we'd been set, and Oliver would find the positives in something that was mediocre – especially if the woman reading it was good-looking and not wearing very much – and then Aaron might be asked to read what he'd written, and Oliver would subtly chip away at it.'

'I see,' said Salt.

'As I say, it's difficult to talk about these things, and I know very well that writing's subjective. But I'm certain that he was writing well, and all he got were little knocks to his confidence.'

'So, what happened?' said Salt.

'We had a couple of tutorials, solo affairs with Tom. I think he came on to one of the women. He had a bit of a reputation and there were women there who had come for more than just tips on writing dialogue . . .'

'Yes?'

'I don't know what Oliver said to him. It was only halfway through the week, but Aaron had his tutorial and that evening he looked ashen and he was very withdrawn. He said nothing in the workshop the following morning, just sat there quietly and, by the evening, he'd gone. Oliver made light of it. He said that his mother had had a fall and Aaron had had to get home.'

'Where did all this happen?' asked Salt.

'In France, a place called Fleurance in the Languedoc.'

'And his name was Aaron, you say? You don't remember his surname, I suppose?'

'Yes,' she said immediately. 'Aaron Bell. I only know because there was a man on the course who lived in Cheshire and he knew of Aaron . . .'

'Knew of him?' repeated Salt. 'How? Aaron wasn't published or anything?'

'It was nothing to do with his writing; it was to do with his brother. Apparently, when Aaron was a teenager, someone was picking on him at school . . .'

'Go on,' said Salt.

'He and his brother were at different schools. His brother, I forget his name, he caught up with this bully in a park somewhere and beat him up very badly.'

'I see,' said Salt. 'That really is very interesting. The only thing I don't understand is, we've had cause to look into this family and there's no record of his brother – his name's Leon, incidentally – having any kind of criminal record.'

'That was the whole point. This man who knew of him had

read about it in the papers up there. It became a *cause célèbre* with the local paper getting involved in a campaign to defend the boy. *Brother takes on big bully* kind of thing, you know, like that farmer who shot a burglar over in Norfolk some-where and all the tabloids got behind him? The magistrates didn't exactly reward . . . Leon, did you say? But when they heard the facts about the way this sensitive boy, Aaron, had been intimidated and taunted, they threw the assault case against his brother out of court.'

'I think I understand,' said Salt.

'I'd told Theo all about what had happened on the course when I got back, and when we saw *Crimewatch* last week, he said I should call you and tell you what I knew about Oliver's behaviour to Aaron.'

'I can't thank you enough,' said Salt. 'You've done exactly the right thing,' she assured the woman. 'Just one thing, though . . .'

'Yes?' she asked.

'Why has it taken you so long to contact us? The programme went out in the middle of last week.'

'I wasn't sure it was the right thing to do, and I didn't want to create any trouble.'

'For Aaron?' said Salt.

'For Aaron, or for anyone else,' said the woman.

THIRTY-NINE

'Your brother?' said Inspector Kavanagh open-endedly.
'Yes?' replied Leon.
'You have a brother?' asked the inspector directly.
'No,' said the young man.

'Leon, don't play games with us, we *know* you have a brother,' insisted the policeman.

'I don't have a brother,' said the gardener.

'Cato Road. In Manchester. You shared a flat with him,' said Salt.

'Yes, I did,' he said.

'So?' said Kavanagh. 'Where is he?'

'He's dead.'

Kavanagh looked to Salt and back to Bell. 'What do you mean, he's dead?'

'Aaron killed himself,' said the young man.

'When was this?' said Salt.

'A bit ago.'

'And what were the circumstances . . . of his death?' ventured Salt gently, completely thrown by the man's assertion.

'Circumstances?' Leon repeated, almost as though he didn't quite comprehend the meaning of the word.

'How did he . . .? What happened to him, Leon?' she continued.

'He drove his car into a wall,' said the gardener. 'Well, it wasn't his car. He hired it.'

'He hired a car to kill himself?' said Kavanagh, incredulous.

'Yes,' said Bell. 'He put four open containers of petrol on the back seat. Then he drove it into a wall. They said he must have been doing over eighty miles an hour.'

'God,' said Kavanagh. 'I'm sorry.'

Salt and Kavanagh had discussed any number of options before speaking to the young man again, but this certainly wasn't one of them. They sat in silence in the conservatory of the bed and breakfast house in the village as Bell claimed some respite from the memory of his brother's terrible death.

He pulled his tobacco from his pocket and rolled a thin cigarette.

Eventually, Salt said, 'We understand your brother was a writer, Leon?'

'Yes,' he said.

'And he knew Oliver?'

'I guess,' he said equivocally.

'He told you about what happened in France?'

'What do you mean?' he said.

'The course he went on, with Oliver?'

'How do you know about that?' he asked.

'Someone who was there has been in touch,' said Salt.

'I knew he was there, that's all,' he said.

'Did he tell you what happened? Between him and Oliver?' said Kavanagh.

'I don't remember,' said Leon.

'Try,' said the inspector, his need to pursue answers to these questions only partly abated by Bell's shocking revelation about his brother's death.

'All I know is that it was a bad time for him,' he said.

'In what way?' asked Salt.

'His writing. That was the big thing for Aaron. But it didn't work out. He came back from abroad depressed. Not long after, he killed himself.'

'On account of his writing?' said Kavanagh

'He killed himself, that's all I know.'

'Your parents?' said Salt. 'They must have been devastated.'

'What do you think?' he sneered.

'You were close? You and your brother?' said Salt.

'No,' said Leon. 'Not really. We were different.'

'In what way?' asked the inspector. Leon gestured to the rolled cigarette in his fingers. Kavanagh nodded his agreement and Leon went to the door and stood there, leaning against the jamb, smoking. 'How do you mean?' continued the inspector. 'In what way were you different?'

'You got any brothers?' he asked. He didn't even look at Salt.

'No,' said Kavanagh. He had a younger brother and a sister, but there was something about this man that made him feel uneasy and he was disinclined to reveal the intimacies of his own life.

'You wouldn't understand, then,' said Bell.

'Try me,' suggested Kavanagh.

'I don't want to talk about it,' he said.

'We checked your room,' the inspector eventually said as Bell leaned there pulling hard on the cigarette in his mouth.

'Yes?' said Leon.

'What do you know about this?' said Kavanagh and put the writers' magazine they had taken from his room on the table.

'What about it?' he said, glancing across at the journal.

'*Writing Today*,' said Salt.

'Yes, I can see that. So what?'

'What're you doing with it?' Kavanagh asked.

'Why? Is it illegal?' He ground out his cigarette end between his fingers and came back into the conservatory.

'What do you want with a writing magazine?' he insisted.

'It must've been Aaron's,' he shrugged.

'Yes?' said the inspector. 'It came to your address. We've checked the subscription list. You're not on it, but it was sent to the flat you shared with your brother in Manchester.'

'So?' he said.

'Why did you keep it?' asked the inspector.

'Why not?' he said.

'Your job's advertised here.'

'Yes? That figures.'

'You've told us yourself you're not interested in writing, but you read a magazine that your brother's once subscribed to, even read the classified ads at the back, and you apply for a job here at the centre. Why do that?'

'Why not?' he said. 'A couple of them came to the flat after he died. One day I read one, and amongst all the ads for secretaries and stuff, there was this job.'

'And you applied?'

He shrugged his shoulders. 'I'm here,' he said.

'Why?' asked Salt.

'I fancied a change.'

'Yes?' said Salt. 'We think you applied for the job so you could get close to Tom Oliver.'

'Why would I want to do that?' he asked.

'I think that's something you have to tell us,' she said.

'We've had a look at the hard drive on your laptop,' said Kavanagh.

'Oh, yeah?' said Bell. 'And?'

'You checked the courses here many times.'

'It's what they advertise them for,' he said.

'Yes. For writers,' said Kavanagh. 'But you're not a writer.'

'And more to the point,' continued Salt, 'why would you Google Tom Oliver so many times before you even came here? As well as many times since?'

'Maybe I Googled Stephen King, too.'

'You did,' said Kavanagh. 'Just the once.'

'You also sent for a course booklet,' said Salt.

'Why not? Good idea to find out about the place,' he asserted smugly.

'Very good idea,' said Salt. 'So why not use your own name? It went to your old Manchester address, but you had it sent under a false name. It's on Keira's list.'

'What's your point?' he said wearily.

'You've got a brother, Leon. Well, you had a brother. He goes on a course with Oliver, but when he gets back, things haven't worked out and he's depressed. Eventually, he takes his life, and some time later you apply for a job here; you get sent course details, but you don't ask for them in your own name. Oliver comes to tutor here, but the man doesn't go home. So, what's happened to him?'

'All I knew about Oliver was from Aaron. He said he was a good writer, but then he came back, and he'd had a bad time. That's all I know. The next month or two, he got depressed. He had some sort of nervous breakdown. I dunno what. And then he killed himself.' He got to his feet. 'Look, I'm done talking about this. I don't want to talk about Aaron. Not now, not at all. I want to go. Now.'

'Yes, you can go for now,' said Kavanagh. 'But don't go far. Alright?'

FORTY

When he was just a kid, little Frank Kavanagh's family had had a German Dachshund, a risible breed of dog whose belly scraped the pavement as its tiny legs struggled to cover the ground. And Kavanagh would hide or go missing – just about anything, in fact – to avoid having to take the thing for a walk and be ridiculed by his mates at the sight of himself with it.

Later, his family briefly owned a Golden Labrador that was, occasionally and of necessity, restrained by being tied to their father's tool box, a solid affair with metal bands around the wooden frame, and made even heavier by the unwieldy tools inside. This toolbox was something of a mystery, given that young Frank had never seen his dad so much as change a plug, let alone use one of the incredibly large and heavy hand-drills or oversize spanners which lay in the box with its faint smell of oil and ancient greasy dust.

Anyway, to stop the Labrador from following Frank and his mates out into the road and down to the local park, they'd once tied its lead to the handle of the tool box and made off.

A few minutes later, as they idled down the suburban road, there was the sound of heavy scraping, followed by a pause, then more scraping, and yet another pause. They looked round to see the dog following them, notwithstanding its slow and intermittent progress as it pulled the solid box along for a few feet, stopped, gathered its strength, and then repeated the manoeuvre.

Apart from those two family pets, the inspector knew little more about dogs than any other member of the public. He'd occasionally been close to operations where they were routinely employed, sometimes looking for a body, more often seeking drugs in a criminal's car, but he'd never taken any particular interest in them. They were, frankly, just another part of the arsenal in fighting crime: computers, surveillance, databases, snipers, Tasers, listening devices. And dogs.

He'd watched as their busy backsides bustled into drug

dealers' cars and lock-up garages and, if the cameras were running and the footage was to be broadcast – on the principle that a fire with no flames was no fire at all as far as news editors were concerned – the frisky little spaniels were always going to come up with a package of Class A dope from deep in the car's interior somewhere.

But that was about it. Today, though, after some unavoidable delay, the dogs that were to scour the local woodland in the hunt for Tom Oliver were, at last, due to arrive. Kavanagh had assumed the place might resemble Crufts' show-ring on prize night. But the inspector in charge of GPDs (General Purpose Dogs) for West Mercia who supervised what were unimaginatively called the 'body-dogs' had decreed that only two dogs would be required. More than this and they tended to confuse one another's scents and were likely to become distracted from the task in hand.

Although his direct contact with dogs and their handlers had been both limited and perfunctory, as with any organization, Kavanagh was well aware of the hierarchy that obtained: firearms support groups (FSG) were the undisputed elite; the murder squad recruited the cream of detectives from CID, and dog handlers were generally regarded with disdain. After all, these were people who not only preferred to spend their time with canine than human kind, but who had, in choosing this path, opted for the slowest of slow-track careers.

Yes, their contracts stipulated that they were entitled to an hour per shift for the 'grooming and training' of their charges, and they received about a hundred and fifty quid a month on top of their salaries for their trouble, but these cops were not destined for high office: the man or woman in the big chair and with the decent view from the top of New Scotland Yard was never going to be someone with a case of Pedigree Chum in the back of their car, of that Kavanagh was quite sure.

'How you doing?' he asked as the PC got out of his van.

'Yes, not bad,' said PC Dorner, as if he already had something else on his mind. 'Been busy; working non-stop in Brum for days. Bloody nightmare.'

'The terrorist business?' asked Kavanagh.

'Yes, explosives search,' said the man as he went to the back of the van and accessed the cage within the vehicle.

'Any good?' said Kavanagh, at this moment rather less

interested in the possibility of carnage in the second city's
Bull Ring than the efficiency of the animal who was eyeing
him warily and was clearly keen to get out.

'Nothing at all,' said Dorner. 'Three days and absolutely
fuck all.' There was little or no variation in his speaking
voice so that everything he said assumed exactly the same
significance.

'Sorry about that,' said Kavanagh. 'So, who's this then?'

'Charlie,' said the PC, and the German Shepherd's ears
pricked up at the use of his name.

'Do you only use dogs?' asked Kavanagh as Dorner opened
the cage and snapped the lead onto the dog's collar in a
businesslike fashion.

'Mostly male,' said the man ruffling Charlie's head. 'There's
a few bitches, but I prefer a dog. Trouble with bitches is they
tend to be a bit too protective. They'd be just as likely to look
after their handler as go and bite the blagger.'

'This fella'll bite on command?' asked Kavanagh.

'Oh, yes, he'll bite,' said the man. 'He'll bite, alright. Do
you know what pressure his teeth close at?'

'You've got me,' said the inspector.

'Four thousand pounds per square inch.'

'Blimey,' said Kavanagh, and then added rather more pointedly, 'But will he find me a body?'

'Oh, yes,' said Dorner. 'His nose is about a thousand times
more sensitive than yours. If there's someone up there,
Charlie'll find them, don't you worry.'

'Good,' said Kavanagh, reassured.

'What have you got for us, then?' asked the PC. 'All I know
is it's a misper. Are you sure he's here?'

'No, not really,' said Kavanagh. 'He's a writer. A bloke
called Tom Oliver. You heard of him? They featured him on
Crimewatch last week.'

Dorner nodded his head. 'Never watch it; missus doesn't
like anything to do with the police.' Kavanagh smiled but the
man registered nothing and appeared to be serious.

'We've checked the friends, family and enemies, all the usual,
but we've drawn a blank and it looks more and more like he
might never have left here,' said the inspector. 'We eventually found his motor down there with his stuff in it.' Kavanagh
indicated the muddy lake bottom a hundred yards away.

'It only went in a few yards, but it was out of sight and it delayed us for a couple of days.'

'And he's a writer, you say?' asked Dorner.

'Yes. Not very well known, and he wasn't very popular: he had more enemies than fans.'

'And you think one of them's left him up here?' the PC added, gesturing to the wooded hills.

'Could be,' said Kavanagh. 'We couldn't wait any longer and started an initial sweep yesterday. It's when we found the owner of the place, an elderly woman who'd had a fall and lay dying up there for a day, maybe two. She'd probably still be there now if we hadn't been out looking for Oliver,' he added soberly.

'And have you got anyone in the frame for this writer's disappearance?' asked the dog handler.

'Yes, we've got a suspect, but he's slippery and he's covered his tracks pretty well.'

'What have you got on him?' asked the man.

'His brother had had some sort of unpleasantness with Oliver; he had a breakdown and eventually topped himself. We think maybe the brother got himself taken on down here so he could get close to Oliver and avenge his brother's death. Trouble is, everything we've got is entirely circumstantial. What we need's a body for some decent forensics.'

'Right,' he said. 'Alright if I get a cuppa first?' They walked over towards the catering truck. 'Terry'll be here in a bit with his spaniel and then we'll quarter the ground and make a start. Only problem I can see is your blokes are bound to have trampled some of the ground doing line-abreast when they came across the old lady.'

'Yes,' said Kavanagh, 'but at least they didn't get very far: she was found pretty close to the house. A lot of the terrain's so steep it's pretty inaccessible for our blokes. And, yes, I meant to say, I've been told there's also a few mine shafts around here, too. So watch out where you're putting your feet.'

'That's no problem,' said Dorner. 'And if your writer's in one of those, there'll be evidence of him going in – unless he was dropped by a helicopter and didn't even touch the sides.'

'I doubt it,' said Kavanagh. 'Bit noisy for that round here.'

'A fried-egg sandwich, please, mate, and a cuppa tea with not much milk,' said the PC to the caterer.

'You've got some of his clothing?' said the inspector.

'Yes, they sent a few things up. But if it's the worst-case scenario – and it almost always is once they get us lot involved – we won't be following scent from his boxer shorts.'

'How do you mean?' asked the inspector.

'Well, that stuff always looks good in the movies, but you say it's over a week ago that your man went AWOL. I reckon it's a different smell Charlie here'll be looking for now. It's the smell of flesh he knows. Anyone's. It's what he's trained for. If there's a body here,' he gestured to the wooded hills behind them, 'it doesn't matter whose it is, he'll find it, I'll guarantee you that.'

FORTY-ONE

'We know that you killed Tom Oliver, Leon,' said the inspector categorically, as if it was the termination of a conversation, rather than the beginning of one.

'Yes?' said Bell. 'So, how come you haven't charged me, then?'

'We'll get to that,' said Kavanagh. 'You killed him down near the jetty, then you put his car in drive and launched it into the water. You did that so that it would buy you some time to deal with his body. No good putting him in the car. He'd be found, possibly very soon if the car didn't sink properly, and as one of the last people known to have seen him, we'd have been all over you. No, better to dump the car and get rid of the body properly. It's an old adage, but true: no body, no murder. But the dogs are here working right now, and so it's really just a matter of time.'

'You reckon,' said Leon with rather more confidence in his voice than Kavanagh might have wished to hear.

The policeman ignored him and continued. 'You know, killing's easy. Happens every night of the week. Vicars do it; schoolteachers; barmaids; seems everyone's at it. I'm surprised there's not more, to be honest, given the stuff that people get up to. You know, the provocation, the emotional turmoil and mental anguish.

'I guess you did it for your brother. He'd had a bad time from Oliver. He sounds like a right malicious bastard. An independent witness has been in touch with us. Someone who was on that course in France, and she says he really screwed your brother over. Is that right, Leon?'

Bell said nothing, wary of being lured into anything by the inspector's conversational manner.

'You wanted to put things right for him. I can almost understand it. But what have you done with Oliver?' enquired the inspector casually

'You tell me,' said Leon. 'You seem so sure of everything.'

Kavanagh smiled, but it was a hollow smile: there was

something in Bell's tone that didn't sit quite right. The inspector walked across to the first-floor window of the Craven Arms police station. The traffic below negotiated the mini-roundabouts, and Wednesday morning pedestrians went about their business, wholly unaware of the drama being played out just a few yards above them. But, with the duty solicitor at his side, if the formal surroundings were intended to intimidate Leon, they didn't seem to be working.

He hadn't even taken the proffered advice and resorted to the familiar stone-walling no-comment mantra, as recommended by his young solicitor.

'You killed him down near the jetty,' began Kavanagh again, his back to the room as he continued to peer down at the traffic. 'It was quiet and unobserved. This was some time after you'd all returned from the pub on that last night. Killing's unpredictable and messy, no matter how it's done, and outside would be best, obviously. How did you kill him, Leon?' he asked, turning to face the young man. 'Your bare hands?' Kavanagh opened his palms and held them upward. 'It takes a lot to strangle a grown man. To feel him writhe and see his face distort as he dies for want of his last living breath.

'Or is that missing statue involved somehow? That would be my guess. And there's a fitting sort of irony there, too: bust of an old tyrant writer kills another – not entirely popular – writer.

'So, down by the lake, bludgeoned to death, the sixty-year-old writer – pissed and pissed off, according to Keira, that night – and the fit young gardener. Unobserved and unheard, everyone else tucked up in bed. You killed him, but then you'd got the question of how to remove his body. Did you know that you were going to kill him?' he asked reasonably, taking a few steps back and sitting down once more, opposite the man.

Leon looked down at the table as the recording tape in the Neal double player whirred round.

'Careful about this: you do know the difference between murder and manslaughter? It's important. Once upon a time, it would have been the difference between you hanging, and your being inside for life.

'Nowadays, you won't be topped, of course, but it'll make a big difference to how long it is before you can nip into a pub and buy a pint again. And that's to say nothing about the considerable grief a decent-looking boy like you is going to have to deal with if you go to a Category A maximum-security nick.

'It's not a cosy set up, you know. Forget all that *Shawshank Redemption* bollocks and some old tosser like Morgan Freeman looking after you. That definitely ain't gonna happen. All you'll find in Long Lartin or Woodhill are some very unpleasant blokes who'll have you crying for your mum by bedtime.'

Leon glanced up at the copper.

'You ever been inside, Leon? Of course you haven't, have you? You got off completely, without even a criminal record when you half beat that kid to death, the one who'd taunted your brother at school. Magistrates threw it out. They reckoned they knew better than the cops. The cops who thought you should at least be taught some sort of lesson about not using excessive violence to square violence.

'Anyway, in the nick, first, they'll take everything you own, and then they'll fuck you rigid, just for the fun of it. The con who runs your wing, he'll pimp you for half-an-ounce of Golden Virginia, and there's absolutely fuck all you can do about it.

'The only reason prisons work is because the cons run them. And if you don't like it – and you won't – and you make any trouble, you'll end up dead, cut to pieces in the shower or, even worse, scalded with boiling water in the kitchen.'

Leon stared back down at his hands folded on the table. The country solicitor appeared more chastened by Kavanagh's homily than the young man was, and stretched his neck and pulled at the knot of his garish tie.

'Murder or manslaughter? The difference is important, Leon. You'd do well to understand that. You should have a serious talk with Mr . . .?'

'Eddings,' said the brief. 'Stephen Eddings.'

'With Mr Eddings here. Maybe you were provoked? Maybe Oliver assaulted you? How about a bit of drunken lechery as defence? I know it's a bit old hat, but it's tried and tested and it's worked often enough before. Yes, you have a chat with your legal representative, and he'll advise you, no doubt. Perhaps you just wanted to talk to Oliver about your brother's death and the events leading up to it, eh? But he got the wrong idea and he said something, or did something? Maybe he even attacked you, thinking you were going to have a pop at him?'

'You don't have to respond to any of this,' interrupted the solicitor. 'These aren't questions; it's just speculation. You are within your rights – and it would be my advice – to say, "No comment".'

Kavanagh ignored the legal man's intervention. 'You put in a plea of manslaughter, arrive at some mitigating circumstances with Mr Eddings' help, and you'd be doing your time in a Category C somewhere out in the countryside. You'd be able to see trees and hear the birds singing. Eventually, maybe even get your own cell. And you'd be with people in for a domestic – "the kitchen knife slipped, Guv. It was just a bit of fooling around that went wrong". Or fraud, or dealing a bit of coke or smack. You'd be with people just like yourself, nothing really unpleasant. What do you reckon, Mr Eddings?' he asked rhetorically. 'With a decent jury, a nice shirt and a bit of a haircut, he might get ten years. Show a bit of remorse, and with a couple of do-gooders on the parole board, you could be out on limited release in five. Really. You hear what I'm saying, Leon? Think about it while you've still got the chance.'

Leon stared steadfastly down at the table and the inspector walked back to the window. 'I think we've covered enough for now. I want you to think over what I've said. And have a good long talk with your solicitor here.'

'Is my client at liberty to leave?' asked the man's legal representative.

'Yes, he is,' said Kavanagh. 'You know he's not been arrested or charged with anything. Not yet. But I want him back here this afternoon, at three o'clock, and we'll see where we are and exactly what we've got then. Alright?'

FORTY-TWO

Stephen Eddings and his client sat in McDonald's across the road from the police station in the precinct. For the solicitor, it was business. Interesting and unusual business, yes, and certainly the most serious case that he'd ever been involved with. But that didn't mean that he wasn't hungry. So, as Leon looked down at his cup of tea with very little interest, the solicitor tried to eat his fries and burger with as much decorum as the young man's situation warranted.

In the incident room across the street, Salt, Earle and Kavanagh were eating bacon sandwiches when the inspector was summoned to one of the many phones that had been installed there.

'It's ACC Hyland,' said the young PC as he passed him the handset.

'Sir?' said Kavanagh.

'How's it going up there, Frank? Any sign of your writer?'

'Not bad,' said Kavanagh. 'It's in the balance, but I think we're getting there. The dog handlers are at work right now and I think our suspect just might be feeling the pressure.'

'Good,' said the ACC. 'Anyway, I've some news for you, Frank.'

'Yes?' said the inspector.

'The complaint against you . . .'

'Yes?'

'It's been dropped.'

'Really?' said Kavanagh. His recent altercation on Crouch End Broadway was just about the last thing on his mind. But he could tell from the ACC's tone of voice that the man felt pleased, almost as if he might have somehow orchestrated the outcome himself. 'So, er, what's happened exactly, sir?'

'Someone came forward. You know, this bloke, he's got a deli on the Broadway, apparently, and when he saw the yellow crime board asking for information at the scene, he actually took the time and trouble to come forward.'

'Blimey,' said the inspector, very surprised by this almost

unprecedented show of public-spiritedness. 'And this witness gave a statement?' he went on.

'Full and unequivocal,' said the ACC, and the senior officer proceeded to read him the salient paragraphs from the document before him. 'His English is better than mine. He's Italian by birth but he's been living here for over thirty years. Anyway, we've had it shown to the solicitor of the bloke who took a swing at you, and they immediately dropped the complaint.'

'Well, I guess that can only be good, sir,' said Kavanagh just a little hesitantly.

'I'd have thought so,' said Hyland. 'It's a result, Frank. Cheer up. You don't sound too happy, but I reckon you ought to pop in to buy a bit of *parmigiano* or a bottle of Asti Spumante from him some time.'

'Yes, sir,' he said. 'Maybe I'll do that. It is good news.'

'See you back in London, Frank, when you've got things tidied up over there. Keep me informed. Goodbye for now.'

'Goodbye, sir,' said the inspector.

'Good news?' said Salt to Kavanagh quietly, drawing him aside from the other officers present in the room.

'Yes,' he said. 'But a little strange.'

'Go on?' she said.

'Someone's come forward, about the Crouch End business, and they've cleared me with a detailed statement.'

'Excellent!' she said. 'So, what's the problem?'

'The problem is that it's the bloke from the deli. You know where we get the . . . what is the name of that cheese?'

'I'm not telling you again,' she said. 'He's probably just taken pity on you because he thinks you've lost your marbles.'

'Anyway,' Kavanagh went on, 'the slightly worrying thing is, his account of what happened bears absolutely no relation to events.'

'How do you mean?' she asked.

'He's given chapter and verse. He says I stood apart and called a clear warning before I pitched in and tried to disarm the bloke with the baseball bat.'

'Really?' she said.

'You and I both know that's not how it happened. I forgot myself, got a bit carried away and was involved before I'd identified myself as a copper. In truth, that bloke might have been a thug, but he was within his rights taking a swing at me . . .'

'How odd,' she said. 'So, what's his motive, then, the deli man?'

'You've got me,' he said. 'Maybe he's got a screw loose or he must be the last person in London who somehow still thinks we're the good guys, in spite of everything.'

'Very odd,' she said. 'But rather touching. So, what now? What're we going to do?'

'We're gonna get up to the centre to see if they've turned up anything, and then we're going to get back to Leon Bell,' he said.

At just gone three that afternoon, Eddings and Bell were already sitting back at the table, with Sergeant Jeff Earle standing in attendance at the door. Kavanagh came in, and Salt followed. The inspector placed a plastic box on the floor near the sergeant and took a seat opposite Bell. Salt sat next to him. The inspector switched on the tape machine, announced the time and the names of those present.

'So, where were we?' he began casually. 'You've killed Tom Oliver, but you've got to get rid of him now. That's always the problem. It's a long way up into the woods to carry a man. Believe me, I know, I've walked it a couple of times. OK, he's no giant, only about twelve stone-odd, but that's still quite a bit of weight to carry at night, up that track in the dark and into the woodland.

'It's too noisy to start the Land Rover. But hey, there's the old flower cart, right outside the front door and with nothing on it but a few plants and a couple of grow-bags. The original wooden wheels disintegrated years ago and it's even got some bike tyres on it now. Perfect. You take the stuff off, put Oliver on it and push him up the track. It's still a bit bumpy and rutted but it's way better than lugging him over your shoulder, eh?'

'Absolute bollocks,' said Bell.

'And any traces of Oliver on the thing you dealt with the next day. You gave it and the jetty a good soaking of creosote, didn't you? I could still smell the stuff the day I got here.'

'Well, at least that's one thing you've got right,' he said. 'I did creosote the flower cart. It's ancient and it needs looking after.'

Kavanagh ignored his plausible explanation.

'I've told you, I haven't done anything,' said Bell.

The inspector gave him a moment and then said, 'You like movies, don't you, Leon?'

'Some,' he said, non-committal.

'What was that old Michael Douglas DVD doing there? It must have been yours. A DVD with not a single fingerprint on the box or the disc inside? You're not telling me some passer-by just dropped *Falling Down* at the spot where you attacked Will Cassin? A bit too much of a coincidence. But why on earth did you leave it there? That does intrigue me.'

'I've had nothing to do with any DVD or attacking anyone,' he asserted.

Kavanagh ignored the predictable response and eventually said, 'You seen *No Country for Old Men*?'

'Yes.'

'What do you reckon?'

'Alright,' he said.

'Only alright?' queried the inspector.

'The end's not right,' he added.

'I agree with you. Good film, but the end's not right,' said Kavanagh. 'We should be reviewing movies for one of the Sunday papers. What's the Coen brothers' best film?' he asked.

Leon almost responded without thought, but stopped himself and said nothing.

'What's their best film, Leon?' Kavanagh asked again.

Bell maintained his silence.

'You know their best film as well as I do,' said Kavanagh. 'You don't need a film guide for this. Everybody knows.'

'Why?' said Bell warily.

'You got a problem saying it?' said Kavanagh.

'I like a lot of their films,' he said.

'Course you do, Leon. Me too. But this is Desert Island Discs for films and you can't have them all. This is that crap bit at the end of the programme where the presenter says: "If you could only take one record . . ." You know the bit. So, come on, Leon, just tell me – if you could only take one Coen brothers' film, what would it be?'

Silence.

Kavanagh leaned across the table. 'Say it,' he said. 'Come on, say it,' and he brought his face very close to the young man's.

Leon looked back at him hard and clenched his fists beneath the table. 'Just say it, Leon. For fuck's sake, just say it,' shouted Kavanagh.

'*Fargo*,' said Bell quietly.

'*Fargo*,' repeated Kavanagh. 'You bet it is. You know just as well as I do what their best movie is. So why the reluctance? What is it you don't care to think about? Is it those snowy Minnesota landscapes? Was it that stuff with William H. Macy on his car lot and his wife and his horrible father-in-law? Thing is, Leon, we don't give a flying fuck if Macy kills his wife or her father, do we? Because our sympathies are all with him. Yes?'

'If you say so,' said Bell. 'I've never thought about it.'

'And who cares if you kill Tom Oliver? The man's a tosser: he's got no friends, and most of the women he's ever been with have left him. He's no loss. Remember the end of the film? Snow. Weatherboard cottage. One of the bad guys – it's not Steve Buscemi, it's the other one, the big fella – out in the woods, what's his name?'

'Stormare,' said Bell, unable to resist. 'Peter Stormare.'

'We hear the sound before we see the scene. Yes? *Eeeeeh*,' screeched Kavanagh as he mimicked the high-pitched scream of a timber shredder in the clear air of those cold Minnesota woods. 'You must remember?' he said, inclining his head a little.

Bell said nothing.

'And then what, Leon?' asked Kavanagh. 'You know what we see? I do, too. I've seen it loads of times. In goes some more of Macy's wife. Into the shredder she goes, and out the other end, blood and flesh speckling the snow as she's mixed with those woodchips. *Eeeeee . . .*'

Kavanagh got up, walked to the door and picked up the plastic box. He brought it to the table, unfastened the clips and opened the lid towards Bell's face so that he couldn't see inside.

The young man pushed himself back into his chair. Kavanagh reached inside the box, lifted out a handful of the dark earth there, held it a foot in the air and then rubbed his hands slowly together as the dry mulch trickled through his fingers and fell onto the table.

'You wanted chip-shop oil,' Kavanagh began quietly. 'You

tried here and there, going as far as Ludlow. One of the chip shops there remembers you. But you're a bit late in the day, Leon. Round here, they've been converting vehicles for a bit now and all the outlets are already committed to supplying canny farmers and the like.

'In the end, you got your oil from a lay-by diner called Billy's Burgers on the A49, the one with the sign that says: "Ugly staff; beautiful food." All legitimate, too. Keira's even got the receipts in the office. Several gallons a week for the last couple of months. Only one problem, Leon: it isn't fish that's been fried in that stuff, it's truckers' breakfasts. Bacon, sausages, eggs and black pudding.

'You're such a clever guy, you're going to shred Tom Oliver and disguise him with so much chip fat as you run him through the machine that no one will ever find him. You'll scatter him in the woods and mulch him in with the flowers in the borders. But do you know what they train the police body dogs on, Leon? They train them to find remains by working on the animal that most closely resembles human flesh: pigs.

'When they took the dogs up into the woods, the mutts went berserk, they were tearing round in circles, not because they couldn't find anything, but because they found Tom Oliver and tons of bacon fat absolutely everywhere.

'We sent samples down to forensics and it took them about an hour to phone and say they'd got Oliver's DNA – and quite a bit of bacon grease, too.'

There was silence in the room.

Eddings eventually said, 'May I speak to my client in private, please?'

'Of course,' said Kavanagh.

FORTY-THREE

'You want to start again, Leon?' said Kavanagh. 'In your own time. Just tell us in your own words what happened.'

There was a long delay with only the sound of the tapes turning. Salt reached over to stop the machine but Kavanagh indicated to her to wait for a moment longer.

'Leon?' said the solicitor at his side.

'I'd come this far to make things right for Aaron,' he began, 'but now that the time was here, it wasn't so easy. I couldn't just do it. Not just like that. Not without knowing him . . . We got back late. We were the last. I hadn't spoken to him in the pub all night. He'd looked completely fucked off the whole time.

'Keira had told me he was pissed off about some other writer who'd come in midweek and put on a good show. She said Oliver was the kind of bloke who couldn't stand being anything but top dog . . .'

'Jackson,' said the inspector quietly. 'Simon Jackson.'

'Yes, that's right,' said Leon. 'So, Oliver's pissed off anyway, and then this woman he's into, she hooks up with some geezer from the Midlands who's on the course that week.

'Back at the house, Oliver asks people to stay for a drink, but everybody just says, "Don't think so," and goes off to bed.

'He says he's gonna get some fags from his room and I'm down here on my own. If I'm going to do anything, it's got to be now. He's going home the next day. But to be honest, I haven't got the stomach for it; if you're gonna hurt someone, you've gotta be fired up, you know what I mean? But this Oliver just looks like a sad, miserable fucker who's pissed off.

'I made some coffee and waited downstairs. I thought he'd fallen asleep, and I'm thinking, You're a lucky fucker, mate, you've just saved your own life. But after a bit I heard him coming down. He says to me he's gotta go outside and throw up. When he comes back in, he says, "That's better," and we sit in the kitchen and he has a beer while I drink my coffee.

'He starts whining, moaning about this woman binning him. The woman on the course . . .'

'Romilly,' added Salt.

'Yes, her.'

'After a bit, we go outside for a smoke and wander down towards the jetty. All I want to know is about what happened in France with Aaron that left him so broken up. I know it's got to be about writing and so I ask Oliver what the problem was with this other writer who came in to read his stuff on the Wednesday.

'He gets really pissed off with my even asking and says it's fuck all to do with me, and then he lays into Jackson and just says if there's one thing a writer can't stand, it's any writer better than himself. "It's the law of the jungle," he says. "Just 'cause people use words and are smart on the telly and all that, it doesn't mean they've not got animal instincts underneath."

'"Is that right?" I say.

'He tells me about rows he's had, falling out with people, agents he's sacked and publishers who've messed him about. I'd read about him and Catherine Wooley in the writing magazine so I knew about some of that stuff.

'Eventually he gets round to telling me about something that happened to him once when he was teaching abroad.

'I said to him, "Look, mate, we've all done things we're not proud of, me too," but he's not hearing me, he doesn't even ask me what I'm on about. He's not interested, except in himself.

"Go on, then," I said. "Tell me."

"Forget it," he says. "You wouldn't want to hear. It's not a very pretty story."

"Try me," I say.

'He says he's teaching a course in France and it's all fine and then this young lad arrives a day late. I remember: Aaron couldn't get the day off from the job centre where he was working as a clerk and he had to join all the others late.

'Oliver's the centre of attention, just the way he likes it, he tells me, but then when they get down to their writing work and all that, it's obvious that our kid's really good.

'He says he wants to tell him to get back on the plane and fuck off back home.

'Although Aaron's not published or anything yet, the book he's working on, Oliver says, it shows a lot of promise, and after a day or two, the other people on the course are taking as much notice of this quiet lad and his work as they are of Oliver, and so he's well pissed off. "So, what happened, then?" I ask him. "You like this story?" he said, looking hard at me, and for a minute I wondered whether he knew that the person he was talking about was my own brother, and he was digging his own grave just by lying there on the jetty and telling me about it.

'All I said was, "You know how to tell a story, Tom."

'"When this boy's work comes up," he says, "I undermine it. Nothing too obvious, but enough to get the others thinking that what he's done isn't that good at all. I blind 'em with science," he says. "Talk about other writers they've never even heard of, that sort of thing."

'"And they can't tell it's good stuff?" I asked.

'"They're not confident enough. So if I suggest something, they follow like sheep," he says.

'"And this lad was crushed?" I say.

'"You know when you touch a snail's horns, that's what he was like. He withdrew. He didn't show up for a meal after that. I felt sorry for him, in a way. Not so sorry I was going to do anything about it, but sorry all the same. Fact is, he'd have struggled in the writing game: his writing was good enough, but it's a tough business and he would have got knocked about by it."

'"So what happened?" I asked him.

'"He came to see me that afternoon. We'd got a one-to-one scheduled, and he asked me to be honest with him about his writing. I told him that I never tell people the truth, even when they ask for it," he says, "because there's no writer in the world who wants to hear anything except that what they're doing is good.

'Oliver goes on to tell me that Aaron insisted, that he wanted to really know, that he admired Oliver and his work and that's why he was there and he wanted his honest opinion.

'Oliver told him that in his case he'd make an exception. Maybe he didn't need protecting from the truth. He said he owed it to him to be honest if that's what he really wanted.

'"It was too good an opportunity to resist," Oliver tells me.

"I cut him to pieces. I told him I could see nothing in his work that was really original, just lots of influences. I told him to carry on if that was his choice, but that in my view, it was not going to work out for him. He wasn't going to be a published writer."

'Oliver goes on to tell me that Aaron left the next day. He told all the others that he'd left a note saying that his mother was ill and he'd had to leave to get back to her.

'"I never heard from him again," he told me.'

'"That's some story," I said.

'"I told you it wasn't very nice," he said, and he was quiet for a while. "I'm not proud of it, to be honest. But when you get older, you learn to know yourself."

'"You'd do things differently this time?" I asked. 'In a way, I was giving him maybe one last chance. To save himself. But he even blew that.'

'"Like fuck I would," he told me. "I'd do exactly the same thing again," he said. "I know more than ever just how strong those feelings are. There's only one thing that matters to a writer, and that's the next book. Everything else can go: friends, family, relationships; we're prepared to lose it all for a decent chapter," he said. "It might be pathetic, but it's true. And the irony is, this kid, he was a real writer, and that's why I could hurt him so much by what I said, and why he took it so hard."

'"You bet," I said. "You fancy another drink, Tom?" I asked him then.

'"You keep all that to yourself," he said. "You tell anyone, and I'll deny every word and I'll sue you for everything you've got, right?"

'After that I went up to the kitchen and looked around. Through in the hall I saw that statue thing. Of the old man who originally owned the place, Osman.

'I came back down to the jetty with the beers. He was lying on his back. "Here's your beer, Tom," I said and he pulled himself up. I handed him the bottle and said, "Cheers." It was the last thing he ever heard.

'I sat there for a while afterwards. I thought about my brother and wondered what he would have thought about what I'd done for him. But you never really knew with Aaron. We were different. I could never do the things he did. But I could do this one thing for him, and so I did.'

There was a long silence in the room. Eventually, Kavanagh asked him quietly, keen not to break the spell of the young man's murderous reverie, 'What did you do next, Leon?'

'I went and got the old flower cart from outside the house, and then pushed him on it up the track into the woods where I'd been coppicing that week.

'I got rid of his motor in the lake, and the next day I used the axe on him and put him through the GreenMech – that's the big shredder we use on the estate – just like the one in *Fargo.*'

Salt winced and there was a further horrified silence in the room as the tape whirred round. 'And the statue?' she eventually asked.

'That went down one of the mineshafts. I dropped it in and it hit the sides a couple of times then splashed into the water at the bottom. It's miles down there,' he said.

'You know when you went over to Hereford that night, to . . .' Kavanagh chose his words carefully. 'To see about Sarah Cassin's husband . . .'

'I hated doing that,' he said. 'He was a completely innocent bloke, but I had to. I watched the house for hours. I saw her. She came out and walked up to the post box. I could have . . .'

'What?' asked Kavanagh.

'I could have hurt her, made sure she couldn't come to the centre the next day, but I've never hit a woman in my life, and I wasn't going to start now, not even for Aaron.

'I watched and waited. And at nine o'clock, I followed him up to the pub to meet his mates, just like Sarah had said he did when I sat in on her doing her reading at the centre that time. And when he walked back, I whacked him. I didn't want to do it, but I had no choice.'

'And what about the DVD? *Falling Down*?' said Salt. 'That was yours?'

'Yes,' he said.

'How come?' asked the inspector. 'Why did you leave it there?'

'It was my way of showing him that it wasn't his fault, or anything. It's a crap film, I know, but what it's saying is that if you push someone far enough, they'll always break. It happened to me when I attacked that kid who was bullying

Aaron at school. It's what happened to Aaron in France. And now it's what I've had to do. I thought maybe he'd watch it sometime, even though he wouldn't understand that it was my message to him. It was like an apology, in a way, for what I'd had to do to him.'

'I see,' said Kavanagh sceptically.

Eventually, Bell pointed to one of the several No Smoking signs taped around the room and said, 'Can I have a smoke? Funny thing is, I feel a lot better for telling you all that. It's been on my mind, you know. A lot.'

'Sure,' said Kavanagh. 'You have a smoke, Leon.'

He leaned over and switched off the tape machine. 'We'll go and get some tea. Leave you to have a chat with your solicitor for a bit. OK?'

'Sure,' he said, and added politely, 'two sugars, please.'